KINGDOM
OF
YESTERDAY'S
LIES

ROYALS OF FAERY

BOOK ONE

HAYLEY OSBORN

LEXITY INK
PUBLISHING

Lexity Ink Publishing
Christchurch, New Zealand

Book Layout ©2019 BookDesignTemplates.com
Cover Design by Covers by Combs
Editing by Melissa A Craven

ISBN 978-0-473-54132-3
also available as an ebook

For Kelly
The best cheerleader for my work I know

PART ONE

IADRUN

ONE

THE BARKING hounds should have sent me rushing up the dirt path and inside our tiny cottage, stopping only to drag the bolt across the door at my back. Our timber walls were thin, but they offered more protection than standing deep in the shadows beneath the only tree in our backyard and waiting for the oversized animals to find me.

My neighbors had heeded the racket already, and moonlight was all that lit the village of Holbeck now. Every candle was guttered, every person likely hunkered beneath a table or behind a couch, with an axe—or perhaps a poker—gripped in one shaking hand.

Everyone but me.

I already knew hiding didn't work; I'd tried it.

Tonight, I would fight.

Ignoring my shaking hand, I tightened my grip on my bow and let my focus rise to the night sky above the woods surrounding two sides of our cottage. The sky was the first place they would come into view.

"Bria!" Mother's loud whisper made me jump, and I turned to find her standing in the door of our cottage, not twenty paces away. The waning moon lit her features as bright as if she were holding a candle. She squinted into the shadows beneath the tree, somehow knowing I was here even though no light from the house or the moon touched me.

The hounds were louder now, though I still couldn't see them. With a sigh, I slid from my hiding place behind the oak. "Go back inside, Mother. I'll be there soon." I kept my voice calm as I cursed to myself. She'd been tucked up in her bed with a headache when I checked on her a few minutes ago, and bed was where I wanted her to stay. The terror in her eyes told me she didn't want me out here right now, but no matter what she said, she wouldn't talk me out of this. I would protect us both this time.

As I opened my mouth to tell her so, her body stilled. I knew what it meant without following her gaze. They were nearly here. Mother had seen them. In the light from the moon, I was certain she'd turned paler than the apron hooked over the back of the dining chair behind her. She took a step back into the cottage.

I nodded. "Go, Mother. Lock yourself in your room and sprinkle salt across the threshold. Or…" I almost couldn't speak for the memories the words brought with them. "Or crawl into the space beneath the cottage."

Her lips hardly moved as she spoke. "You'll come soon?"

"Soon," I repeated, watching her sink back inside the house as she searched the sky. A rogue thought skittered through my mind. Depending on how the next few minutes went, that might have been our final conversation. I shoved the thought away, focusing on *them*. Thinking like that was the fastest way to make it a premonition.

The hounds led the raucous procession, beasts almost as tall as a small horse. Their wiry coats were black, brindle, white and anything in between, and their lips curled back showing off their sharp fangs every time they barked. But it wasn't the hounds I feared. It was the mask-clad riders that followed in their wake, sitting high on the backs of their galloping steeds.

The Wild Hunt.

They came from Faery, and they passed by on their horses at least once a month, but sometimes as often as nightly, fae criminals employed by the Unseelie King. They dragged innocent people from their homes to become slaves to the King, or a soldier fighting for him in the years-long war between the Faery Kingdoms of Seelie and Unseelie.

It was my fault they had Holbeck in their sights tonight. I'd lost myself in my work this morning and hadn't realized I was singing. I'd been loud enough for Selina to hear, which meant I was loud enough for them to hear, too. If they didn't take me as punishment for breaking the only law they policed in the human lands, they'd take the newborn next door because I'd led them straight to him. The Wild Hunt stole newborns almost as often as they kidnapped adults.

No one in Holbeck expected them to pass us by tonight, though. Not after my singing and the recent birth of the baby just a few weeks ago. Tonight, there were too many reasons for them to stop.

Like the rest of the town, before darkness came tonight, I'd sprinkled a line of salt at both doors into our cottage and across all the windows. I flexed my grip on my bow, searching for the leader amongst the riders on horseback. If I found his heart with my arrow, we'd get a reprieve. They'd have to return to Faery to find a replacement, and with any luck, that replacement would be less intent on taking infants from their mother's arms. Or girls who sung by mistake.

Of course, if I missed, I'd likely end up a slave.

I readied my bow and gave a last glance over my shoulder at our cottage.

My heart stilled. The door was ajar.

In Mother's haste to hide—and probably because of the fog from her headache—she'd left our home open to the Wild Hunt. I glanced between the door and the hunters. Did I run to close it and hope they didn't see me, or did I trust my arrow would hit their leader before any of them reached my home?

It wasn't the loss of my own life or my possible Faerie enslavement that kept my feet planted on the ground. It was Tobias, the baby next door. That child had fought hard against the coughing sickness that almost stole him from his family. Now he was getting better, he deserved the chance at a normal life. If I didn't stop the hunters, they'd steal the child. Then again, if I didn't shut and bolt that door, they might steal Mother.

I cursed beneath my breath. No matter how much I wanted to keep Tobias safe, my first responsibility was to Mother, and she wasn't safe with that door open. I'd check she was hidden and make my stand from inside the house—we lived close enough to our neighbors that I could make a killing shot from our kitchen window.

Clutching my bow and one arrow in one hand and lifting my skirts in the other, I sprinted for the cottage. My hands were so slick with sweat, my arrow almost slid from my fingers. I gripped it tighter, my eyes on the cottage door.

The hound's barking grew frantic.

They'd seen me.

One of the hunters shouted a command, his voice a low growl above the din of the dogs. The air moved, and I knew without looking that the rest of the hunters were urging their horses to move faster. Now they had someone to chase, they wouldn't stop until the hunt was over.

My boots smacked against our dirt path. I was no longer worried about stealth, only speed. I could barely catch my breath and the running was only partially responsible. The hunter's voice had sent a jolt of terror through me that constricted my lungs.

The chase was on. For me.

The light from the moon disappeared as a cloud, or perhaps the hunters, drifted in front of it. It didn't matter. I'd lived in this cottage most of my life. I could find my way around these grounds in pitch darkness if I had to.

I risked a glance over my shoulder. The first of the hounds was on the ground now, close enough I could hear his claws scratching on the dirt path as he raced toward me. I leapt up the steps and sprinted through the back door, careful not to break the line of salt at the threshold—salt hadn't worked last time, but I wasn't too cynical to try again. "Mother. Hide and do not come out!" Wherever Mother was, she remained silent. I'd never been so grateful.

I grabbed the handle and pushed the door to shut it, just as a wild-eyed snarling hound stuck its head through the gap. Using my shoulder and all my weight, I leaned on the door, but the hound was stronger than me. It pushed back until the door was wide enough to sneak through the gap, where it stopped, nostrils flickering as it sniffed the air. The hound was even larger up close than it seemed in the sky, its back so tall I could ride it and not have my feet touch the ground.

Its cinnamon fur was wet around its gaping maw, showing off canines that could easily tear a chunk from my arm or leg. A low growl rumbled from the back of its throat as it took in the living area of our cottage.

I pressed my back against the wall, my breathing ragged while I fumbled with my bow. If I didn't shoot the hound, I'd have no chance of turning and making a killing shot out my kitchen window at its master as he came for the baby next door.

The hound bent into a crouch. Ready to attack.

With shaking hands, I fired off my shot.

The animal yelped, the arrow nicking its front leg. Blood blossomed, running in a thin line through its shaggy fur.

I pulled another arrow from my quiver. My heart pounded so loudly in my ears, I could no longer tell what was happening outside.

A noise in the door made me turn.

Upon the back of his black horse and unbothered by the salt sprinkled across the doorway that should have stopped him, Xion Starguard, the leader of the Wild Hunt, rode into our cottage.

TWO

XION STARGUARD was everything my nightmares were made of. Like the rest of the Wild Hunt, he wore a mask fitted so perfectly to his face it portrayed the facial expressions it should have hidden. Magic, no doubt. Xion's mask was a perpetually smiling skull, the openings for eyes, nostrils and mouth yawning pits of nothingness. His fae ears were long and pointed—the tips protruding from the long strands of his inky dark hair. He wore clothing of black, from the knee-high boots over his pants to the cloak thrown over his shoulders and a sword strapped to his waist.

I have no idea how he and his horse fitted through our door—probably magic—but he ducked low as he crossed the threshold, keeping his head bowed so as not to hit the ceiling once inside. He and his horse took up most of the space in our tiny cottage. I could touch his mount's nose if I took a step forward.

He met my eyes, and the mask creased into something disdainful. "Salt doesn't work." From upon his horse—its color so deep it could have disappeared into the night—his gaze fell on his barely injured hound. "How dare you!" His deep monotone boomed around our cottage, echoing and otherworldly, angrier now than it had been a moment ago.

I didn't care if he was upset about his dog. It wasn't dead, and his kind possessed healing magic that would have made my job as assistant town healer infinitely easier could I access it. I tried to nock my bow, my shaking hands making it impossible. At Xion's command, my slippery palms allowed the arrow to slide from my grip and float toward him. It stopped halfway between us and the point slowly turned until it angled back toward me. The threat was clear, and though I didn't know how he would make that arrow fly fast enough to hurt me without a bow, I had no doubt he could—and would. My imagination also suggested he'd likely have some fun hurting me first.

With nothing to lose, I met his eyes and drew another arrow from my quiver.

Xion raised one eyebrow, his question clear. *Was I certain I wanted to do that?* He slid from his horse, his feet making a hollow thud on our floor. His eyes never left me, and he waited.

Of course, I was certain. Certain I wanted to do everything I could to keep from dying or having him drag me to Faery as a slave. He didn't know much about humans if he thought his presence was enough to make us give up and give in. Or perhaps he did. Perhaps when faced with the leader of the Wild Hunt, most people did exactly that.

All these thoughts flew through my mind in less than a second as I again nocked an arrow, my hand suddenly steadier. I danced on my toes, ready to duck out of the way the moment the arrow he controlled began to fly.

As I pulled the string back, something moved behind Xion—Mother, sneaking out of her bedroom.

He must have seen my eyes move and turned just as Mother slammed a vase into his temple. The blow was hard enough to rock his head back. Tiny rivulets of blood flowed from somewhere in his hairline to make a slow trail down over the white surface of his mask.

I released my arrow. We had him. Between the two of us, we'd saved the baby and ourselves.

Before the arrow could reach his heart, a wind whipped up inside our home. Like a miniature tornado, it picked up our chairs and table, cutlery and plates from the bench, the candle and candle-holder. And my arrows. All of it whirled in a circle around the three of us and Xion's horse and hound—neither of whom seemed bothered in the least. A second later, a burst of blue light lit the cottage so brightly I had to close my eyes. By the time I opened them again, every piece of furniture we owned was flying toward Mother.

Like a doll in the ocean, she stumbled backward in the current of furniture. Xion sent a coffee table crashing into her skull, followed by a chair striking her leg, which hit with a sickening crack. She slammed into the wall and slid slowly down, the rest of the furniture stopping at her feet.

I thought she was dead, but she opened her eyes and, using her hand on the wall for balance, Mother dragged herself back up. She took a step around the furniture, pulled a long-bladed knife from her sleeve and lunged at Xion.

Before the knife could even scrape his skin, the room again exploded in bright blue light and Mother dropped like a stone, falling heavily onto the coffee table that had hit her head moments ago.

"No!" I reached for another arrow, but there were none left. I couldn't recall if I'd used them all, or if Xion Starguard had taken them from me as part of his living room tornado. It didn't matter. Mother was lying on the floor with blood dripping from her nose and her head lolled to one side. And there was an angry and powerful fae standing between us.

Outside, the hounds barked again, and hooves thundered across the ground. Xion's mount whinnied and stomped her feet. He glanced out the open back door, his lips tightening. The rest of the hunt—the ones who had come nowhere near me—were ready to move on. It was as if it called to him. To both of them.

With a curl of his lip, he scooped up his hound as if it were no bigger or heavier than a rat and hoisted himself up onto his mount.

A butter knife glinted on the ground in front of me. I lunged for it, wrapping my fingers tightly around the shaft.

Xion Starguard looked down at me in disgust. "Your mother will die for attacking me. Do you want the same fate, little human? Or do you prefer to return to Faery with me?"

I wanted not to react, but the menace in his voice made me step away, my back hitting the wall behind me. I shook my head. I didn't want to go to Faery, but I didn't want Mother to die, either. "Please," I whispered. "You can't let her..."

"It's already done. Think yourself lucky I don't drag her back to Faery with me. Had you not injured my hound, I could carry you instead of her." He glanced at the enormous dog laying across his lap.

"Then, I'm glad I did," I spat, braver now I was two steps farther from him. Losing one parent to Faery was bad enough. I wasn't losing the other that way.

The skeleton mouth on his mask fell open, before abruptly returning to that never ending smile. The leader of the Wild Hunt wasn't used to people standing up to him. A deep growl came from the back of his throat that made the hair on my arms stand up. "You are lucky, human, that it is only the child we require tonight, or I would have great pleasure in dragging you to Faery with us. You may not fare so well next time we meet." With another quick glance over his shoulder at Mother, he rode out the door.

My hands clenched, and I started after him as if I could keep up with his horse that was faster than the wind. He'd hurt Mother. He should pay.

"Bria." Mother's voice stopped me on the spot. Her eyes were closed, but her lips moved as she called my name. "Bria. It's okay. We're okay."

She was right. We were alive, and that was all that mattered. I ran to her, pushing the furniture aside and dropping to my knees beside her.

Outside, the sound creeping through our open doors and into my consciousness, my neighbors were keening. The baby was gone. I had stopped nothing. All I'd done was occupy the leader for a few minutes and injured Mother in the process.

"That was brave of you," whispered Mother.

I shook my head, my vision distorting as I thought of the baby. Selina would be devastated. So would her parents.

Mother's hand wrapped around mine, her grip stronger than I expected. "It's okay, Bria. I'm fine."

I blinked and inhaled a deep breath. She wasn't fine. Her leg was broken—I didn't know how she'd stood on it to attack Xion with the knife—she had a gash from her shoulder to her elbow, an open and bloody wound on her opposite bicep, and blood streaming from her nose. But she didn't seem to be dying, no matter what Xion Starguard had said.

I could heal those scrapes and bruises. I was good at that and it would give me something to focus on, other than the baby. "I need to make a splint for your leg. Then we'll get you into bed." Once she was comfortable, I'd take a lamp into the woods to search for some yellow vine and swamp petal for her other injuries.

Mother's head dropped back against the coffee table and she closed her eyes. "Thank you, Bria."

The sun was already rising by the time I returned from the woods with the herbs I needed for Mother's injuries and convinced her to take them. I lay down for a few minutes rest before starting on the chores for the day, which now included putting our cottage to rights after Xion Starguard's furniture tornado, only to be woken by the pounding of a fist on the door. I dragged myself from my bed, my eyes scratchy, to find Mrs. Plimmer and her young son on the threshold. They lived at the other end of town—the rich end, with the publicans and store owners. We only ever saw them down this way when they needed a healer. "Good morning, madam." I smiled, knowing it wouldn't be returned.

She looked past me into the cottage. "Get Aoife." Her voice was crisp, and she pronounced Mother's name O-fee.

"It's pronounced Ee-Faa, and my mother is unavailable today. Can I be of assistance?" I used

the same haughty tone, too tired to ignore her
rudeness the way I usually did. The entire village
spoke to me this way. They had all my life. Re-
calling Mother's wish that I overlook it, I plastered
a smile on my face. She was here for help.

The woman's eyes moved between me and the
mess our home was in. I pulled the door in behind
me to block her view. "What do you mean
unavailable? Aoife is never unavailable."

That wasn't entirely true. Mother often took
time out for herself, secure in the knowledge that
I could look after her patients just as well as she
could. It was just that usually she was available
to take over should someone as difficult as Mrs.
Plimmer call. "I'm afraid she is today." I glanced
at the little boy standing a step behind his mother.
There were tear stains on his cheeks and he held
his left arm pressed against his chest. "If you're
here about Jonty's arm, I can help you." I opened
the door for them to come in, wondering if they'd
believe the Wild Hunt had made the mess.
Though if the town gossip mill was working, they
likely already knew.

Mrs. Plimmer turned on her heel. "No
need. Jonty will be seen by a proper healer,
not some half breed trying to pretend
otherwise." There were no other healers in
Holbeck. Only Mother and me.

I smiled through gritted teeth, wishing the insult didn't hurt. I'd heard it so many times I should be used to it. Everyone in Holbeck knew Mother, and most of them remembered Father. No one actually believed I was part fae. They used those horrible words to comment on the deformity I'd had since birth that affected both my ears but not my hearing. The top half of each ear was folded in on itself, halving the length and making hard, fat, ugly rolls of the cartilage. My ears didn't look fae. But they didn't look human, either. Mother said people were wary of anything different, and I should be kind and never give them any reason to think I was something I wasn't.

I drew in a tight breath. "I'm just as human as you, Mrs. Plimmer. And Mother likely won't be available to see any patients for a few days, so if you don't want Jonty in unnecessary pain, bring him inside now." My words fell on her back as she walked down the front path. She wouldn't come inside. As she opened the front gate and stepped out onto the street, I called, "I'm available whenever Mother's busy, Mrs. Plimmer. Come back any time."

With a deep sigh, I dumped boiling water into the kitchen sink. In the week since Xion Starguard injured Mother, she'd come down with a fever that wouldn't break. The wound on her bicep was red and angry in a way I'd never seen before, and no matter which herbs I used, I couldn't heal the wound or bring down the fever. I'd tried everything, even purchasing a stick of begio root from a passing traveler, which cost more coin than we made in a month, but to no avail. I was almost out of options.

I eased my hands into the hot water, trying not to think about the wood that needed chopping, or the garden that needed tending, or the fact that in two days, we'd be out of meat and I'd have to go out hunting. Plus, Mother's patients needed to be seen.

But ignoring one thing led to thinking about another, and an image of Father flashed through my mind. I tried never to think of him, but since it was the Unseelie King's hunter's who'd taken his life, he hadn't been far from my mind since Xion Starguard rode his mount through our back door.

The hounds came first that night. Back then, I hadn't known they were the hounds of the Wild Hunt. I hadn't even known that the hounds warned us to get inside and lock the doors. Mother knew. She rushed me inside, screaming Father's name as she ran.

He was hunting in the woods behind our cottage and not yet home. We thought he must have made a big kill because he was late. He heard our shouts and yelled back, telling us to get inside and hide, that he was almost there. Mother and I crawled into the tiny space beneath the cottage—the dirt cold against my skin—and waited. She wrapped one arm around me and, with a finger to her lips, instructed me not to make a sound.

I was so scared. All I wanted to do was press my head against Mother's chest and have her wrap me in the safety of her arms, but terror held me still. I couldn't even squeeze my eyes shut.

Father's running footsteps were fast and heavy against our dirt path. The back door opened, then closed again, and I heard his heavy breathing. I remember letting out my breath and smiling at Mother. And wondering why she didn't smile back. Father was okay. He'd made it. Metal screeched on metal as he slipped the bolt into place, and I waited for him to lift the hatch hidden beneath the dining table and join us in our hiding place. Once Father was here, nothing would be scary anymore.

There was a tremendous crash as both the front and back doors shattered at the same moment. Mother and I jumped, and she placed a hand over my mouth in case I screamed. I didn't. Not because I was brave. Because I was so terrified that any sound I wanted to make died in my throat.

"Myles Ridgewing!" A loud and otherworldly voice boomed. "We've been searching for you."

"You've got the wrong person." Father's voice, though not as loud, was strong and sure. "There's no one here by that name."

I nodded, my blanket of fear lifting a little. It wasn't Father they were after. Yes, his name was Myles, but our family name was Tremaine. They had the wrong man.

The intruder made a noise I thought was supposed to be laughter, but sounded nothing like it. "And yet, you're the one for whom we search."

Father's feet sounded on the wooden floor. Just one single step. I imagined him moving forward, but in hindsight, and after facing Xion from the Wild Hunt, I'm sure he was stepping back. "I'll not go with you. Not alive, anyway."

Another laugh. "Dead it is, then. My instructions are to return you any way possible."

Father's footfall sounded again, another pace back.

"And Aoife. And—"

This time, it was Father who laughed. It was as hard as the laughter of the intruder, and a sound I'd never before heard from him. "Aoife died

years ago. But I'm sure you know that already."
That was a lie—Mother was still very much alive.
"And even if she hadn't, you have no jurisdiction
over either of us."

"Perhaps not. But I have orders. And you know
I always follow my orders. Come with us."

"Never."

There was movement in the room above, scraping and crashing like our furniture was being
tossed around the room. Wind passed through the
gaps in the floorboards and across my face, making me shiver. There was a thud. Then another.

I shifted, finding a gap in the floorboards to
peek through. Father lay curled in a ball on the
ground with not one, but five fae, standing in a
wide berth around his body.

I silently urged him to stand and fight back.
He was the strongest person I knew. He had to get
up.

With impossibly slow movements, he rolled
onto his back and opened his eyes. "Take me. Or
kill me. Just get it over with."

I shook my head. No. Neither of those were
options. He should fight. He should do everything
he could to stay with us. This wasn't how Father
behaved. He loved us. He'd do anything to be here.

Mother moved enough to catch my eye. She
put her finger to her lips. She was right, of course.

If I screamed at Father to fight back, we'd all die.

There was another thud, and I peeked through the gap to find Father on his knees with his arms up in front of him, palms out, as if that would stop the fae from attacking. None of the men around him moved, but Father's body convulsed. He fell backward, his head hitting the wooden floor with a horrible cracking sound. As I watched, he blew out a last breath of air.

I put my hand over my mouth to stop from crying out. Father was dead!

The leader laughed, like he enjoyed watching the life ebb from Father. "Bring him with us."

Footsteps crossed the floor of our cabin, boots echoing on the wood. A fae male, tall and gangly legged, bent and picked up Father's lifeless body, throwing it over one shoulder. As he bent, I glimpsed long black hair and a skeleton mask. The mask worn by the current leader of the Wild Hunt, Xion Starguard. To this day, I still despised what I thought next. I was only a child, but the way the muscles in his arms flexed mesmerized me. He was unnaturally graceful, his movements fluid in a way I'd never before seen. I couldn't look away and it made me sick.

I shook my head, pushing the memories away. When I let them take over like that—and I rarely did—I felt like I was eleven years old again and trapped beneath the cottage. A fine sweat broke out on my skin and anger pulsed through my veins. The Wild Hunt were murderers, but Father should have fought harder. Or fought at all. Then maybe he'd still be here. I'd faced Xion Starguard and lived. He might have too, had he tried.

I took some deep breaths to calm myself, my hands gripping the kitchen bench so tightly that my knuckles were white. One day, I'd pay the Wild Hunt back for the pain they'd caused my family. But first, I would make Mother well. And to do so, I'd use every weapon at my disposal.

"Bria?"

I looked up to find the back door cracked, and Selina's pale face watching me through the gap. She still looked dazed and broken—a week wasn't nearly long enough to get over losing the baby brother she'd wished for all her life. I'd apologized a million times, and every time she told me it wasn't my fault. She could tell me a million times more, and it still wouldn't ease my guilt. I would never utter another word in song again. I should never have done it that day.

"Are you all right, Bria? I knocked, but you must not have heard."

I sucked down a deep breath and nodded, offering my best friend a smile. The past week had been much worse for her than it had for me, but to fix any of it, I needed her help.

"Want to come outside with me?" She beckoned with her head.

"Of course." I smiled in her direction. We'd been there for each other for the past eleven years. My pile of dishes could wait a little longer.

I wiped my hands on a towel and followed her out to the twin swings in our shared backyard. Father had hung them from the oak between our cottages not long after Selina moved in when we were both six years old. The same oak I'd tried to hide beneath when the Wild Hunt came a week ago.

She sat in silence, as she did so often lately, the swing swaying softly around her planted feet, her long auburn hair falling over her shoulders.

"How are you doing?" I asked, spreading my dress around me as I sat. I needed to work up to asking for her help to save Mother's life, which felt cruel since she was still dealing with her brother's death.

She lifted a shoulder, tears pooling on her lashes. I already knew she didn't want to talk about herself. She'd come to me for distraction. "How's Aoife today?" Not that talking about Mother would distract her much.

I shook my head. "No better." She was worse than she'd been the day after it happened. Worse than yesterday, even. I took a deep breath, crossing my fingers like a child and hoping I could count on Selina. "I need to go to Faery."

Selina's watery eyes widened. She shook her head. "Bria, no! You can't."

Human's who went to Faery most often never returned. The magic of the land made them forget where they came from and made them a perfect target for the High Fae that ruled the magical realm to take them as slaves.

I took a deep breath. I'd thought of all the reasons not to do this, but I always came back to one thing. I was a human healer—and a beginner, at that. My skills were good, but I was no match for fae magic. If I wanted Mother to live, I had to reach out to those who had other—better—methods of healing. "I have to go. Magic made that wound on her arm, and probably the fever, and the same magic is preventing her from getting better."

Selina shook her head again. More slowly this time. She knew me well enough to realize this wasn't a spur-of-the-moment decision. It didn't mean she wouldn't attempt to talk me out of it. "True, but at what price?"

I leaned forward, catching her eye. "Does it matter? What would you give to get Tobias back?

What would you give for the Wild Hunt never to have taken him?"

"Everything. Anything." Selina let out a deep sigh and ran her hands down her face. "But if Mother's magic couldn't keep Tobias safe, what chance do you have against the Unseelie King?"

Little, probably. And when Selina put it like that, I began to doubt the sense of my plan. Selina's mother was one-sixteenth fae. Her great-great-grandmother had been fae, sent to live in exile in the human world. The family had no contacts in Faery, and Selina's mother had only just enough magic to hide her children if the Wild Hunt came calling—at least, she thought she had. Last week had proven otherwise. Selina, to her disappointment, had received none of that magic passed through the family line.

Still, maybe there was hope. Maybe I had a weapon the Unseelie King would never suspect. "What if the king didn't recognize me as human?"

Selina stopped swinging, her eyes narrowing. "You have a plan." Somehow, she laced both hope and despair into those few words.

I nodded, twisting the swing to face her. I was almost smiling, relieved to talk about this the plan that had been forming in my mind all week. Hopefully the two of us could iron out any bumps I might not have considered. And there was always the slight chance I might even have time to search for Tobias while I was in Faery. I reached into the pocket of my white apron and pulled out an envelope, passing it to Selina.

She stared at the thick textured paper a moment before taking it in her hand and running her fingers over the gold embossed letters on the front.

Briony

25 Hardbrook Lane

Holbeck

The envelope was unopened, but we both knew what it contained. The same envelope had been arriving for years, always five days before All Hallows Eve. It was addressed to the previous owner of our cottage using only her first name. Briony No-Last-Name had left no forwarding address. Every year, Mother threw the letter in the bin the day it arrived. Every year, I asked her about it and she told me she didn't know how to forward it on.

Two years ago, filled with curiosity, I took the letter from the bin and brought it out to the swings beneath the oak where Selina and I sat now, and we opened it together. The card inside had been just as glamorous as the envelope that carried it, with a flowing script embossed in gold.

> *By decree of the Unseelie King,*
> *you are invited to the*
> *Masquerade Ball*
> *All Hallows Eve*
> *at the Unseelie Court*
> *Dress Formal*

The Unseelie King's masquerade ball was the party everyone wanted to go to. The guests were fae from the three Unseelie Courts that he ruled over—Winter, Autumn, and Darkness. Each year, he granted one favor to a person picked at random from his guests on All Hallows Eve. Two years ago, Selina and I had stared at the card with open mouths, before stuffing it back inside the envelope, pushing down the seal and running inside to throw it back into the rubbish bin I'd rescued it from. Neither of us had ever spoken another word about it. Until now, when I was holding this year's invitation in my hand.

"But the ball is tonight." She stared at the unopened envelope between her fingers, her voice uncertain.

I nodded, trying to look confident. If Selina believed I thought I could do this, there was more chance she'd agree to help.

"And you will pretend you're Briony No-Last-Name." It wasn't a question. One look at the envelope and Selina knew what I was planning.

"He'll know you're not her. You don't even know if you resemble her." She shook her head, her lips pressing into a thin line. At least she'd forgotten about Tobias for the moment. "This is a bad idea."

"Would it still be a bad idea if I could bring Tobias home when I came back?" Low blow, but I really needed her help. There were things only she could offer which would give me a better chance of succeeding.

Selina drew in a breath, her eyes again turning glassy. She shook her head. "I want him back more than anything. But I don't want to lose you as well. I can't." She reached for my hand.

I gave her a weak smile. "At least it's not in Seelie, right?" I wouldn't even be considering this if the masquerade was in Seelie—the other kingdom of Faery. The Seelie Queen didn't tolerate humans. Those who made it all the way across the Unseelie Kingdom to her border were killed on sight. The Unseelie King was cruel and cunning, but the Seelie Queen was a tyrant. There was no way I'd ever willingly walk into that part of Faery.

Selina nodded. "Right."

"Does that mean you'll help me?" It didn't. But we could go around in circles talking about this, and I wasn't changing my mind. Getting the king to grant me a favor was my best chance at saving Mother.

Without removing her eyes from the envelope and with a sigh in her voice, she asked, "What do you need?"

I licked my lips, unsure if our strong friendship went as far as I was about to ask. "A dress." I swallowed before elaborating. "One of the fae dresses that used to belong to your however-many-times-great-grandmother." Selina's mother had an entire wardrobe filled with fae dresses she'd never worn but refused to throw out. I understood her not wanting to get rid of them— they were stunning dresses worn for only the most formal of occasions. Occasions that never happened in Holbeck.

Selina smiled—weak and watery, but the first I'd seen from her in a week. "I was hoping you'd say that." She stood and took my hand. "Come. Before Mother arrives home from work."

THREE

THE DRESS we chose was pale blue and strapless. Diamantes sparkled around the top of the fitted bodice and at the waistline before giving way to three layers of tulle, each a slightly darker shade of blue. Selina's mother's collection also contained several masks, including a silver one with feathers on one side in the same blue hues as the dress. And to top it off, Selina found a set of diamante hoop earrings for my ears.

I had no suitable shoes, so Selina loaned me a pair of hers that were beautiful, strappy and silver. I was half a size bigger than her, but since both our feet were tiny, these were the best I could hope for.

I sat at Selina's mother's vanity table, watching my image in the mirror while Selina pulled my hair from my face to pile it on top of my head in an updo that would mark me as human as plainly as if I'd carried a sign stating the fact. "You can't do my hair like that. Bring it down. Over my ears."

Selina tutted under her breath. "You're much too sensitive about your ears. No one will care what they look like."

Untrue. And doubly so given what I was planning. "Except if I'm walking into the court of the King of the Unseelie fae." They would definitely notice my ears.

Selina's cheeks reddened. "Oh. Of course. I just meant..."

I knew what she meant. We'd had this conversation before. I always wore my hair pulled into a low ponytail at the back of my neck, covering my ears and secured by a clip Mother and Father gave me when I was a child. I'd learned early in life that because we lived in fear of the pointed-eared fae, anyone who looked neither fae nor human was not to be trusted.

Selina lived in hope that would change for me one day. She was one of the few people who didn't care how I looked. I smiled at her reflection in the mirror. "I know. But for tonight, they remain hidden." I swallowed. This was the perfect moment to bring up the other thing I wanted to say. "There was something else in the envelope that first time we opened it." I wasn't sure if Selina ever saw the extra gift inside, but I'd spent two years wondering what the two tiny flesh-colored triangles were and always came up with the same answer.

I leaned forward and scooped up the envelope, opened the seal and tipped the triangles out onto my hand. "Any idea what these are?"

Selina frowned at me in the mirror, pulling a portion of my hair up onto my head and fastening it with pins she had clasped between her lips. She lifted one shoulder, speaking around a pin. "Do you?"

I licked my lips, aware of how this sounded. "Ear tips. To make human ears look like fae ears."

Selina's mouth popped open, the pin dropping onto the wooden floor with a ping. She withdrew her hands from my hair and moved until she was looking directly at me rather than at my reflection. "What?"

"Think about it. Would the king send an invitation year after year to a person who never replies? Or would he stop the first time they snubbed him? Or maybe he'd march right up to Briony No-Last-Name's cottage and ask her directly why she refused to attend his ball, then drag her back to Faery and punish her for not bowing and scraping the way he expects." I shook my head. "What if the invitation didn't come from the king? What if it comes from Briony No-Last-Name's husband or lover who was stolen away to Faery by the Wild Hunt as a slave?"

Selina's eyes narrowed. "A slave will hardly be able to get hold of one of the king's personal invitations."

I had considered that. "Maybe he is a slave, but he's been there so long he's proven his loyalty and he can get his hands on exactly that. Maybe he knows someone who could help disguise his lover so he can spend a single night with her. We have lived in this house for sixteen years. Her lover must have been in Faery all that time, or he'd know she was no longer here." I held the tiny triangles up in front of Selina's face. "What if these are to disguise human ears?"

Selina screwed up her face. "Ew. That's revolting."

"Is it? I thought you'd see it as romantic. The lengths he's gone to just to see his lover again." Selina loved a romantic story, and in my head, I'd thought this was one.

"Not that part, the fake ear part."

I had slight misgivings about that. Apart from the ickiness of looking like one of them even for a short time, I had no idea where these came from or if the magic within them should be trusted—if they even contained magic.

But the benefits of possible fae ears for tonight far outweighed every one of my misgivings. "It'll be fine." I raised one tip to my ear.

Selina stopped me with a hand on my arm. "What if you can't take them off?"

I added that to the list of things that could go wrong, though it still wasn't enough to dissuade me. If I ended up with fae ears for the rest of my life, it was a small price to pay to get the king's favor and make Mother well again. "I'll deal with it if it happens."

"I don't like this." Selina shook her head, her lips drawing together into a thin, tight line.

"Your displeasure is noted." I raised one of the tips to my right ear and rested it on top, holding my breath as I waited.

Nothing happened.

Selina smiled, the air coming from her lungs in a whoosh. "Not ears, then."

My shoulders fell and I nodded, not yet willing to remove the triangle. If they'd been ears, tonight would have been so much easier, but it didn't matter. It didn't matter because I was going anyway, ears or not. I needed that medicine for Mother.

A sharp burning pain ripped across the top of my ear.

"Bria!" Selina crouched beside where I lay on the floor—I didn't even remember falling down. "Are you all right?" Her eyes roved over my face. "Oh, stars. Your ear. It's..."

"What...?" I took her hand and pulled myself up to sit.

"Umm..." She pointed at the mirror, helping me back into the chair in front of it.

The burning had already subsided, leaving nothing but the echo of pain. I glanced in the mirror and gasped. It had worked. The tip had attached the way I hoped it might and for the first time in my life, my ear wasn't deformed. Sure, it now looked fae, but not in the huge pointed way of the wild hunters. The top of my ear was small, pointed delicately at the end. I turned my head, looking from every angle. I'd expected them to look as ugly as my normal ears, but they were beautiful. They were no longer deformed. "I can't even see where it joins."

Selina's face appeared beside mine in the mirror. Her forehead creased in a frown. "Can you get it off?" She swallowed hard, trying not to show how much my pointed ear disgusted her. And failed.

I nodded, though I wasn't sure. Why would I take it off? It looked wonderful. "Hand me the other one."

I braced for the burning pain as magic fitted the fake ear tip to mine. Even knowing it was coming, it stole my breath, but this time I remained on my feet. The second ear fitted every bit as well as the first. I couldn't stop admiring them in the mirror, I was so grateful to look normal. Or normal-ish.

Selina dropped a deep blue gem on the vanity where it landed in front of me with a clatter.

I twisted to look at her. "Is that a time gem? Where did you get it?"

Selina put a finger to her lips even though no one else was home. "It's Mother's. You can't go into Faery without it. You won't know when to leave, you'll end up confused and you'll be easy pickings for the fae to trap you there."

A human could last about five hours on their own in Faery before they lost all track of who they were and where they'd come from. There was no way I needed five hours to gain the king's favor. And even less chance I was taking something as valuable as a time gem with me, no matter how good it would be to have a warning when it was time to leave Faery. "That's very generous, but—"

"Take it. Or I'll tell Mother what you're planning." She tilted her head to one side and crossed her arms over her chest. When Selina made up her mind about something, there was little chance I could dissuade her.

"What if something goes wrong and I can't come back?" The time gem was probably the most valuable thing Selina's family owned. "Your gem will be gone, too. You'd have no way to—"

Selina picked up the gem and placed it in my hand, closing my fingers around it. "If that happens, then I'll be certain we did everything possible to get you out of there. I won't have to sit here and look at that thing and wish I'd given it to you." She shrugged. "And Mother will be mad at first, but I know she will agree with me."

I looked at it in my hand, then slipped it into the pocket in the folds of my dress. Selina was right. The gem would make tonight's mission so much safer. I hugged her. "Thank you."

Selina brushed me off and picked up her comb and hair pins. "You might see Prince Fergus tonight. In the flesh."

I looked down at my hands to hide my distaste. Prince Fergus Blackwood might be the only person in both worlds who didn't differentiate between humans and fae. He took anyone as a lover—and usually took a different lover every night. The women he chose wore his favor as a badge of honor.

In the coming weeks and prior to his nineteenth birthday, the prince was expected to announce his engagement at the first in a long line of ceremonies to prepare for his coronation—which was likely years away—though as far as anyone was aware, he had not yet found his princess. Selina wasn't the only person who secretly—or not so secretly—wished to be the girl the prince chose. "I'll be sure to keep my distance."

A wry smile rose on her face. "You say that now, but I bet you'd change your mind if you met him. I hear he's very charming. And rumor says he's good looking, too." She clipped another piece of hair in place and then stood back and surveyed me in the mirror. "I think you just might pass as one of them."

The trail through the woods that would lead me to Faery was well worn, even though those from Holbeck rarely walked it. Ours was the closest village to the only entry point to the kingdoms of Faery, and the villagers of Holbeck knew better than anyone the dangers of crossing it. Every year, hundreds of people spent the last of their human coin in our town on the night before they crossed to Faery, where they hoped to make their fortune.

Most were never seen again. Occasionally we heard they'd become slaves.

I always wondered why no one attempted to talk them out of going. Tonight though, I understood. Tonight, I was willing to risk all I had because the fae had something I couldn't get anywhere else.

Babbling water soon reached my ears, slightly louder than the soft whoosh of wind through the trees. The brook meant I was close, and I stopped to tie on my mask. Somewhere near the river was a fae guard, and behind him, the gates to Faery. Mother had told me once that the Crossing wasn't obvious. That is to say, there was nothing marking the entrance to Faery. The guard was more obvious—but only when he wasn't hiding himself on the Faery side of the border. He was, however, picky about who he allowed through.

I wasn't worried. I was dressed for the masquerade and had an invitation in my hand.

Until I reached the brook and discovered there was a long winding queue standing between me and the Crossing.

The Unseelie King's All Hallows Eve masquerade wasn't a secret, but I'd never realized how popular it was among humans, each of us wanting something only the Unseelie King could give.

The queue was close to a hundred people. Every person—male and female alike—was dressed as elegantly as me; gowns of every color, long and flowing. Suits in blacks and greys, with colorful bow ties. All had walked to reach this place in the woods, and every person wore a mask covering their face.

I nodded to the woman in front of me and settled in to wait as raised voices from the front of the queue reached me. Two females were arguing with the fae guard, their arms making wide gestures as they fought to make their point. I strained my neck to watch.

"We were invited!" the taller of the two insisted. She was wrapped in layers of red fabric, her wide skirts swishing each time she moved. A leaf had caught on the bottom hem and followed her movements. "The crown prince personally asked us to attend."

The fae guard looked down his nose. "Then the prince would also have given you a written invitation. Without that, you may not enter." His gaze shifted to the person behind them, a woman on her own. "Next."

The two at the front planted their feet. "We have to get in there." These were the first words the other woman had spoken. Her lilac dress was understated compared to her friend's. Strapless and fitting, it fishtailed from the knee.

The woman in front of me turned with a wry smile and I realized she was less a woman and more a girl. Perhaps around my age. And fae. What had she been doing on this side of the Crossing? "Someone seems desperate." Her golden hair was half piled on her head, half curled down her back. Between her locks, the pointed tips of her ears jutted. Her yellow gown hugged her figure, drawing the eye to a body most women would be jealous of. Despite those pointed ears, her blue eyes behind her mask were friendly.

I nodded, knowing I'd beg in the same manner to get through those gates if I had to. "There must be something she wants desperately."

The girl lifted one eyebrow. "A husband?"

There was something to her tone that told me I was missing something. "She plans to ask the king to find her a husband?" I wasn't in a position to judge someone else's wish, but it wasn't something I'd ever ask the Unseelie King for. A fae husband? No way.

The girl laughed, then frowned. "You're serious? You don't know why all these women are here tonight?"

"To ask the king to grant them a favor?"

She shook her head. "The king has instructed Crown Prince Fergus to find a bride. He has until Winter Solstice Eve to name her or the king will find someone for him. Tonight is one of the last formal opportunities for women to put themselves in the prince's path. Of course, I'm sure there will be plenty more informal chances." She sniggered. "But in the meantime..." Her eyes rolled along the line ahead of us.

"Everyone here is hoping to be that person?" I was shocked. I knew others dreamed of this, but I'd never imagined so many would actively chase it down. "Prince Fergus doesn't want a human bride." At least, I assumed he didn't. Tolerating humans in his bed was one thing, but marrying one was surely quite another.

The girl's look was conspiratorial as the guard moved aside and let the two women at the front of the line through, sans invitation. "You and I know that. The humans don't. They think they're heading for a life of riches and privilege." She laughed, and it was neither a joyful sound nor kind.

It took me a moment to realize she was speaking to me as if I was one of her own. Fae. The disguise was working. But my momentary happiness was tainted by the knot that formed in my gut as the two human women sauntered through the invisible gates and out of sight. "They will make them slaves?"

The girl shrugged. "Happens every year to some degree. There are more of them this year because they all believe they have that special thing the prince wants. How long have you been away?" She changed topics without stopping for a breath.

I sighed, perhaps a little dramatically, hoping my answer was enough to keep her from asking unwanted questions. "Too long. And not long enough."

A sad smile crossed the girl's lips as she turned away. "I wish I could be gone *too long*."

Apart from the row of stone markers that ran from the babbling brook all the way east to the ocean, the border with Faery was unremarkable. The Crossing was marked by two large trees between which one had to walk to move between the lands. There might have only been stone markers along the border, but the invisible wall ensured no one—human or fae—could travel across it at any place except The Crossing.

The Guard checking our invitations was always here, but not always visible. Mother said he had a hut on the other side of the border where he sat and waited for people to cross.

The wait to reach the front of the line seemed unfathomably long. Each person or couple went through the same charade as the first, using some new excuse where their missing invitation might be before the guard finally relented and let them through. I hoped the prince offered his hand in marriage to one of them. I hated seeing so many walk willingly toward such a horrible fate.

By the time I was almost at the front, I realized there were only two of us with an actual invitation. The guard's eyebrows lifted when the girl in front of me produced hers, and again when I showed him mine.

To reach the kingdom of Seelie, it was a hard left turn at the Crossing. Unseelie was any other direction. I wasn't certain, but it seemed as if the guard pointed the two of us with invitations in a different direction than he had for everyone else.

I knew the moment I'd crossed into Faery for I was no longer in the woods, but in a stone-walled tunnel.

The girl in yellow was already gone and the tunnel was empty by the time the guard allowed me through, but there was only one way to go, so I followed along, trying not to think about all the humans who'd come before me. And definitely not thinking about what might happen should anyone see through my disguise.

The tunnel smelled musty and was lit by lanterns hanging high on the walls. They didn't flicker, not even as I passed directly beneath them—my shoes slipping on the smooth dirt floor—and I could only assume the light they cast was powered by fae magic. The stone walls were covered in bright green moss, and through the high ceiling vines—or perhaps roots—grew. The roots reached out, trying to twist themselves around me. I stifled a cry and ducked around them, my pace slowing as I scanned the tunnel to make sure I didn't walk into one unnoticed. I could only imagine what they'd do if they caught me.

Music played in the distance. The sound made me stop, and I closed my eyes to listen for a moment. Nowhere in the human realm of Iadrun were we allowed to listen to music, though I'd been lucky enough to hear once in my life. Then, like now, I'd listened with closed eyes and a full heart. Music lightened my soul in a way nothing else could. That it was outlawed by the fae just gave me another reason to dislike them.

My hand brushed the time gem—the keeper of time that would remind me to leave Faery—in my pocket and my eyes flew open. I had a limited period to get this done. There was no time for standing around listening to anything.

I rounded a bend and the tunnel opened, filling with bright light, and I found myself on the edge of the ballroom. I'd thought I was far underground, but above the brightly lit dance floor was a ceiling made entirely of glass through which thousands of stars shone—more stars than I'd ever seen in the sky, and so bright. Where the ceiling wasn't made of glass, strings of lights dangled, swaying gently on some unseen breeze. At the other end of the room, standing on a low stage, a group of fae made music from instruments I'd only read about in books—violins, violas and a pianoforte—while couples danced elaborate moves, all in time with each other. Closer to this end of the room tables were piled high with food, and many fae stood nearby with plates and napkins brimming over. The room ended in a mezzanine that looked out over many more people dancing and eating below.

To my right, the king perched on his throne upon a dais raised high enough that he could look out over top of every head. Beside him sat a young woman, her gown made of pale white beads—a dress so stunning, it put my exquisite outfit to shame.

I'd imagined a long line in front of the king as he listened to everyone's request, before deciding which favor to grant, but there was no one else around him. I drew in a deep breath. I didn't mind going first.

A human girl dressed in nothing but two flimsy scraps of material—one tied at her waist and the other tied over one shoulder—walked up to me with a tray of drinks in her hand. As I tried to work out if she was here willingly, or if she was a slave, she smiled. "What's your poison, lady? We have every drink you ever imagined."

I shook my head glancing at the glasses on her tray, every color under the sun—bright green, turquoise, red, and even one that was yellow and orange with steam coming from the top—while I wondered again if she was here against her will. By her tone, it didn't seem so, but it was hard to tell.

She lifted her tray in front of my eyes and I shook my head. Everyone knew a human should never accept a drink while in Faery in case it was enchanted with fae magic which would steal your senses. "I just had one." I smiled.

"Let me know when you're ready for another." She was already walking away as she spoke, heading for two fae men standing a few steps in front of me and looking over the dance floor. "What's your poison?"

Both men turned to face her, their eyes making slow paths down her body. One said something too low for me to hear, and both of them broke into bawdy laughter.

The human girl shifted uncomfortably. "What's your poison?"

The man closest to me licked his lips, his eyes on her chest. "I'd quite like a piece of you. What do you say? Shall we find a dark corner?"

The girl smiled, but there was fear in her eyes. "I'm sorry, lord, but I must work tonight."

His eyes remained on her chest as he spoke, making me feel uncomfortable. "I'm sure you won't be missed. We won't be long." He nudged his friend, and they both laughed.

"I'm sorry, lord, I can't." She turned, starting toward another group of guests. The girl wasn't sorry, anyone could see it. She was terrified of being made to do something she didn't want.

The man followed her, reaching out and pulling the ties of the cloth at her shoulder. Her hand flew up to stop the material falling, while the other hand wobbled, trying to keep the drinks stable on the tray. The man's nostrils flared, and he spoke in a low voice. "Drop your hand."

She lifted her chin and shook her head.

Whether in Faery or in Iadrun, this wasn't okay. I stepped between them, looking at the girl and hoping my voice didn't shake. "Ah, there you are, Daisy. My guests have arrived and are awaiting your service."

The girl bobbed her head, gratitude filling her eyes. She turned to leave, but the man moved in front of her. He looked at me. "I'll thank you to keep out of this, unless you want to take her place in that dark corner?" His eyes raked down my body.

My hands shook, but I clasped them behind my back, refusing to let him see how a glance at his pointed ears terrified me. I'd dealt with bullies before and I knew that was exactly what he wanted. "I'll go nowhere with you. Daisy, my guests." I hoped I sounded authoritative. I'd never demanded anyone do anything in such a manner, but damned if I was letting this creature drag the girl away against her will.

"Keep out of my business." He spoke through gritted teeth. With a glance at the girl, he said, "Drop your hand." When she didn't, he reached out and poured his drink over her head.

As she jerked away from the flow of the liquid, one glass on her tray wobbled and then fell, knocking into the glass beside it and toppling so the entire tray smashed on the floor.

"You little tart! You did that on purpose! It's all over me." The man had two splashes of turquoise liquid on one shoe, nothing else. His cheeks turned a mottled red, and I had the feeling this would not end well for the girl. As I tried to come up with a way to fix the situation, another man arrived. He moved so smoothly, he could have been floating. I wasn't convinced he wasn't. His face was hard, and he stared at the mess on the floor with disgust. Then his cold eyes rose slowly to land on me.

FOUR

I COULDN'T breathe. Could barely think. The man was staring at me. Did that mean he knew I shouldn't be here?

The man's dark hair was smoothed and braided, proudly showing off the long and pointed ears that sent shivers along my spine. He was dressed all in black—waistcoat, pants and shirt— the only splashes of color being the aqua bowtie at his neck and the gold rings adorning his fingers. It was difficult to tell his age beneath his black mask. He seemed about my age, yet carried himself with the confidence of someone much older.

"Get out of here," he said. He didn't need to ask me twice. With a glance at the girl, we made a quick retreat.

The man in black moved his attention to the girl's attacker. He threw an arm around the other man's shoulders. "Theo! Is that you? I can't believe it!"

Theo stopped mid-rant and turned to Dark Hair. He blinked. Even beneath his mask, I saw it. I should have moved farther away, but I was glued to the spot, watching. "L-lord," stammered Theo. "It's been a long time." The last syllable raised slightly. Not quite a question. "When did I see you last?"

"No, no." Dark Hair guided Theo away from the girl. "I don't want to talk about me. Tell me what you've been up to."

"Where to start. There's so much to say." Theo grinned at Dark Hair, letting himself, and his friend, be guided away.

I released my breath. The girl was safe from his unwanted advances. For now, at least. I turned to find her picking up her tray. The smashed glass and ruined drinks that were spread around her feet moments ago had disappeared. Care of Dark Hair, I guessed. "Thank you," she whispered, rushing away to collect more drinks.

I scanned the ballroom one last time, working up the nerve to approach the king. My eyes fell on the man that must be Prince Fergus. He stood across the room, near the orchestra. Like the rest of the guests, he wore a mask covering half his face, but it was pointless when he also wore a circlet on his head proclaiming his royal status. His suit was navy blue, his tie a brilliant magenta, and his black mask looked like a wolf. He cut a striking figure. If looks alone were enough to choose a husband, then the girls in the queue into Faery had the right idea.

He seemed to enjoy the attention he was receiving tonight. No surprises there. Everything I'd ever heard suggested he loved the limelight, and there was plenty of that tonight. Pressed tightly around him was a circle of women—and a few men—five deep. He laughed and talked with many of them, turning on the spot as someone else caught his attention. I didn't imagine he'd take well to marriage, not after having the freedom to do as he liked all his life.

I drew in my breath. The king. That was why I was here, and time was ticking. I had to leave when the gem in my pocket vibrated, if I wanted to get out of here with my senses intact.

I started toward the only person who might save Mother, my heart almost beating out of my chest. I'd grown up on stories of the cruelty of this man. He didn't look nasty. He looked bored, lonely and old.

I approached the king from his left, but he wasn't looking my way. His eyes narrowed as he stared across the ballroom and it might have been my imagination, but it seemed as if the thousands of lights above flickered with his movement. He clicked his fingers, and a guard appeared from somewhere behind him. The king spoke a few words in his ear and the guard marched into the middle of the dance floor where he tapped on the shoulder of a blond-haired fae man in a black tuxedo and a pink, bird-like mask. The fae smiled and followed the guard back to the king. Almost everyone in the room watched while trying to appear like they were doing anything but.

"Your name?" The orchestra quieted enough to hear the king's voice above their sound.

"Cymon." There was a wobble in the fae's voice. I wondered if he'd done something he shouldn't have or if he was just terrified to speak to the king.

The king gave a slow nod. "Cymon. And why are you here tonight?" His voice was soft, cajoling and sweet.

"To enjoy this splendid party. At your request, of course." The wobble was there again.

Another nod from the king. "May I see it?" The king's voice lowered a level, and it seemed as if the entire room leaned closer to hear what he said next.

Cymon's head tilted. "See it, your Highness?"

Another nod. "Yes. My invitation."

Cymon patted his pockets, and I suddenly understood why the guard at the entrance to Faery had asked to see the invitations. Why he'd returned mine to me after a quick glance at it. "I ... ah ... I seem to have misplaced it." There was no hiding the quiver in Cymon's voice this time.

"Misplaced it?" The king's voice was lower than a whisper, danger falling from every syllable. "How is that possible?"

Cymon shook his head so fast I thought his brightly colored mask might fly off. "I don't know, your Highness. I'll find it, though. If you would allow me to look?"

The king's eyes rolled over Cymon and he gave another nod. I thought he would allow the fae to hunt for his invitation.

Cymon must have, too, because his shoulders loosened, and he took a step back.

Faster than I could see, the king gave a flick of his wrist. Invisible hands clamped around Cymon's ankles, picking him up and dragging him, upside down, across the room, to hang him over the edge of the mezzanine, meters from where I stood.

Cymon screamed. "Please, I'll find it. I'm meant to be here. You'll see." He wriggled in the invisible grasp, unable to free himself.

I glanced at the crowd, searching for someone who might help the careless fae. The woman he'd been dancing with had tears running down her cheeks, but most everyone else looked on in scarcely hidden glee.

"I do see. But rules are rules. If you can't find your invitation, then you're no better than the rabble who come here from the other side of the border. And since you're no better than them, you can go play with them." With a blink, whatever magic gripping Cymon's ankles, released. There was dead silence in the ballroom, even the orchestra stopped. At the wet sound of Cymon's body hitting the ground far below, the crowd cheered.

The king almost smiled, and, as if signaled to do so, the orchestra again began to play.

I stared at the crowd, then gave a quick look at the king, my heart hammering in my chest, and my legs weak. The king had killed that fae without breaking a sweat. Without even leaving his throne.

I wouldn't let it bother me. I was here for a reason, and this might be my moment. I should walk up to him now, tell him what I wanted. I should do it while he was still thinking about the fae who'd crashed his party without an invitation. Maybe, with his mind on something else, he'd be more likely to agree to help me.

With a deep breath, I started around the edge of the crowd. The weight of the king's gaze fell heavily upon me. Those eyes, ice blue and cold, were enough to make me want to turn tail and run. I wouldn't though. This was about Mother, not me.

The words I wanted to say ran through my head as I walked. I'd have no time for stammering or stuttering. I imagined such a thing would get me the same treatment Cymon had faced. I had to say what I wanted as fast as I could, before he had the opportunity to cut me off.

I forced a smile onto my lips. "Good evening, your Highness. And what a lovely evening it is."

The king looked me over and gave a slow blink. A bead of sweat ran down my back and my palms were clammy. He might dismiss me here and now, and that would be my chance ruined. "Indeed."

I blew out a sharp breath of relief. He hadn't sent me away or picked me up by the ankles. I wasn't sure if it was my imagination, but it seemed as if the lights brightened and the chatter in the room diminished as I greeted the king. As if the entire ballroom were leaning forward and listening to this conversation. "You are looking particularly dashing tonight, your Highness." I didn't think he was dashing at all. Not up close. He had the sharp features all fae seemed to share, but his age made them more pronounced. His high cheek bones gave his cheeks a sunken look, and his jaw was too defined to be beautiful. The pointed ears protruding between strands of grey hair were the longest I'd seen, and I couldn't let my gaze linger on them lest he see how terrified the sight made me. His cold eyes combined with the scar on his right cheek added up to someone I'd prefer never to look at. I just hoped the king didn't divine that from my words.

The king inclined his head, his eyes crawling over my face.

"There you are." The voice came from behind. Someone stopped beside my right elbow and wrapped a firm hand around it. I turned to find Dark Hair, grinning down at me with friendly eyes and a perfect smile, as though we'd known each other for years. "Have you eaten?"

I tried to pull away from him, keeping my movements discreet. I had no intention of making a scene. When he wouldn't release me, I smiled politely. "I have eaten, thank you. I'm just about to—"

The king reclined on his throne, his eyes swinging from me to Dark Hair. "Go to the dance floor?" Dark Hair used my elbow to turn me away from the king before guiding me through the crowd of dancing fae. His fingers dug into my arm, the pain making my breath hiss.

"Let go of me," I whispered, pulling at my arm again. "I don't want to dance."

He turned on that beaming smile. "Of course you do. Everyone wants to dance at the masquerade ball. It's the entire reason we attend."

I gave a quick yank on my arm and pulled free. "Not me. I have other things to do." I turned back toward the king. We were already in the center of the crowded dance floor, and leaving wasn't as easy as he'd made getting here seem. I elbowed my way through the throng and had almost reached the edge when Dark Hair stepped in front of me.

"Do you have a death wish, lady?" His body blocked all chance I had of seeing the king and knowing whether he was watching in horror, or if he hadn't given us another thought since we walked away.

"No. I have a favor to ask the king."

The man's lips pressed tightly together, their fullness momentarily disappearing. "That's what I mean. It's a death wish to ask the king a favor tonight."

"But…" I shook my head, my brow furrowing. That wasn't what all the stories said. Tonight was the one night he granted favors. Tonight was the only night he might save Mother. "That can't be true." My tone was far from convincing.

"Can't it?" He took my arm, leading me between dancers, to the mezzanine side of the room where tables and chairs were set up and fae sat talking, laughing and drinking. He guided me to the balustrade, which he leaned casually upon, looking out at the sea of people below. Cymon's body was already gone, the mess cleaned up. Guests again danced as if nothing horrifying had happened.

I shook my head. I wasn't in the mood for dancing, or watching others dance, or whatever this fae wanted from me. Before I could walk away, his hand was on my back, forcing me to stay beside him. He turned me around until I looked out over the people dancing below. "Look. Then look again."

My heart was racing. I didn't know what game he was playing, I just knew I needed to be anywhere but right beside him. I needed time alone to assess my next move. As I searched for a way to take my leave, my eyes landed on a red dress in the middle of the dance floor below. And a pale lilac dress beside it. The girls from the front of the line.

For half a second, I was relieved for them and the knot in my stomach loosened. The girls were safe, and they had made it to the party. Granted, the prince was up here, but maybe they'd find their way up soon. Or perhaps he'd go down there.

Then the fae's words echoed in my head.

Look again.

The girls were dancing, certainly. Their feet moved so fast I could barely see them. Their skin shone with sweat and the smiles I thought I'd seen on their faces weren't smiles at all. They were grimaces. "They're enchanted." My voice fell flat.

"That's what the king does to humans who come here to ask for favors tonight. Just imagine what he would do to fae who should know better." He threw me a smile. "But, of course, you knew that."

My breath came so fast the scene in front of me wavered. "I need to sit down."

The man smiled, the movement of his cheeks moving his understated black mask. "You need to do nothing of the sort. Can't you see the king is still watching you after the scene you made at his feet. The only thing you need to do right now is act like you're having the time of your life." He wrapped a hand around my arm and pulled me back to the dance floor, where he took my right hand in his left and placed his other hand firmly on the small of my back, leaving me with no option but to lay my left hand on his shoulder.

He was tall. I had to reach up to find his shoulder. He was a strong lead, spinning me left then right and leaving me with little chance of making the wrong step in this dance I'd never seen before but which everyone else on the dance floor knew perfectly.

"Why are you helping me?" I also wanted to know who he was and what he wanted from me in return, but couldn't bring myself to ask.

"Because it would ruin my night to watch the king tear a pretty lady apart limb by limb." He spun me in a fast circle and all I could do was hold him tight.

"I don't believe you," I hissed when we stopped spinning.

He lifted one shoulder. "That's your choice, but I tell the truth. How long have you been gone?" He asked it like he knew me.

My heart fell. "Who says I've been gone at all?" Was it that obvious I didn't know how to act here in the Unseelie Court?

A smile played at the edge of his full lips and behind his mask, his brown eyes danced. "No one currently living in Faery would ask the king for a favor on All Hallows Eve. He doesn't do that any longer."

"Clearly." My tone was dry, and I worked hard to keep the dismay from my face. There was truth in his words. It was why no one else had approached the king, why he wasn't listening to person after person ask him to grant them a favor.

He spun me around again. "Plus, I've never met you before, and you seem unwilling to let go and have a good time. So you mustn't be from around here."

His tone was light, and despite myself, some of my tension eased and a smile played on my lips. I let it stay, hoping the smile would make him think I was enjoying myself. Dancing in the arms of a handsome fae wasn't the worst way to spend an evening. "And you know everyone that ever set foot in the Unseelie Kingdom?"

"Of course not." He grinned. "But I never forget a pretty face."

I snorted at his mediocre attempt at flattery.

"You don't like compliments, lady?" He looked down at me as we moved around the dance floor. "Or is it just that you didn't like that one?"

The smile I was trying to keep a hold on threatened to explode. I hadn't expected to dance at the masquerade. I certainly hadn't expected to smile while I was here. Yet this man had somehow achieved both in a matter of minutes. "Didn't your mother ever teach you that women like to feel special? They don't like it when you roll out compliments you've used a hundred times before."

"Ouch." He drew in a loud breath as if I'd truly injured him. "It sounded like I'd used that one before, did it? Well, I'll be sure to use something less common the next time I compliment you."

I smiled at the ground. Oh, he was smooth. Not that there would be a next time. Still, I let myself enjoy the feeling, knowing that tomorrow I'd return to being the girl with the ugly ears.

"And for the record," he continued, watching me as he spoke, "my mother died years ago."

I stopped dancing, but he pushed his hand into my back, urging me to continue. "I'm sorry." I hadn't known, but I felt like a heel for suggesting his mother should have taught him something she couldn't possibly have.

He shrugged, his eyes settling on the prince, now dancing with a woman in a pale pink dress. "It's okay. I got over it a long time ago." The smile had left his voice, and he sounded distant.

I followed his gaze, desperate to change the topic of conversation. "Do you think he'll find a bride tonight?"

"I think..." He paused, watching the grinning prince spin his partner in two quick circles. He certainly looked to be enjoying himself. "I think he'll tell us all when he's ready and not a moment before." Copying the prince, he spun me in a circle before moving me diagonally across the dance floor, somehow avoiding a clash with the dancers coming toward us. "Tell me." He leaned in to speak in my ear and a shiver ran up my spine. "What was so important you needed a favor from the king?"

I shook my head. There was no chance I was spilling that information. "It's personal."

That smile returned to his face, and the horror I'd felt about mentioning his mother eased. I wondered what he looked like beneath that black mask. His smile was certainly a thing to behold. "Maybe it's something I could help with?"

I stared up into his waiting eyes. Brown with flecks of gold. This wasn't even a consideration, and I should tell him so. Only one of the ruling royal family could heal Mother. Only they held strong enough magic. There were just two males in that family; one was sitting upon his throne and the other was dancing with a woman in pink. This man could not help me.

The top of his mask moved as if he were frowning. "Unless you've done something so bad, I'll have no choice but to report you to the king?" He shook his head, his voice softening. "Can't be that though, since you were going to the king yourself."

"What does it matter?" Suddenly, I no longer wanted to be in this man's arms, spinning across the dance floor in the Unseelie King's ballroom. His question was like a bubble popping, reminding me I'd failed to get the thing I'd come to Faery for. I glanced at the door I'd entered the ballroom through, wondering if I could make a run for it and whether the dark haired fae would even allow it.

He lifted a shoulder. "Call me curious." His eyes narrowed and, as if he'd noticed my own misgivings about this conversation, a hardness crept into his voice. "I could always force you to tell me."

Magic. He could use magic to find out everything he wanted to know. Or I could offer him the very least detail and hope it was enough to sate his curiosity. I swallowed. "I know a human sick from fae magic. The human is important to me. I don't want them to die."

His eyes narrowed. "A boyfriend? Husband?"

"No." I shook my head. "Nothing like that. More like a ... father figure." The lie was rough on my tongue, but it seemed safer that he learned as little as possible about me. I didn't want him to track me down after this night.

He smiled, though it didn't seem as easy as it had before. "Okay, I get it. Not a boyfriend."

"I hoped the king might save him. But now I know he won't, there's no point in staying." I removed my hand from his shoulder. "Thank you for the dance, but it's time I left."

"Are you not enjoying yourself?" He was holding me as if we were still dancing, even though both our feet had stopped moving. Dancers moved past us in waves, circling around us as if we were an island.

I gave him a tight smile, the sound of Cymon's body hitting the ground still loud in my ears. "How could anyone enjoy this?" Except, there were hundreds of fae here who were enjoying it. Admitting I didn't want to be here might be as good as admitting I was human.

His eyes rounded, then he burst out laughing. The fae couple dancing beside us looked over and my dance partner spun me around, giving me no choice but to cling onto him. "A woman after my own heart." He cast a quick glance in the king's direction. "Just one more dance? Then we'll call it even and you can run back to your human. Or wherever it was you came from."

"Even?" What in the stars did he think I owed him for?

"For saving you from the wrath of King Aengus."

It was tempting. When I danced with him, I felt like a princess. I'd never felt special like that in my life. No one had ever given me that chance. I opened my mouth to agree to one final dance, but the gem in my pocket vibrated.

How was it time to leave already? It seemed as if I'd only been here a few minutes. I pulled from his grasp. "I'm sorry, I must go. Thank you for the dance. And for saving my life."

His gaze went to the king and his face—what I could see of it—tightened. With flaring nostrils, he stared at the man before speaking quietly to me. "Just go with this, okay? It's in your best interest. And don't make a scene. The king is watching." Before I could respond, he dropped his eyes to mine and cupped his hand to the side of my head, lacing his fingers in my hair.

For the smallest second, I stared back at him, unable to break his gaze. Then the gem vibrated again, pulling me to my senses. He looked like he was about to kiss me, and there was no way that was happening.

I shook off his grasp and ducked beneath his arm, my eyes on the exit to the tunnel. I didn't care if the king was watching. I was leaving.

One of the rings on Dark Hair's fingers caught on the ring in my fake ear. I tugged on it, hoping this delay wouldn't stop me from getting away while Dark Hair stared at me with wide eyes. He shouldn't be surprised at my rapid departure. If this was how he acted around all women he'd just met, he should expect the same reaction. I pulled again, freeing myself with a jolt.

Burning pain ripped through my ear, worse than the pain when the magic attached to me. I bit down on the scream that wanted to fly from my body, covered my ear with my hand, and ran. The exit wasn't far, but there were fae in the way. I pushed past them or dodged around them, my heart thudding so loud it drowned out the music. My dance partner now knew exactly what I was. He would not let me leave, just as I would not sit around and wait for him to make me his slave.

I sprinted as fast as I could in my stupidly high heels, and I wasn't nearly fast enough. I knocked some glasses from a tray carried by the same girl I'd seen when I first arrived. They fell to the floor with a crash. Every pair of eyes in the room swiveled to me, every mouth opened in surprise. I sprinted harder, expecting a hand to wrap around my arm and pull me to a stop any moment.

Even when I reached the tunnel, I couldn't relax. The shiny packed earth was impossible to run on. I was too slow, and I had to get out of these shoes. I stopped, leaning against the stone wall as I slipped my shoes from my feet.

Footsteps echoed behind me.

I hooked the straps over my fingers and ran again. One shoe slipped from my grasp. For a second, I thought about stopping and picking it up, but there was no time.

"Wait!" My fae dance partner called, closer than I wanted him to be.

I sprinted faster, but I might as well have crawled for all the good it did me.

I couldn't take another step toward home because he was suddenly standing in front of me.

FIVE

I DON'T RECALL what happened after that. I think I tried to duck around him. Truly, the next thing I remember was sitting at the table in the main room of our cottage with a vial of turquoise liquid gripped in one shaking hand, my single remaining shoe in the other. In my rush to leave Faery, I'd forgotten all about Tobias. I hadn't even tried to search for him. Selina would be so disappointed.

I placed the vial on the table so I could read the beautiful flowing hand of the note attached to it.

The perfect pick-me-up for
injured human friends. F.

Dark Hair believed his magic was strong enough to help me. How I hoped he was right, but

I'd save my gratitude until Mother was up and about again.

"Bria?" Mother's weak voice floated from her bedroom.

I pushed to my feet. The sun was brightening the eastern sky, and I hadn't yet slept. My first patients would soon start banging down our door.

I padded into Mother's room. She took in my elegant hair and stunning dress and pushed up onto her elbows. "Oh, Bria. No." She shook her head. "Please tell me you haven't been to Faery."

I forced a smile onto my face. "I have the cure to your injury." I held up the vial, tucking the note into my pocket. "You'll feel better in no time."

She dropped back onto her pillows. "You shouldn't have done that for me. What did you promise the king in return?" Her voice was weak, but her eyes were concerned. Or perhaps scared.

I forced the smile wider, worry niggling in my gut about what exactly I might have to do because of the vial I now held in my hand. There was no way I was telling Mother I didn't know if I'd agreed to anything. "Nothing. I didn't speak to the king. I found someone else who believed he could help us." I sat on the edge of her bed and held the vial to her lips. "Drink, Mother. This will fix you right up." I hoped so, anyway.

Mother swallowed the liquid down, her eyelids growing heavy a moment later. I rose to leave, and her hand caught mine. She licked her lips twice, her words a quiet whisper when she got them out. "Thank you, Bria. I'm so proud of the woman you're growing into."

I patted her hand and waited until her breathing grew slow and even. As I walked from her room, already thinking about which patients might be back for a follow-up visit today, there was a tap at our back door. I opened it to find little Jonty Plimmer staring up at me. His face was taut with pain. He still held one arm pressed tight against his body, while the other arm clutched a wriggling chicken. "Did you mean it when you said I could come back any time?"

I looked over his shoulder for his mother. It was strange that he used our back door. Although it was only a matter of walking around the side of the cottage, most guests came straight off the road to the front door. I smiled down at him. "Of course. Are you having trouble with that arm?"

He nodded solemnly. "It hurts. I have to keep up with my chores, but I can't use my hand and Mother won't bring me to be fixed because..." He bit off his sentence, but I already knew what he was going to say.

"Because she doesn't like me."

Jonty looked at the ground, his head bobbing. "Can you help me?" He nodded at the chicken. "I can give you Becca as payment."

"Becca?"

He beamed, his eyes meeting mine. "She's mine. I raised her since she was born. She's the best layer we have." His face saddened as he realized what he was saying. He had to give away the animal he loved to make himself better. All because his mother wouldn't give him any coin, or even her permission, to visit me.

I took Becca from his hand and put her in the empty coop beside the door. A laying hen would be divine. My mouth watered as I imagined the yoke of freshly poached eggs soaking into a slice of warm bread.

I crouched in front of him. "Here's the thing. I can bind up your arm and put it in a splint which will stop it hurting so bad, and I can give you some dalliagrass to chew for the pain, and you'll feel much better. But your mother will notice the splint and know you've been to see me. What do you think she'll say?"

He ignored my question, listening to the point that mattered most to him. "You can take away the pain?"

I nodded. "Most of it. You still must be careful while it heals."

He straightened. "Mother will be mighty angry. But it'll be worth it. I can handle her."

"And one more thing." I smiled and directed him inside. "I can't take Becca. She'd miss you too much."

His face dropped. "But I have nothing else I can pay you with."

Considering we sometimes only received a handful of seeds for the vegetable garden from patients needing far more care than Jonty, he wasn't the only one. It would be nice if we were paid better for what we did, but Mother and I weren't healers for the money. We did it because we wanted to help people. There was no way I would send Jonty away still in pain. "Do you know what? You've paid me enough just by showing me how brave you are, coming here today alone and offering Becca as payment."

Mother didn't get better that day. Or the next. A week later when she'd had only a mouthful of watery soup to eat all day, I was about to curse the unknown name of the dark-haired fae who'd tricked me into thinking he could help, when Selina rushed into our cottage.

"Have you heard?" She poked her head around the back door. Her lips were pressed tight, and there were creases around her eyes.

I looked up from the poultice I was making for the infected heel of a man waiting in Mother's office. "Heard what?" I couldn't even make myself sound interested. Yesterday, Selina's mother had come over, sat me down and told me the thing I knew, but was doing my best to ignore. The wound on Mother's bicep was worse than ever, the broken skin now so large it covered her from shoulder to elbow and looked like something was eating her from the inside out. Mother didn't have much longer to live. Ever since, I'd felt as if a little of myself was about to die, too, and even working with Mother's patients didn't bring me any joy.

Selina cast a sympathetic gaze at the closed door of Mother's bedroom. "Maybe we should talk outside? I'd hate to disturb her."

"I have a patient."

Selina snorted. "Someone who prefers Aoife and is rude to you even though you're a better healer than your Mother and probably your patient's only option?"

That was pretty much how the initial conversation with the man had gone. I hadn't even had the energy to fight him on it. I knew I could save his foot, but when he told me he would never let someone as ugly and untrustworthy as me touch any part of his body, I swung the door shut in his face. I had bigger things to worry over than someone who needed my help but didn't want it.

The man was silent for about half a second behind that closed door. As I walked toward Mother's bedroom, he pushed the door to our cottage open and demanded I help. No apology for the way he'd spoken, just entitlement. And though I would have loved to keep him waiting while I sat and talked with Selina, I also wanted to get the stupid idiot out of my home. "I'm almost done. Just give me a moment. I'll meet you out back."

I didn't think I'd ever been as rude to a patient as I was to that man. I applied the poultice, told him he'd need to visit again tomorrow, and no, Aoife wouldn't be available to see him. Then I opened the door and shooed him out.

Selina sat waiting on one swing, a children's book clutched across her chest and tears on her lashes. She'd saved for weeks to buy that book for her little brother before he was born. "Want me to read it to you?" It was Selina's favorite fairytale about a princess who was strong and powerful but whose people deemed her too ugly to become their Queen. Their cruelty hurt the princess, so she ran away to rule a new kingdom where they didn't care how she looked.

Selina shook her head. "I know you hate this story."

I did. I hated it because the very first time Father read it to me, he told me the story was a lie and that the princess had died, killed by the hatred of her people. I'd never gotten over that and was glad Selina didn't want me to read it. "What haven't I heard?" I asked, picking up our conversation from the kitchen as I took a seat.

The worry that created creases around Selina's lips returned. "Prince Fergus found his bride on All Hallows Eve. They're bonded."

Bonded was a fae term I hated. It meant magic had decided two fae belonged together and once bonded, they spent the rest of their ridiculously long lives together. Supposedly, a bonded pair could combine their magic, making them stronger than they were individually—as if they needed that. I hated the term because the elite of Holbeck used it when they found someone they wanted to wed. They weren't bonded at all, they probably weren't even in love. It was as though pretending to be fae somehow made them better than the rest of us. Besides, I never understood why the fae would allow magic to choose their partner—the old-fashioned way of getting to know someone first and falling in love seemed like the only way to do it.

As for Prince Fergus now being bonded, it didn't surprise me. There'd been a non-ending supply of women putting themselves forward for the job at the masquerade. It wasn't something I could make myself care about. Not at the moment. Maybe not ever.

As I opened my mouth to say so, Selina said, "Then he lost her again. She left before he could..." She shrugged.

That was a little more interesting. Not much, but enough to keep me inside this conversation. "Before he could what?"

"Ask for her hand, I guess. The king has spared no expense and searched all of Unseelie for her, but no one's seen her since that night."

I shrugged, my attention waning. "Sounds like she doesn't want anyone to find her."

Selina's eyes lit for just a second. "Or maybe they don't know who they're searching for. Prince Fergus didn't see her without her mask. He knew she was the one just from speaking with her. Isn't that romantic?" Typical that Selina would see the romance in this story—it included the prince, after all. "They have one of her shoes. They've traveled through Unseelie trying it on foot after foot, but it didn't fit anyone. Now Prince Fergus isn't sure if she was fae or human, so they're on their way to the Crossing to do the same here in Iadrun." She drew the syllables of the last word out—Ee-ah-drun—as if she wasn't sure she wanted to speak her next words. She glanced at her feet before meeting my eyes. "Could it be you?"

I snorted. There was no way. "I would have told you if I danced with the prince."

"You lost a shoe."

My heart beat faster as realization dawned. I *had* lost a shoe. And I'd run off without leaving my name, just like the prince's new bride. I shook my head. It couldn't be me. "I didn't go near the prince." But what if they'd picked up my shoe by accident, thinking I was his runaway bride? Worse, what if my dark-haired dance partner had handed it to the prince and told him it was his bride's shoe as some cruel joke? The same way he'd joked about giving Mother the medicine she needed. I rested my forehead against the rope of the swing. Both those options were far more plausible than I wanted them to be.

"They were my shoes." Selina's voice was almost too soft to hear.

I swallowed. Her shoes. Meaning, if the king's messengers made it to Holbeck without finding the runaway bride, and if the shoe they had was the one I'd lost—the one I'd borrowed that had been a fraction too small—then the shoe would fit Selina and she'd be mistaken for the one the prince wanted to marry. I forced light into my voice. "It will be fine. Our names weren't on the guest list. They have no reason to come to Holbeck." I would have believed my own words had I not witnessed all those girls entering Faery without an invitation.

Selina stopped swinging and twisted to face me. "I know I tell you all the time how much I'd love to be Prince Fergus' bride..." She shook her head. "I don't want to live in Faery. Or marry someone I don't know. I don't want to be the prince's wife."

I lifted my lips into what I hoped looked like a smile. There was no way I'd let her go if it came to that. If they arrived in Holbeck before they found the woman they were searching for, and if Selina tried that shoe on before me, I'd step forward and tell everyone it was me who'd worn the shoe. I'd show them the dress and mask I wore that night and deal with the consequences. But it would not happen. It just wouldn't. I squeezed her hand. "It will be fine. They'll probably find her before they make it here."

It was another two full days before the king's messengers—the Wild Hunt—arrived in Holbeck.

They appeared just after the sun reached its peak, their huge hounds heralding their entrance.

From the far end of town, they made their way from house to house. Selina and I waited on the swings behind our cottages, our hands linked while we silently wished for some other foot to fit that blasted shoe. We wished to hear the hounds' barking grow quieter until it disappeared, taking the Wild Hunt far from here. We wished for the king to call off this stupidity. We might as well have wished the sky rain down flakes of gold.

Selina's mother paced nervously inside their cottage, while my mother knew nothing of what was about to happen, as close to death as she was.

We stayed where we sat even when, through the windows in Selina's cottage that looked right through to the street, we saw Xion Starguard swing down from his mount and stride up the path to her front door, four hunters in his wake. I hoped Selina's mother might ignore the knocking. If no one came to the door, perhaps the Wild Hunt would move on to another village and forget about us. But Selina's mother would never risk angering the Wild Hunt, not so soon after losing her child to them. She didn't realize that showing them out to where the two of us sat might mean she would lose another.

Xion stopped in front of us, his eyes first rolling over Selina, then me, while his hunters and their hounds spread themselves around the edge of our yard, their backs to the woods, to watch. His lip curled when our eyes met. I imagined he was re-membering the last time he was here. I felt much the same level of disdain for him, except mine was mixed with a whole pile of fear.

"You first." He pointed to Selina. The shoe—Selina's shoe—dangled from his fingers, tiny in his huge hands, and the mate of the one I'd worn to the masquerade.

"If you don't mind, I'd like to go first." I toed off my boots.

Xion's eyes moved to me and his words were slow. He looked down his nose, leaving me in no doubt he felt speaking to me was beneath him. "Last I checked, it was me, not you, in charge of this ridiculous woman hunt. Or am I mistaken?" His voice was low and without inflection.

I shook my head, no words forming. The power in his voice made my hands shake, and I pushed them beneath my thighs.

He turned to Selina. "You will go first."

I watched the shoe swaying in Xion's hand while my brain churned through ways to make sure no one forced Selina to marry someone she'd never met.

Xion crouched in front of her, and with gentler hands than I ever imagined him to possess, took her foot and slipped it into the strappy shoe.

I held my breath and closed my eyes, waiting for the words I knew would follow. *We've found her. This is Prince Fergus' bride.*

When those words didn't come, I opened my eyes to find Selina smiling while Xion shook his head. "Sorry, miss, but this can't be your shoe. You won't be marrying the prince." This task painted him in a completely different light than the two times I'd encountered him before. Raw power still rolled off his muscular body, but today he was cordial, polite even.

Selina ducked her head. A movement that could have looked like she was upset, but that I suspected was her hiding her relief.

I shook my head at the stupidity of the process, looking at the shoe on Selina's foot. The shoe that had once belonged to her had been tried on so many times in the past weeks, and by so many women, that the leather straps were now stretched and gaping. For her to wear this shoe now, the leather would need another hole punched in it for the buckle to slip through.

Xion removed the shoe and looked at me. "Your turn."

My heart gave a giant lurch, and I forced myself to draw in a single calming breath. It would be okay. The shoe had never fit me that well to begin with. This could not be a match.

"Your foot." The eye holes on Xion's mask narrowed with impatience. Perhaps his cordiality only went as far as Selina.

I held out my foot. He rested it in his lap and slid the shoe onto it, clasping the buckle. His hand rested upon my ankle as he worked. I watched, waiting for the words he'd said to Selina, the words he'd said to thousands of women over these past few weeks.

His fingers tightened on my ankle and his voice was so quiet, I wasn't sure I'd heard. "But ... you're human." His gaze met mine, confusion creasing lines into the forehead of his mask.

My heart dropped deep into my stomach. I shook my head, my voice as quiet as his. "I'm not her. I've never even met the prince." As I spoke, he released my ankle, and I saw what he meant. The shoe fit as if it were made for my foot. Straps that had gaped on Selina rested perfectly against my skin. The length was exact. Even the sparkling silver color complimented my skin tone.

I shook my head again. The prince might as well have been in a different room to me, he was so far away the night of the masquerade. "It must be a mistake. Someone's playing a joke. Or ... or there could be hundreds of other women with this exact shoe size. You just need to keep hunting." I pulled my foot from his lap. "I'm not her." If I kept saying it, he might believe me.

Xion nodded, and for a moment it seemed as if he agreed. Until he spoke. "It can't be anyone else. The shoe is spelled to fit only the one that wore it that night." His eyes narrowed as he looked over my face. "Ears."

I knew what he was asking. He wanted to see my humiliation. The thing I never showed anyone. If it proved I wasn't the girl the prince wanted as a bride, then I'd choke back my embarrassment and let him see.

He brushed my hair away from my left ear and I closed my eyes, hating his hands on me. I knew the moment he'd seen my deformity because he sucked in a deep breath. My cheeks heated. I already knew I was hideous, I didn't need scum like him reminding me. I pulled from his grasp and dragged my hair back over my ears.

Selina's mouth was set in a tiny circle, and her eyes kept bouncing from me to him. She reached out her hand and wound her fingers through mine. Her touch settled my breathing.

"Everything all right?" One hunter called from beside the back door to my cottage.

Xion blinked, his face—that mask— unreadable. "Fine." He got to his feet. "We're done here. Neither of these girls are the ones, and there is no one else left in this village who hasn't tried the shoe. Go ahead to the next village and announce our arrival. I'll be along in a few minutes. Once I've removed this shoe."

The hunters filed past without another word while Xion bent and unbuckled the strap. His movements were slow, and he watched his men from the side of his vision. The moment they climbed on their horses and rode from our town, he yanked the shoe from my foot, pulled me to my feet and dragged me into my cottage.

SIX

I PULLED against Xion's grip. As we reached the steps up to the cottage, Selina jumped to her feet. "Wait! What are you doing with her?"

"She's perfectly safe with me. I just have a few questions for her." Xion's voice left no room for argument, though I hoped Selina might. I didn't want to be alone with this man. It didn't matter that he'd said I couldn't be *her*. Or that he'd released his men to go to the next village. I'd seen that shoe on my foot and it had fit better than any shoe had ever fit me.

Xion opened the door and pulled me inside, depositing me on a seat at the dining table. "Who else is here?"

I shook my head. "Just Mother. But she's..." I shrugged. He was the one who'd hurt Mother. He knew exactly what her current state of health was.

With a single nod, he scanned the room as if I might have hidden someone behind the potted plant, before folding his arms and staring down at me.

I glared at him, refusing to show my terror, even as he leaned in and brushed my hair aside for the second time.

He straightened, his eyes roving over me before he shook his head, speaking to himself. "You can't be her. It's not possible to make those things look normal." By things he meant ears, and by normal he meant fae.

I pulled my hair down over them. He wasn't saying anything I hadn't heard a thousand times already. It didn't matter how many times I heard them, the words always hit like a punch to the stomach. He smirked, as if he knew he'd landed a verbal hit. Then he pulled a leather pouch from his pocket and tipped something into his waiting hand. With his spare hand, he gripped my chin so I couldn't move. Then, gently, he touched my ear.

A sharp burning pain ripped through me and I cried out. He had the ear tip I'd lost at the masquerade and he was forcing it onto me. His grip was firm and no matter how hard I fought, I couldn't move from his grasp.

Selina banged on the door, her fist making it rattle on the hinges. I opened my mouth to scream again and beg her to come inside, but Xion was quicker. He released my chin and put his hand over my mouth, his voice low in my ear. "If you want her to live, tell her you're fine."

My breath caught in my throat. This man killed and maimed without a second thought. I would not allow Selina to be his next victim. I nodded, and he lifted his hand allowing me to speak. "I'm fine, Selina. I tripped over my own feet." I glanced at Xion, eyebrows raised. Was that good enough?

He shook his head. Not a good enough excuse.

I drew in my breath. "We're just talking. There's nothing to worry about. I'll come over as soon as he's gone."

There was a long silence from the other side of the door. Selina didn't believe me. I knew she wouldn't. I only hoped her fear of the Wild Hunt would be enough to make her do as I asked. She didn't want to leave her mother with no children.

Sure enough, with a sigh loud enough to hear inside the cottage, her footsteps faded away. Xion released his hold on me, his eyes on my newly formed fae ear. He seemed already to have forgotten Selina. "This is powerful magic. Who made it for you?"

I shook my head. "I don't know."

"Do you wear them often?" His lips curled as he spoke, as if it was so revolting that a human would trick a fae with magic that he almost couldn't say the words. Or perhaps he was just upset that I would dare wear pointed fae ears to disguise myself as one of them.

Part of me wanted to rail against that arrogance that said they were better than us. The rest of me didn't have a death wish. "I've only worn them once. Today makes twice."

"At the masquerade." There was a sigh in his voice, the only time I'd heard any emotion from his low monotone.

"Yes," I whispered.

He ran a hand through his long inky hair, pacing away before turning and stalking back. "You must come with me." He wrapped his fingers around my arm.

I pulled away, shaking my head. "No. I have commitments here. I don't want to marry that horrible prince and live in that awful place. I can't be bonded to him."

The eyebrows on the mask lifted. "I thought you said you hadn't met the prince before."

"I haven't." The closest I'd ever been to him was across the room at the masquerade.

"So you can't be bonded to him, can you?"

I stared at him. Was he agreeing with me?

He sighed at my blank stare. "You'd have to meet him twice—at least a year and a day apart—to be bonded to him that way. Does that clear things up for you?" His voice was filled with sarcasm, the mask responding to his facial movements as if it weren't a mask—forehead creasing and cheeks moving. I was so intent on watching to see how that might be possible that I almost missed his words. "You're nothing to the prince, and he certainly doesn't want to marry a human. There's been a mistake." He stalked closer. "But you gave up all rights to choose anything the night you tricked your way into Faery and spent the evening pretending to be fae at the masquerade."

I lifted my chin. He wanted to call me out on tricking people? "I'd have thought you would have respected that. You fae love to trick humans, don't you? Or is it not so much fun when the boot is on the other foot?" I hoped he'd see I was too lippy to be a princess and leave me behind.

His face hardened. Even through the mask, I could see it. "There's trickery, and there's outright lying." He wrapped his hand around my arm again. "And no one respects a liar."

I didn't care what he thought of me. I was not going to Faery with him. And I certainly would not live the rest of my life there. I had to look after Mother in her last days. "Then you'd better leave me behind in case I upset the prince with my bad habits."

"The prince has many of his own bad habits. Perhaps you two will find them a common talking point." He pushed me out the front door where his horse waited, chewing on flowers from Mother's garden.

I stood beside the massive black beast that Xion Starguard rode through the sky night after night. There was no way I was getting on that thing. I dropped onto my knees in the grass, my arm pulling in his grasp.

"Get up." His gaze was on his beast and he made soft clicking noises with his tongue.

"No."

He turned, blinking long and slow. This time when he spoke, his voice was measured, almost daring me to disagree. "Get. Up."

I narrowed my eyes. Perhaps that made me a fool, but I didn't care. "What do you want from me? If I'm not to be his bride, then leave me here, I'll tell no one the shoe fit." Who would I tell? Who would even believe me?

"You have just become a colossal pain in the prince's ass and leaving you to live your life in ignorance is no longer an option. Now get up off the ground and get onto the horse."

"No." I shook my head. "You can't make me."

"Can't I?" Anger flashed in his eyes. Wind whipped up and with a flick of his hand, Xion immobilized me.

Immobilized.

No longer in control of my body.

I could breathe. And blink. But no matter how hard I tried to move, my body wouldn't obey.

Another flick of his hand and my dress disappeared, making way for a pair of charcoal riding pants tucked into knee-high boots, and a black long-sleeved shirt with a scooped neck, and I was suddenly on the back of his horse. I tried to throw myself off, but the only place that happened was in my imagination—my body didn't move a fraction.

Xion seemed to know what I was trying to do— I had no idea how. "I wouldn't bother," he said as he climbed on behind me, one arm going around either side of my body as he took the reins.

"Please don't do this," I begged, grateful the magic holding my body hostage allowed me to speak. I needed to be with Mother. I didn't want her to die alone. "I never even met the prince and

I guarantee he won't like me. He will be revolted by my ears. Please don't make me marry him." He'd said I wouldn't have to, but my guess was that was a lie.

"Oh, I agree, he won't like you." His head moved and I could almost feel him looking down his nose. "You're not exactly from the right stock for a royal bride." Meaning I was too human. And probably that my body was too broken and ugly to be one of the royal family. He laced disdain through his words, but they lit a glimmer of hope inside me. Perhaps he hadn't been lying when he said I wasn't to marry the prince.

And if the prince didn't want me as a bride, then surely I could stay home. "Leave me here. Pretend you never saw me."

Xion clicked his tongue and shoved his heels into the horse's sides until we started to move. "Believe me. If that were an option, I would gladly leave you behind."

I pounced on that admission. "Do it. No one will know. I won't tell. Leave me here."

Another long silence followed as the horse ambled past our cottage and toward the woods, some strange magic making his feet silent on the ground. "It's not that simple."

"It is! You just have to make it—"

"Quiet!" The word burst out of him with a growl and I jumped. Or I would have, had I been able to move. His tone suggested anything other than complete silence would be unwise. So, I focused on the woods looming in front of me and switched to thinking how I might escape.

We rode to the little brook where I'd lined up to enter Faery a week earlier. With no one else around, I didn't see the guard until we were almost past him, sitting on a stool, reading. He barely glanced at Xion, waving one hand to allow us through, and we trotted into Faery.

I braced, expecting the same tunnel I'd walked into before, the one that led directly to the king's ballroom where, travelling on the back of this horse, my head would be very close to scraping the ceiling. There was no tunnel. Only more woods. Thicker than the human part we'd just left, tree trunks sparkled in the sunlight while the autumn leaves upon them were brighter than any in Iadrun—orange, burgundy, red and yellow. The birdsong was louder and coarser here, and the insects that buzzed past my face left behind trails of colored light. Between the trees, glowing butterflies floated out of reach. It was beautiful, but everything this side of the Crossing was a trap. According to Mother, things my imagination had never considered lurked in the woods of Faery. Things that would gulp me down for breakfast.

I tried not to think about what might be hiding nearby, because at some point I would have to run through these woods. I would escape from Xion and I would return to Mother.

Since I couldn't move, my only weapon was my tongue. Which I used as often as I could, trying to wear Xion down. "Tell the prince you lost me. Tell him I told you I needed to use the bathroom and ran. Stars, tell him I didn't attend the masquerade. Just let me go." If he used his imagination, I was certain there were plenty of excuses the prince would believe when Xion didn't bring me to him.

Apart from the soft shuffle of our bodies with every step the horse took, and the noises from the woods, there was silence. Xion might refuse to speak, but that didn't mean I had to. "Why aren't we flying? That's usually how you get around, isn't it?"

There was a long pause before he responded, his voice deep and low. "Because right now, I don't want anyone to see us."

"Don't you have a spell for that?" I muttered, barely able to contain my sarcasm. My rear ached from sitting in one place so long and I couldn't even scratch my nose. If he could do all that with magic, surely he could conceal us from whoever he was hiding from.

"Why didn't I think of that?" His sarcasm wasn't even remotely contained.

"It was just a suggestion."

A deep sigh followed his silence. "I can only hide us while we're on the ground."

"You're saying there's a spell on us right now? No one can see me?" And no one could rescue me. Not that anyone would. Selina was the only likely option, and she'd have to find a way—and the will—to come into Faery first.

"Unfortunately, it's not being seen that's my main problem at the moment." His legs moved as he guided the horse with his knees.

"It isn't?" I didn't think someone like Xion Starguard had problems. "What is your main problem, then?"

He sighed again, and I could almost see him lifting his eyes toward the sky. "The noise one of us is continually making."

I tried to twist around to face him, just to see if he was kidding, but the magic still bound me. "You think I talk too much?"

"Got it in one."

"Let me go. Then you won't have to listen. Just imagine how angry the prince will become, listening to me day and night." I wasn't a talker, not really. But I could make it seem like I was if it helped me out of Faery.

A humorless laugh rumbled from his chest. "I'll deal with the prince's anger any day over the incessant squeaking of your voice."

Squeaking? My voice didn't squeak. "I'd have thought you had a spell for that, too."

"Don't tempt me."

We rode in silence after that. The woods grew thicker with each passing minute. So thick, no sun penetrated, and a chill grew in the air. I tried to note the trails we travelled upon, in case there was ever a chance to escape.

I didn't think of Mother, or Selina, because thinking of them reminded me that the only place I might ever see them again was in my memories. I also tried not to think of what may happen when we finally reached Prince Fergus. I wasn't the woman he was expecting. Would that anger him? Whichever way I looked at it, there seemed a high possibility I'd end up his slave.

"Is this my punishment for singing?" The Wild Hunt only took Tobias that night, when they should have taken me, too. There had been plenty of opportunity for Xion to whisk me away while he was in our house, yet he hadn't. Since I'd never met the prince, perhaps this kidnapping was really about my singing.

"For singing?" Xion didn't seem to know what I meant.

"Yes. The day you took the baby, I forgot myself and was singing in the woods."

There was silence behind me before he finally answered. "The Hunt came for the baby that day. No one else. I was unaware you'd broken that rule."

I wasn't sure if I should be relieved or not. I hadn't brought the Hunt to Tobias. But now I'd admitted what I'd done to the leader of the Hunt. I pressed my lips together and vowed not to speak again.

We rode for what felt like hours without a stop. I needed to go to the bathroom but didn't bother asking because I knew what his answer would be. I'd as good as told him a bathroom stop would be the perfect time to escape. There was no way he would allow me to relieve myself in the bushes.

"What's wrong?" he growled. The spell keeping me still had loosened a little the farther we got from my home. I guess he'd noticed me wriggling.

"Apart from the fact that I've been kidnapped and am currently bound by magic against my will?"

A beat of silence. "Apart from that."

It was my turn to hesitate, but the reality was, I couldn't hold it much longer. "I need to use the bathroom," I mumbled.

He shook his head. I felt the movement through the arms that he wound around me to grip the horse's reins.

I was tired and scared, and that small movement brought my anger on. "Your nag won't mind when I wet myself all over his back? You won't mind sharing a saddle warmed with my—"

"Obsidian is a Huntiano." I felt his stare on the back of my neck. It was as if he expected I would be impressed. "He is the finest horse in all of Faery."

I wasn't impressed. I knew nothing about human horse breeds and even less about fae horses. "Well, whatever he is, he's about to be very wet if you don't tell him to stop soon."

A long silence followed. I made the small wriggling movement that the magic allowed and finally heard a long sigh. Xion clicked his tongue and pulled on the reins. The moment the horse stopped, he swung down to the ground and looked up at me, waiting for me to do the same.

I glared at him. "Magic, remember?" There was no shortage of bite in my voice.

He smirked as if he had been waiting for me to remind him, then flicked his fingers. Immediately, the resistance I'd felt when I tried to move disappeared. But I had no time to balance myself before I slid from Obsidian's back to land in a heap on the ground, my pride hurting worse than my body. Xion snickered.

What an ass. I jumped to my feet and sprinted for the nearest tree. When I was done, I stood up, retied the strands of hair that were curling around my face into my hair clip, and looked around. The woods were so thick, I could only see Obsidian because of the movement he made as he bent his head to nibble on the grass at his feet. If I was going to escape, this was the time.

I took a step away, listening for Xion's footsteps coming after me. Nothing. Another step, followed by another pause. No movement from Xion. In fact, I was fairly sure I could still see Obsidian, waiting where I'd left him. My pace increased. When, after twenty steps, Xion still hadn't come after me, I jogged, then sprinted, my heart in my mouth.

I was doing this. He didn't know I was gone.

I was free.

I'd hide in the woods until night fell. Then I'd make my way back to the Crossing and back to Mother. All I had to do was keep quiet. And keep running.

Suddenly, Xion appeared on the trail in front of me, hands on hips. One moment there was only woods, and then he was there, black cloak flaring out behind him.

I changed direction, swerving hard to my left before crashing between trees and bushes, crushing flowers beneath my boots.

I'd only taken two steps before he was standing in front of me there, too. He reached out and wrapped his hand around my arm.

"Let go of me!" I pulled away and ran three steps.

This time, when he caught hold of me, he wrapped both arms around my body, lifting my feet from the ground and squeezing tight enough to cut off the air to my lungs.

"Put me down," I wheezed, wriggling in his grasp.

There was a sneer in his voice and he spoke in my ear. "Why would I do that? I enjoy the feel of your body pushed up against mine."

Yuck. "Be grateful you're holding my hands, or you'd be nursing a broken nose right now." I sounded braver than I was, but I could look after myself in a fist fight. I'd had to learn to defend myself against bullies since the day I started school and I'd won my fair share of fights. Even so, I doubted my skills with my fists were a match for anything Xion Starguard and his magic could do.

A skeleton couldn't have eyebrows, yet it looked very much like the mask over Xion's face was lifting one eyebrow. "You've got a smart mouth, girl. I wonder if you've got the skills to back it up."

Nope. I'd already decided I didn't. But that wasn't what my smart mouth said. "Put me down and see." I narrowed my eyes, hating the way he looked down on me. "But if I were you, I'd take a few steps back to avoid a fist to your nose."

His dark eyes ran over me, and I could almost see him calculating my next move. He knew I was hoping to give myself a few extra seconds so I could run if he released me. Which meant there was no possible way he was loosening his grip.

But to my surprise, he said, "Very well." He bent his knees and dropped me back onto the ground.

If running was what he expected, I'd give him something else instead.

The moment he released his grip on my arms, I spun to face him, drew my hand back, bunched it into a fist, and aimed at the bridge of his nose. My hand skidded across his cheek before hitting where I'd aimed. There was a satisfying crunch as bone cracked beneath my blow.

Then, before he could cry out in pain, before I could turn tail and run, his mask slid from his face and fell with a thud onto the dirt path beneath our feet.

I was no longer staring at Xion Starguard.

I was looking up into the handsome and mask-free face of Prince Fergus Blackwood.

SEVEN

AS THE MASK fell, Xion's long black hair was replaced with a shorter shaggy mop that reached his shoulders. The eyes that had been nothing but black holes behind the mask, were now brown, flecked with gold. A sheen of sweat covered the prince's handsome face and a steady flow of blood dripped from his nose. His lips rounded in surprise as he stared at the mask lying on the leafy forest floor between our feet.

I shook my head, trying to reconcile what I was seeing. Xion Starguard and the heir to the Unseelie throne were the same person? I searched my memory to see if I should have known this already, but I didn't think it was public knowledge. I also wasn't sure what the protocol was when suddenly faced with an Unseelie Prince. Or if protocol even mattered given he'd kidnapped me and I'd probably broken his nose.

He walked a few steps away before turning, waiting for me to speak.

"You're the prince?"

"Sometimes." His voice was soft, unsure. The polar opposite of the icy monotone that had been in my ear these last few hours. He dabbed at his nose, the blood disappearing as he held his hand to it.

"And sometimes you're the leader of the Wild Hunt." It wasn't a question. Didn't need to be. The evidence was lying at my feet. Yet, I needed to hear him confirm it. Prince's rarely ran around hiding their identity.

He nodded, his eyes going to the ground.

"Why?"

His head shot up. "Why not? Why shouldn't I do what makes me happy, like everyone else in the world?"

A chill went down my spine. *Do what makes me happy.* The Wild Hunt's sole purpose was to steal humans. Or kill them. "And the king is just as happy that his heir is running around with the most dangerous people in Faery?"

"Most dangerous?" His eyebrows rose, and he stalked back toward me.

"The rehabilitated criminals."

A flash of amusement crossed his face. "That's who you think makes up the Wild Hunt?" He shook his head, chuckling.

His laughter made my gut harden. None of this was funny. "Oh, you, who so bravely hides his face behind a mask—before dragging our loved ones from their homes—thinks it's hilarious that we might consider the perpetrators of such crimes to be some of your worst criminals? Because that is not a huge leap."

His laughter cut off. "You think that's what we do?"

"I know it is," I shot back. "I've seen you. Twice now."

"You must spend your time with some truly despicable people then." His voice was low, all traces of amusement gone.

That hard thing in my gut turned to white hot anger. I stepped toward him. "The people you took while I watched were far from despicable. They were good—one was only a child. Yet your people hauled them, kicking and screaming, away from their families. So, I ask again, how does your father feel about you running around with that type of person?"

Prince Fergus swallowed, his eyes dropping to the ground. A cool breeze blew through the woods, bringing autumn leaves of red and orange down from the trees above. The farther we'd traveled into the woods, the more like autumn it appeared.

"The king doesn't know?" My voice was a whisper as I considered what this meant.

There was a long silence. A muscle in his jaw worked, and he turned away, speaking into the woods. "No one knows. Except my sister, the rest of the Wild Hunt. And now you."

My heart gave a little leap, and I worked to keep the smile from my face. I was saved, unless he wanted his dirty little secret shared with everyone I came across while he held me here in Faery. "Good." I gave a brisk nod, moving to stand next to him. "Then you'll be returning me home."

His head shot up. "Pardon me?" He spoke slowly, his tone dangerous. I had no doubt he knew exactly what I was suggesting.

I met his eyes, no longer frightened of him. If his secret was as big as it seemed, he'd do whatever it took to keep me quiet. "Now that I can share your secret with the entire world, you'll be wanting to return me to my old life to buy my silence."

The step he took toward me was menacing. "You think..." He paused, swallowed loudly, and then continued to speak through gritted teeth. "You think I'll allow you to return to your home? That I'll risk leaving you there in the hope you won't tell everyone what you've learned today? Or that knowing what you now know makes a scrap of difference?" He shook his head, leaning over me with flared nostrils. "I could end your life in a moment." He clicked his fingers, the movement casual and cold at the same time.

I squared my jaw, trying to mask all emotion on my face. Put like that, I was now in a worse position than I'd been moments ago. If he was going to kill me—and it was looking likely—I would keep fighting until my last breath. "Send me home and I'll never breathe a word to anyone."

"I don't trust you." He glared down his nose.

The feeling was mutual. I drew myself up. "Nor I you. But if you keep me here in Faery and make me marry you just so you can become king, I will tell everyone we come across that you are Xion Starguard." It wasn't like I had anything to lose. Chances were, he would kill me either way.

He shook his head, his lips curling into a sneer that looked exactly like the sneer on Xion Starguard's mask. "Who would believe you?

You're nothing but human scum. I am the Prince of Unseelie."

My heart raced and my hands shook. He had to be bluffing. If he wanted to kill me, he'd have done so already. He needed to make a deal with me if he wanted this to remain a secret. And I was certain he very much wanted that. "They don't have to believe. I only have to create the smallest hint of doubt in the smallest pocket of people. Once I do, you'll be watched like a hawk until you finally make a mistake and show everyone that the *human scum* was correct." He stared at me, nostrils flaring. I pointed my finger at his chest. "You know I'm right."

The tightness around his lips softened. "I will not make you marry me. We're not bonded. I lied about that."

My mouth dropped open. It wasn't that his confession wasn't pleasing, more that I couldn't imagine why he'd say such a thing. "Why would you do that?"

"For many reasons. None of which concern you." He shook his head, his eyes moving across my face. "What exactly are you hiding from?"

I lifted my eyebrows. This was a change in the conversation's direction that I hadn't expected, and a question with an obvious answer given he'd kidnapped me. "You, of course."

His eyebrows shot up. "Me?"

"Why are you surprised? As Xion Starguard, you came to my home, killed my father, injured my mother and took my best friend's baby brother. As Fergus Blackwood, you decided you wanted to marry me without ever speaking to me or asking consent..." I paused and turned away from him as a horrible notion wriggling into my brain. "Tell me it wasn't you I danced with at the masquerade?" Surely it couldn't have been. He was alone. And the man with the circlet on his head had looked more like a prince than the man I danced with at the ball.

He was silent.

I met his eyes, knowing the answer. The eyes I was staring at right now were the same color as the eyes of the dark-haired fae. Then there was the medicine for Mother. Only those with the strongest magic could help her, and as a royal, Fergus Blackwood would be one of the strongest fae in the Unseelie kingdom. "It *was* you."

He licked his lips. Not an admission. Or a denial.

If he wouldn't deny it, I would. "No. You had a circle of women around you, all elbowing their way forward to claim the next dance. You danced with them. Not me."

He drew in a long breath, looking off into the growing darkness of the woods to my left. "That was my best friend, Jax. He has ... magic ... that can make him look like me. He enjoys the dancing and the women, whereas I hate it."

I shook my head. None of what he was saying added up to equal anything I knew about him. "You leave a string of women in your wake everywhere you go. Everyone knows it. That masquerade was your perfect party."

He turned away, taking a few steps and running his hands through his black hair.

"Why would you hide that way, Prince Fergus?" This made no sense. That masquerade was all about him. Why would he have someone else take his place?

He drew in a deep breath and let it out slowly. He turned, his eyes going to the mask I'd knocked from his face, still lying on the red and orange leaves where it had fallen. "Knowing what you do about me, is there no reason you know that might take me away night after night? A reason I might want no one to know about."

The pieces fell into place. "You pretend to be with a different woman each night so you can go with the Wild Hunt?" My eyebrows rose. How he must love the Wild Hunt. "Don't the women get mad? Don't they tell everyone?" We didn't know each other well enough for this conversation, but I couldn't stop myself from asking. It was all so outrageous, yet I could feel the truth of it.

"I think they wonder if there was something wrong with them that caused me to leave before anything happened between us. They know there have been many women before them and all of them claim to have had the best night of their lives. They don't want to be the only one who failed." He smirked. "And I never kiss and tell what happens—or doesn't happen—between us." He looked me over. "While we're sharing secrets..." he paused like he didn't want to speak, before forcing the words from his mouth. "I know you are one of us. Fae."

I snorted. "Did you drink too much faery wine? Because..." I shook my head. "No. Just, no." His suggestion was so far from possible that I couldn't even list all the reasons it wasn't true.

His gaze was solemn. "This isn't just a feeling. Nor is it a game. I *know* you are. Without the shadow of a doubt."

This time when I shook my head, it was with less force. I wasn't fae. It was something I knew with complete certainty. But his confidence made my belief waver. "I'm really not." My mind worked in a hundred directions, trying to find his reason for saying such a thing. "If this is about the pretend ears and us getting married—"

"It's not about that," he snapped, walking away and stopping to stare into the darkening woods. "You removed my mask." His voice softened, so I almost couldn't hear it above the rush of the wind in the trees.

This was dramatics. Removing his mask proved nothing. "It was only a mask." And it wasn't like I'd tried to do it. "It pretty much slipped off of its own accord. Anyone could have done it."

He spun around, his nostrils flaring, all softness gone. "No. Anyone could not have done it. It is spelled, so it is impossible for any human—and most fae—to remove it."

"So why could I?" He was making things up to suit his own agenda.

He shook his head. "Believe me, that is something you don't want to know."

I shrugged. Fine. If it wasn't a big enough deal to tell me all the details, then it wasn't a big deal at all. "Perhaps you're just not as good at spells as you believe you are." I didn't even know why I was debating this with him. I wasn't fae.

He stalked toward me, his graceful movements marking him as the lethal hunter that terrorized our villages night after night. Even without the mask, it took all my resolve not to shrink away. "I am one of the strongest fae in all of Faery. My ability to weave spells is not the issue here."

I drew myself up. "And I am not fae. So go find yourself some other explanation." I snapped at him the way he was snapping at me. This wasn't up for discussion. Whatever he was trying to trick me into wouldn't work.

His arm shot out and he clamped his hand onto my chin and turned my head until he could see my left ear. All my life I'd been told the deformity was a birth defect, that there was nothing anyone could have done about it. But with Prince Fergus staring at the mess that was my left ear, another idea—one I didn't want to consider—surfaced.

What if I wasn't born this way? What if Fergus was right, and I was fae? Could Mother or Father have done this to me? Perhaps they'd found me wandering the woods alone as a child and had taken me in. Of course, they would have gotten rid of the ears. Had they not, everyone would have known they were bringing up a fae child. I shook my head, speaking as much for my benefit as his. "You're wrong. I'm not fae, and my parents would never have done whatever you're suggesting." I pulled from his grasp.

He dragged his hands down his face, his voice softening. "I'm not lying to you." He frowned, eyes running over me like it was the first time he'd seen me. "What's your name?"

"Bria. Tremaine."

He inclined his head. "I'm not lying to you, Bria Tremaine. There is no possible way for humans to remove the masks of the Wild Hunt. And there are only a handful of fae able to do it. It's one of the best parts of the job for me. No chance of ever getting found out." His lips quirked into the smallest of smiles, gone almost before it appeared.

"Until me."

The ghost of a smile ran across his face again. "Yes. Until you."

I shook my head, unsure if I was trying to convince myself or him. "I can't be fae. I've been to Faery only one other time, and that was the night of the masquerade. And I have no magic." I turned to him, trying—and failing—to hide the desperation from my voice. "I'd know if I had magic, right?"

"Usually. But if you've lived all your life away from Faery, perhaps your magic hasn't had the chance to mature. Also, the longer you spend away from Faery, the weaker your magic grows. So, I guess there's a chance that it's too weak to notice."

I shook my head again. I couldn't be.

"You never suspected?" He tilted his head to the side as if he couldn't see how that was possible.

"I had no reason to. Still don't." I didn't believe. I wasn't fae. But my ears...

He moved a step closer, sympathy filling his eyes. "Could either of your parents be fae?" The implication was obvious. If one parent was fae, I was, too.

I shrugged. "You tell me. You killed them both."

"To be fair, I didn't kill your mother. The magic I used when she was injured would have caused an infection that would keep her from healing properly."

An image of Mother lying in her bed hit me in the heart. She might have taken her last breath already, while I was standing here with the uncaring fae who had done it to her. "You're an ass, did anyone ever tell you that?"

"I don't believe anyone ever dared." His lips flickered. "I am a prince, you know."

His voice seemed light, and though I thought he might have been joking, his reminder hit the mark. I might try to barter for my life, but the prince could end me with the click of his fingers. Probably literally. Tears welled in my eyes.

As I told myself to get a grip, he shuffled his feet, leaves crackling beneath them. "Sorry. That was insensitive. It's a nasty habit of mine." Fergus

Blackwood was an insensitive dick; it wasn't exactly breaking news.

"Please let me go back home. Allow me to be with Mother in her last days." I hated the way my voice broke, but I couldn't stop it. Because of him, I was desperate and running out of options.

He shook his head, an apologetic smile on his lips. "I can't do that."

I blew out a breath. "You mean, you *won't* do that."

"Can't. Won't. Same thing." He lifted a shoulder. "The rest of the Wild Hunt is still searching for the girl who fits the shoe."

"So, call them off. Tell them you found me. Tell them you don't like me after all, that I annoyed you and you killed me." Option after option spilled from my mouth in my desperation to see Mother again.

"And when someone realizes you are still living at your cottage in Holbeck, how do you think that will work out for either of us?"

Not well. For me, anyway. I felt like a trapped animal looking into the eyes of my future killer. And that made me lash out. "Or is it that the Wild Hunt won't listen to you?"

His jaw stiffened almost imperceptibly. "They listen." The edge returned to his voice. Not as pronounced as earlier and gone after another deep sigh. "I just ... may have piqued the king's interest by stealing you away into Faery and hiding from the Wild Hunt for the past few hours." The final words were a mumble. He stuffed his hands in his pockets and looked at the ground.

"What, exactly, does *piqued the king's interest* mean?" Because it didn't sound good to me.

"It means that he'll want to know where I've taken you and why. And he won't stop until he finds out. Most likely starting with questioning your family and friends." He stared at me a moment and his eyes rounded as if he'd just realized something. "Did you use the potion I gave you at the masquerade?"

I nodded, my voice growing snarky. "Of course. On Mother."

He let out a loud curse. "It didn't work." He shook his head, his pacing becoming brisk.

It was a statement rather than a question, but I answered anyway. "Mother's worse than ever in case you hadn't figured that out. Thanks for asking."

He swallowed. "I thought ... you said..." He shook his head, stopping still. "If she were human, she'd be cured. You said she was human. You said it was for a man." I couldn't decipher the tone in his voice. Desperation? Regret?

"She *is* human." How many ways did I have to say it?

"But her condition hasn't improved." He wasn't asking a question, yet I had the sense he wanted me to disagree, to tell him I was joking and she was better.

There was nothing to disagree with. I shook my head.

Fergus began pacing again. Four steps past me along the wooded trail, four steps back. Even though night was almost here, he didn't trip in the darkness. "That potion used on someone of fae birth only hastens their end."

My eyebrows rose. "Hastens their end? You mean the potion is killing her? And I can't be with her while she dies?"

He lifted a shoulder, a picture of fae arrogance. "She was going to die anyway without the potion. Humans have no way to heal fae magic."

He didn't need to spell that out. I knew without a doubt that I had to get back to her. I licked my lips. "Prince Fergus, please let me go to Mother. I just want to be with her when she passes. After that," I shrugged. "I'll come back and do whatever you ask of me here in Faery. Get married. Prove I'm fae—or not. Anything." My voice died. "Just let me go to Mother."

He frowned. "You want to watch her die?"

"I want to be there to make her comfortable in her last hours. Is that so hard to understand? I'm sure you'd want the same, and that you'd use your immense power to ensure no one stopped you if you found yourself in my position."

"Huh." He looked out past me into the dark woods.

I waited for him to say more, but he seemed uninclined. I took it as encouragement. "You don't have to take me. I'll walk. Just point me in the right direction." Said aloud, that didn't sound quite the same as in my head. It sounded like I was trying to escape again. "Or you can come with me." *Just let me go back to Mother. Please.*

He stared into the darkness of the woods as he spoke. "Why don't you ask me for your mother's life?"

I blinked. "I didn't realize I was in a position to bargain." It was a question worded as a statement. "But if that's an option, I'll do anything. If you can save her, name your price."

Fergus turned to me. "Remember how I said we had piqued the king's interest?"

"I believe you said it was you who had done that."

"Quite." He closed his eyes in agreement. "I think we may both be of interest to the king at this moment. He noticed you at the masquerade."

Fergus lifted an eyebrow. "Acting strangely. He might not know your name, but you can bet he's trying to find out. Then, Xion Starguard goes searching for his son's future bride—the same girl who created a fuss at the masquerade—and disappears. No one in the Wild Hunt has seen him in hours." He watched me, waiting while I connected the dots.

"The king thinks I'm ... dangerous?"

"Who knows what the king thinks?" There was a trace of bitterness in Fergus' voice. "You can be sure he's thinking about you though, trying to work out if you're friend or foe. I also have this strange..." He shook his head. "I don't know. Whenever I think about your cottage, I get this..." He put his hand to his stomach. "Tight feeling in my stomach. Like something is wrong." He blew out a breath, some tension in his shoulders going with it.

"Does that happen often?" I wasn't sure how seriously I should take him. About any of this.

"Me thinking about your cottage?" There was almost a smile on his lips. "Never. And neither have I had this bad feeling about a place before."

For a moment, Fergus Blackwood seemed almost human. Until I caught sight of those pointed ears poking between the strands of his black hair. He was fae, and I didn't trust him.

There was no danger at my home. Despite what he said, the king surely had much more on his mind than to waste his time thinking about me. "I need to go. I'll do whatever you want of me after. Just, please, let me go back."

Prince Fergus watched me, the growing moonlight casting half his body in shadow. Finally, he nodded. "You have to be careful, but very well. You can go."

EIGHT

BEFORE I could think twice, I threw my arms around him. "Thank you. I promise I'll come back. You don't have to worry."

For a moment, his hands rested on the small of my back, then he extricated himself from my grasp, turned and walked along the trail toward his horse.

I stared after him as he disappeared into the darkness. Was that it? I could leave? He hadn't given me directions, but I could manage without.

I hoped.

I started along the trail in the opposite direction than he'd gone, my step light, even though the full darkness of night now covered Faery.

"Bria Tremaine." Prince Fergus's voice floated toward me.

I turned to find him sitting atop Obsidian. Only it wasn't Fergus seated on the horse. He was Xion again, complete with skeleton mask.

"I am the leader of the Wild Hunt. If we're to travel in the dark of night, we'll travel as hunters." He beckoned with his head, holding something white in one hand as he jumped from the horse.

"What about people seeing us?" I walked toward him, trying to work out if this was a trick. Using the horse would be so much quicker, yet he'd been uninclined to get off the ground earlier.

"It's night. No one will question seeing the Wild Hunt out at this time of day. Our whereabouts are much less likely to get back to my father. Put this on." The white thing in his hand was a mask shaped like a cat, its mouth open and teeth bared. He held it out.

"You're giving me a mask?"

"I'm loaning you a mask. There's a difference." He waited until I took it. "It's already spelled for you. Just hold it to your face and the magic will do the rest."

I stared at it, unsure if I wanted to put it on. It felt like in doing so I would approve of everything the Wild Hunt did, and I could never do that.

Seeing my hesitation, Fergus's voice hardened. "Put it on. Or we stay here."

Suppressing a sigh, I held the mask to my face. This was for Mother.

The moment it touched my face, the mask attached to me, sucking my skin so hard it felt like my face might rip away from my body at any second, the sucking sensation worse by far than the stabbing pain of the ears attaching. It hurt so much I couldn't breathe. Or scream. Then it stopped. Just like that. The pain was gone as if it had never been. I touched my face to find the mask in place, fitting perfectly to the contours of my cheeks and chin.

Fergus' smile was sardonic. "You look ... truly evil. Perfect for the Wild Hunt."

Obsidian was a different horse with darkness surrounding him. He seemed unable to keep his feet still. Perhaps it was the night calling to him, or just the fact that he knew Prince Fergus would take him out to ride when the night grew deep.

Not only did Fergus provide a mask for me, but he magicked up a horse, too. From thin air. One moment it was just Obsidian stomping his feet in front of us, the next there was a slightly smaller version of Fergus' enormous horse standing there. Apart from white rings around the bottom of her two front legs and her smaller size, the two could have been twins.

"Her name is Raven." He indicated I should climb on.

I was an okay rider, but horses had never been a big part of my life. Had Mother insisted our patients pay us for our healing skills using coin, we could have afforded one each and a spare. But because people paid with whatever they had, we often had an abundance of the thing we needed least. And a lack of ability to purchase anything useful, including horses.

It wasn't riding her that had me pausing just out of reach of Raven, it was that her back was without a saddle. I'd never ridden bare-back. That was an entire set of skills I had yet to attempt, let alone master. It had been fine with Fergus behind me on Obsidian. I'd actually felt quite secure. I shook my head. "I ... ah ... can't we both ride Obsidian?"

A smirk settled on his masked face. "Because you prefer to be pressed up against me?"

I glared at him and eyed Raven again, my cheeks heating. "Surprisingly, no. I thought you might be concerned about me escaping on my own mount."

Fergus chuckled. "Sure you did."

With little choice—because there was no possible way I was ever riding with him again after a comment like that—I called Raven over to a fallen tree just off the trail. Trying to look like I wasn't completely out of my depth, I hoisted myself onto her back and took hold of the reins.

I was barely seated before Raven took three steps along the trail and then pushed up into the air. I wrapped my arms around her neck and squeezed my eyes shut as the canopy of treetops loomed, but somehow Raven found a space between branches and only a few leaves brushed my arms and legs as we passed through. When I cracked my eyes open, we were high in the sky, the woods a block of darkness below. She ran as if she were on the ground, as if there was earth beneath her hooves. Magic held me on her back. Not the magic that had gripped me tight when Fergus brought me into Faery, but magic that held me as secure as if I were seated on a saddle. I sat up, using the reins rather than Raven's neck.

"Hold on tight," called Fergus from over my shoulder. "There are some good updrafts above this part of the woods."

Wind pulled at my hair and clothes, and the ground raced by so fast it stole my breath. Still, I couldn't close my eyes. I didn't want to miss anything—Faery from up here was stunning. Where the woods ended, lights of every color twinkled. No one in Faery had to live their nights in darkness, terrified the Wild Hunt would come for them. I wanted to hold it against them—him—and I probably would once my feet were on solid ground again, but right now all those colors against the darkness of the night were mesmerisingly beautiful, and the wind on my face was such a rush, I couldn't hold anything against anyone.

Raven swooped down without warning and my stomach dropped. I gasped and though I wanted to scream, a laugh burst out of me instead. I wasn't sure I'd admit it to anyone, but riding Raven was exhilarating and invigorating in a way I'd never experienced before.

Fergus and Obsidian appeared beside me. He leaned forward, speaking above the rushing of the wind. "Did you just … laugh?"

"Yes!" I laughed again. I wasn't even embarrassed at the giggle that escaped my mouth. "Did you expect me to wrap my arms around Raven's neck, close my eyes and scream in fear?"

He watched my face—my mask—a moment before he answered. "Well ... yes." Mild amusement flashed across his mask.

I shook my head. "I've never felt anything like this. The wind rushing past, the power of the horse beneath me, the view—"

"The wonderful company." He grinned. Somehow, his mask didn't look quite so scary right at this moment.

I held back my grin, debating whether to tell him that the company was the least amazing thing about this. "It's so freeing!"

All traces of laughter left his face and his mouth dropped open. He recovered himself after a moment, giving a single nod. "It is the most freeing thing I've ever done."

Travel via the horses of the Wild Hunt was fast, the ground rushing past at a speed I'd never before encountered, and we were at the Crossing in no time. No one needed to tell me we'd reached the border—it was plainly obvious. From Faery, the border was a sparkling glass wall as high as the eye could see. Even at night, lit only by the moon, the wall twinkled. "It's beautiful," I whispered.

"Doesn't quite look the same from Iadrun, does it?" Fergus asked.

I shook my head, as Raven drifted down toward a three-meter gap in the wall at ground level.

She landed softly on the ground, galloping a few steps before slowing beside a stone gatehouse where the guard who'd let me through the night of the masquerade sat reading by torchlight. He glanced up and waved us through, putting his head down to read again, the look on his face saying he did not want another interruption tonight.

Fergus sat tall and straight as he directed Obsidian along the trail, leaving me to follow behind. I watched his stiff shoulders before calling, "Do you really think the king will be waiting at our tiny cottage?" It seemed like an over-reaction to me. Nothing looked out of place. Certainly there was no reason for his tensed body and grim face. I still had trouble believing the Unseelie King would take an interest in my home. But then, until a few moments ago, I'd never imagined I'd ride a horse through the night skies of Faery with the leader of the Wild Hunt who was also a fae prince, so what did I know?

"I hope not," he answered, his voice soft.

The moment the cottage came into view, I wriggled off Raven, ripped off my mask and ran toward it.

"Bria!" The prince's voice was low but contained enough urgency to stop me mid-step.

I turned, unable to keep the frustration from my voice. "There's no one here. Everything looks exactly as it always does." I turned back, desperate to check on Mother, then thought of something. "Unless you can magically tell there's someone here?" I had no idea what he could do with magic, but given the way he made the horses fly, it seemed as good a reason as any for his reluctance to move forward.

He shook his head. "Magic can't tell me that. And I agree, there seems to be no one else here. But something's ... off. Can't you feel it?"

I couldn't. The cottage doors and windows were all closed, the way they should be at this time of night. No light escaped from the rooms within either our cottage or Selina's. Everything was exactly as it should be. And he was stopping me from seeing Mother with his worrying. "Perhaps you're just not used to entering a house where someone is about to die without your assistance."

He grimaced, shifting on the back of his horse and looking at his hands. "Perhaps that's it."

I spun around and started for the cottage at a trot.

"Bria!" Selina sprinted out her back door and across the yard and wrapped me in a hug. "You're okay! I've been so worried about you. I didn't know what to do." She pulled back, reaching down to grip on of my hands. The moonlight shone in her eyes. "I have so much to tell you."

I glanced between her, my cottage and Fergus, sitting on the back of Obsidian at the edge of the woods. I couldn't talk to Selina at the moment. Not with the leader of the Wild Hunt so close. I needed to keep her safe almost as much as I needed to be with Mother.

I extracted my hand, trying to ignore the crestfallen look on Selina's face. "Can we talk later?"

"S-sure. I just never got the chance to tell you earlier, but I saw Tobias' grave."

My heart disintegrated. It couldn't be true. Even if Tobias really was dead, his final resting place would be in Faery. There was no chance she'd ever see it. "Are you okay?" I'd have given anything to make her a cup of tea and sit down to talk about it with her.

She nodded, more light in her eyes than I'd seen in weeks. "It was in the woods next to a sparkling tree with fiery leaves. I've tried to find it again since, but I keep taking the wrong turn. I won't give up though." She held up the picture book she loved so much as she moved back toward her cottage. "I want to read to him, one last time." She glanced at the back door to my cottage. "I checked on your Mother. She's the same as she was."

"Thank you," I whispered, relief washing over me.

"You'll come and see me in the morning? Once you've finished with your patients?"

I nodded, guilt filling every pore of my body. There would be no patients. Just me sitting with Mother as she died, and then a promise that would pull me back to Faery. I called to her back. This could be the last time I saw her. "I love you, Selina."

She turned with a smile, walking backward as she spoke, "Love you, too!"

I stumbled into the cottage, my mind only half on the danger Fergus had mentioned. The rest of my thoughts were taken by Mother. And by Selina thinking she'd found Tobias' grave. Her description of the grave sounded like it could be in Faery, but that made no sense. Fae didn't bury their dead, they burned them. If Tobias were already dead, no one in Faery would have taken the time to bury him. But I couldn't remind her of that, because thinking about what else they might have done to him was worse than pretending he was already in the ground.

As I ran in the back door, the front door of our cottage flew open. I tensed, searching the room for a weapon. Fergus had been right. It wasn't safe here.

It took me a moment to realize it wasn't the king, or anyone from the Wild Hunt bursting into my home. It was Mrs. Plimmer. She marched inside without waiting for an invitation, pointing at me as she advanced. "Thief. No good half-breed thief!"

"Mrs. Plimmer." I sighed. Now was not a good time. I wasn't even sure I could remain civil. "You need to leave. Come back in the morning."

She pulled herself up straight. "Leave? Not without my property, you ugly-eared pretender."

Anger rose inside me, but I pushed it down. *She's baiting you.* I could hear Mother's advice as clearly as if she were standing beside me. *People like her just want a reaction, then they want to use that reaction to drive us away. Don't react, Bria. You're better than that.* I smiled at Mrs. Plimmer. "Your property?"

"Yes, you smug little harlot. You stole our chicken." Mrs. Plimmer puffed out her chest as if she'd dealt a winning blow.

My eyebrows shot up. I'd expected Mrs. Plimmer's anger because I'd fixed Jonty's arm. I hadn't expected her to be upset about a chicken. Nor could I find it inside me to care. "I did no such thing." With each passing second, it was growing more difficult to remain pleasant.

"Trinity Archer saw you place our chicken in your coop. Right, Trinity?" She turned to look through the open front door and I realized she'd brought people with her. Five stood outside, arms crossed and waiting. For what, I was unsure. Probably for a chance to hurt me. Or at least have me confess to thievery so they could drag me to the village gaol.

Trinity stepped up to the threshold, but not over. "Yes, ma'am. I was in them woods over there. Saw it with my own eyes."

"And did you also see Jonty pick the chicken up as he left and take her home with him?" I turned to Mrs. Plimmer. "Did you check your own chicken coop before marching over here?" There was a bite to my voice that I didn't even try to contain.

"Listen here, you foul-looking tart. My chicken was seen—"

The back door of the cottage flew open, banging against the wall behind it, and a man strolled in, his casual movements at odds with the slamming door. He was tall and broad with a balding head, and wore black pants, a black cloak and knee-high boots. His concerned eyes met mine, and it took a moment to realize this was Fergus Blackwood in disguise. His face looked different, but his build and clothes were the same. And the eyes, they were definitely his. It had to be him.

The anger on his face made everyone take a collective step back. He stalked over to Mrs. Plimmer, graceful and predatory, stopping so close she had to tilt her head back to see him. "What ... did you just call Bria?"

Mrs. Plimmer's chin lifted. "I called her what she is, a foul-looking tar—"

"Take it back," Fergus bellowed, his voice suddenly so loud, I jumped.

Mrs. Plimmer jumped too, but her eyes remained defiant. She lifted her chin higher. "Or what?"

"Or I make you." The level of his voice dropped to become soft, daring her to deny him. There really wasn't any space between the two of them, but somehow Fergus moved closer.

Whatever she saw on his face was enough for Mrs. Plimmer. She yielded a step, quickly followed by a second. Another couple of steps and she'd be out the door and gone.

Fergus must have thought so too, because he stalked after her, his voice menacing. "Take. It. Back." He was different tonight from how I'd seen him in the past. As Xion, he was cold and calculating, yet always calm. Tonight, Fergus was angry, and it was white hot and volatile.

Her tongue shot out over her lips and she glanced my way. "I'm sorry," she mumbled.

"Pardon me?" Fergus put a hand to his rounded and human-looking ear.

Mrs. Plimmer's nostrils flared, and a red dot appeared on each cheek. Her eyes shifted between the two of us. "I'm sorry for calling you such awful names."

He looked at me and I nodded. "Bria accepts your apology," he said. "Now leave. And don't come back for her help unless you're dying, and you have coin to pay."

Mrs. Plimmer shot out the door, her friends already gone.

I shut the door at her back and turned to find Prince Fergus looking as he usually did, black hair falling over his shoulders, brown eyes glowing with anger. He glared at the door as if he could see through it and was still staring at Mrs. Plimmer. "You shouldn't let her talk to you like that." His voice was strained.

"Yes, well, it isn't as if I have much choice in the matter." I enjoyed working as a healer. I was good at it. If I didn't take the insults, I didn't get the work.

He stepped toward me, leaning down until his face was hovering above mine. His voice was soft. "You didn't even try."

I looked away because he was right, I hadn't tried to stop her. But the moment Fergus arrived,

I'd stepped back and let him handle it. And I'd done it because I enjoyed seeing terror on my tormentor's face that I'd never been able to inflict—even during those fist fights at school, I might win, but no one was truly scared of me. It had been nice to have someone on my side for once.

I hated how much I liked that feeling.

"Thank you," I mumbled. "For sending her away."

He blew out a breath, any leftover rage disappearing with it. "Anytime."

I shook my head, almost letting out a sarcastic laugh. There was no way the Unseelie Prince meant those words. Rather than call him on it, I changed the subject. "You can change your look."

He shook his head, his features softening until he was almost smiling. "Not well, and not for long. My friend Jax can do it better—he's a puka, a shapeshifter. I have to rely on an enchantment, but it worked well enough for what I required." He paused, his smile growing. "Why? Do you prefer looking at me when I'm like that?"

I snorted, unable to bring any bite to my words. "I'd prefer not to look at you at all, but here we are."

This time, when his smile grew, it remained. "I'll take that as a yes."

A blush inched up my cheeks. There was no way that was true. Prince Fergus in his usual form was very easy on the eye with his high cheek bones and defined jawline. The problem was, he knew it. To my relief, he pulled his skull mask on. "What are you doing?" There was no need for masks now.

"Making sure your mother doesn't recognize me as the prince."

"Oh, right." It suddenly occurred to me that he'd placed a lot of trust in me, by bringing me here. Already, I could have told several people his secret. Yet it was he who'd stood up for me and was now giving me time with my dying mother.

I started for her closed door, my heart beating in time with my boots as they tapped on the wooden floor. "Mother?" I knocked, but there was no answer. I pushed the door open and walked in. A shaft of moonlight fell across her body as she lay in bed. Her eyes were closed, and her chest rose and fell slowly. I lit a candle so I could see her properly and immediately wished I hadn't. The wound eating her skin had spread across her chest, but even so, the weight on my shoulders shifted as I realized she was still alive. I'd made it home in time.

"She lives." Prince Fergus stood behind my left shoulder. I hadn't even heard him enter.

Mother's eyes flickered open, focusing on Prince Fergus, rather than me. She licked her lips. "The Wild Hunt. Come to take me at last." Her voice lacked the strength I was used to hearing, but no one would mistake it for fearful. It made me proud that she would look Xion Starguard in the face without cowering, even if I was beginning to wonder if he wasn't quite as bad as I'd always thought.

"Mother," I whispered. It was so good to hear her voice.

Fergus stepped across the room toward her, his movements too fast for me to react. He crouched at her bedside and gripped her chin with a grasp so tight, her skin turned white where his fingers pressed. His other hand shot out and pulled her blonde hair away, revealing a human ear. Mother didn't so much as flinch, and had it not been for the way her eyes widened when he launched at her, I might have thought Xion Starguard didn't scare her at all.

"Now do you believe me?" I demanded, finally jumping into action. A surge of anger shot through my veins. Mother was ill, and this was not how a dying woman should be treated. "She's not fae. Her ears prove it." It still didn't prove I wasn't. But since neither Mother nor Father were fae, I couldn't be, either.

Fergus's only answer was to angle Mother's head for a better view of her ears as he spoke a mumbled sentence beneath his breath.

The moment he began to mutter, Mother found the strength to fight. She wriggled beneath his grasp, tossing her head from one side to the other in an effort to escape. She'd been sick for so long, I wasn't sure where she got the energy, but she bucked and kicked like her life depended on it. Fergus, unfazed, continued to hold her chin and mumble.

"Stop." I pushed his shoulders, trying to dislodge him. What he was doing to her was wrong on so many levels.

"Do not push me." Fergus's words came through gritted teeth, his eyes never leaving Mother's face.

I shoved him again. I may as well have shoved the timber wall of the cottage for all the good it did.

He stretched his arm toward me, palm facing out, demanding I not come any closer.

I didn't need to. I could see what he'd done perfectly well from where I stood. Mother's human ears were gone, the round tops replaced by the sharp points of fae ears.

NINE

I SHOOK my head, refusing to believe, my eyes locked on what Fergus had done to Mother. "This is a trick. You used your magic to make her ears like that because you couldn't bear to be wrong." Or perhaps it was the guttering candlelight that was making me see things.

He shook his head slowly. To my surprise, there was none of the glee I expected in his voice, just resignation. "It's not a trick. All I did was remove a glamour." He turned his hand over. In the center of his palm, a tiny glass jar of red liquid appeared. With considerable calm, he unscrewed the lid and forced it into Mother's mouth. "Swallow it. The potion will reverse the effects of the other potion you took."

Mother let the liquid sit in her mouth for a moment before dropping her shoulders and swallowing it down.

Fergus held his hand above the wound on her bicep and as I watched, it knit together, healing until it became a faded scar.

But the healing wasn't the most remarkable thing in the room. I couldn't stop looking at Mother's ears. This wasn't possible. I knew Mother, and she wasn't one of them. She was kind and compassionate. And pretty. And she'd never had ears like the ones protruding from her hair.

"Xion Starguard." Mother's head once again rested back on the pillows. With closed eyes, she spoke. "The boy whose smirk haunts my dreams. Thank you for choosing to save my life." She drew in a breath, her blonde hair fanned out around her head.

"I had a point to prove." Fergus cut a glance in my direction.

"You have proven nothing. This is magic, a trick. I'm not naïve enough to think those ears are real!" Because believing that meant I had to reassess my entire life.

"Oh, you should believe, Bria Tremaine. It's not my magic at work on your Mother."

I clenched my fist, wondering if I dared smash it into his nose again. I wanted to.

Mother shifted on the bed, pulling herself to sit up, her voice stronger than it had been in weeks. "It's true, Bria. I'm fae. The same as him."

Fergus cast a told-you-so look over his shoulder.

Mother caught the movement, her eyes narrowing. "Xion Starguard. You think you're special, untouchable even. You pretend to forget, but I know your secret. I know why you wear that mask."

Fergus stared at her, then got to his feet. He shook his head, not as if he were repelling her words, but as if he needed to clear his mind. His eyes jumped from Mother's new ears to the living room outside her open bedroom door. Perhaps he never fully believed she could be fae, either.

"No." I shoved his shoulder, and he stumbled back. "This isn't real. Whatever game you're playing here, we want no part of it. The only fae here is you."

His lips tightened and he gave a nod, took a long look around the room, then started for the door, mumbling beneath his breath something about having been at the cottage before.

"Xion." Mother called to him before he made it to her bedroom door. He stopped without turning. "Can I ... can I remove your mask?"

He turned, looking at me.

I shook my head. She couldn't. She'd see he was the prince. "Mother. Sorry, but you can't do that."

"It's okay." Fergus watched me as he moved closer to Mother. "It will be fine, Bria."

I looked between them both, an overwhelming need to sprint from the room overtaking me. I might have forgotten how to breathe.

Fergus squeezed my arm on his way past. "It's okay." He crouched beside the bed, angling his face to Mother.

She reached out, her fingers sliding beneath Fergus' chin where she hooked them beneath the edge of his mask and pulled.

I braced for her reaction, for what Fergus would do because of it, but nothing happened.

The mask didn't budge.

"Well?" I asked. If she was going to do this, she might as well get it over with.

"I'm trying." She brought her other hand up, pulling with both.

The muscles in Fergus' neck stood out as he braced against her.

I shook my head. "You're weak. You've been in bed too long and lost all your strength." But I heard how wrong I was. The mask had almost flown from Fergus' face at the slightest touch from me. Weak or not, she should be able to remove it. She was doing this for another reason. "What is it you're trying to say, Mother?"

Fergus got to his feet, looking at me the moment Mother dropped her hands. "Remember I said—"

I put a finger up, stopping him. I didn't want to hear from him right now. I wanted to hear from Mother. The things she'd neglected to tell me over the years were piling up.

"No human can remove a hunter's mask. And only some fae can do it." She lifted her eyebrows. "Have you tried?"

I looked past her, shaking my head. I didn't even want to know how she knew that. "Are you saying you're human?" My voice didn't sound like my own.

She shook her head. "I'm not."

She wasn't human. And using the same story as Fergus, she was telling me what I didn't want to hear. I blew out a breath, my voice flat. "And neither am I."

She shook her head again.

I turned to Fergus, but at some point, he'd escaped from the room, leaving the two of us alone. "Why can I remove his mask when you can't?"

"That is something you really don't want to know."

Oh, but I did.

Before I could say so, Mother reached up and took my hand. "I will answer all your questions,

Bria. Just give me half an hour. I need a little more time for Xion's potion to work." Her head fell back against the pillows and her eyes filled with tears. "I should have told you what you were a long time ago. Your father wanted you to know." She shook her head. "I didn't think it was in your best interest."

I felt numb, like I was watching this happen to a stranger. Things like this didn't happen in real life. I didn't want to be fae. I wanted to be Bria Tremaine, healer from Holbeck. "None of this is about my best interest, Mother, or you would have told me years ago." My voice was flat. Mother was fae, and she was hiding out in Iadrun while pretending to be human. This was about her. "I think you're scared, and you're hiding from something." And it had to be something big. Not only had she hidden what she was, she'd mutilated my ears to hide me from that same thing. No one went to such extremes without reason. "So what is it, Mother? What are you hiding from?"

She shook her head, tears spilling from her eyes and running down her face. "Bria. I can't..." Her eyes fluttered closed as if she thought she'd given enough of an answer.

She hadn't. Not even close. "You can't what?" She'd lied to me all these years, and now she was hiding behind the weakness of her injury rather than offer an explanation? "Tell me what you're hiding from? Or explain why you would mutilate part of my body when you used magic to hide your own ears from everyone?"

Her mouth fell open. "Bria." I barely heard the words, only saw her lips move.

"I'm right, aren't I? You couldn't bear to do it to yourself, but you still did it to me." I shook my head. "You could have told me all of this, Mother. You could have explained it before any of this happened, and I'd still have loved you. Now..." I shrugged. I couldn't even look at her. "You're not the person I thought you were. And since you seem better than you have in weeks, you can look after yourself." I walked out of her bedroom.

"Bria! Stop. Where are you going?" Her feet landed on the wooden floor as I opened the back door.

I didn't answer. Not because of the tears that were now streaming down my face. Or because of the anger pulsing through my body. But because I didn't know where I was going. Selina was the only friend I knew well enough to run to, yet I couldn't run to her with this.

I started for the swings—my usual place of comfort—to find Fergus already there, sitting on the swing Selina usually used. Part of me had stupidly hoped he was gone, out of my life. No such luck. His elbows rested on his knees and his head lay in his hands, something made possible by his height—I could never have sat like that on the swing and had my feet on the ground. Moonlight dappled his form as it shone between the leaves of the giant oak.

"Still here?" I asked, sinking down onto the swing beside him. I wished my voice had more venom. But it wasn't him I was mad with.

He lifted his head, the mask still on his face, and blinked as if he'd just woken from a dream. His voice was soft. "You know it takes a lot of magic to hold a spell like the glamour she was wearing. Especially here in Iadrun. She probably had very little magic left over."

I sighed. The fae in my life needed to stop talking in riddles and give me some straight answers. "Meaning?"

"Meaning maybe she did what she thought was best for you." He touched his ear.

"No." I shook my head and pulled my hair back from my ears so he could see them. "There is no way this was best for anyone."

"I just think you should hear her out. Maybe she believes she had a good reason."

I glared at him, hating that I could hear the sense in his words.

Fergus suddenly stiffened and climbed to his feet. "Do you hear that?"

Barking echoed in the distance. I glanced across the fields to the edge of the woods where we'd left Obsidian and Raven. Both horses were tense, stomping their feet and whinnying. "The Hunt?"

He let out a long, low whistle and turned on the spot, looking around our moonlit back garden. "Where do you hide? When there's, you know, danger?"

He was still part of the Hunt. I wasn't telling him that. "We run into the woods."

His long, slow blink told me he didn't believe me. "Not helpful." He whistled again, and the cinnamon-colored hound I'd injured last time they were here came bounding out of the trees and across the fields.

Fergus' worry put me on edge. Seeing that hound made it worse. I balanced on my toes, ready to run if that animal so much as looked at me. Perhaps I could scurry up the oak tree before the animal attacked.

But I seemed to be the least of the hound's worries. She bounded over to Fergus, her tail wagging so hard her body almost bent in half. Fergus crouched, and the dog rolled onto her back for a belly rub, long legs pointing to the sky. Damn thing didn't look half as terrifying like that.

"Are they coming here?"

Fergus straightened. "I believe so." His words were careful.

There was something he wasn't saying. "For me? Or you?" I was the one who fit that damned shoe, but Fergus was currently missing from the Wild Hunt. I really hoped they were on their way to pick him up.

"Officially, me. But Buttercup thinks—"

I snorted. "Buttercup?"

He glanced at the hound lolling at his feet.

"Seriously? You call one of the hounds of hell *Buttercup*?" That was the name for a tame little terrier. Not the thing that had come at me with snapping jaws and dripping saliva.

"Don't judge what you don't know."

I shrugged. I knew enough about that animal to know she didn't suit the name he'd given her.

"Buttercup thinks they're after you. Or your mother. We need to leave." Buttercup sat up, nudging her head into Fergus' thigh. He scratched behind her ears.

"You two can talk to each other?"

He nodded and tapped his temple. "In here."

I sighed. I didn't even need to listen to Buttercup. If the Wild Hunt were returning to my cottage, no matter how hard I wished it weren't true, logic said it wasn't Fergus they were coming for. My glance fell on Raven and Obsidian. They were our ticket out of here. "I'll meet you at the horses." Without giving him the chance to disagree, I ran for the cottage, ready to throw Mother over my shoulder and drag her out to Raven if I had to. But I stopped suddenly when I found her out of bed and dressed, her cheeks rosy with health. Whatever Fergus had given her had worked fast.

The dining table was covered in a pile of long-bladed knives, swords, a cross bow, axes, spears, and about twenty other unnamable weapons I didn't know we owned.

She glanced up as I slammed the door. "You should have gone with him."

I lifted my eyebrows, surprised she knew he'd left. "I am. We are. Come on. There's a horse that can take us away from here."

She raced the short distance from the table into her bedroom and pulled another long-bladed knife from under the bed, the handle covered in strange writing. I had no idea how I'd never known it was there. "I can't guarantee your safety here."

I took hold of her as she ran past, gripping her shoulders to make her stop. She had so much energy. I didn't know where it had come from.

"We're leaving. We don't need to stay and fight."

She shook her head. "Too late. Hear that?" She paused, the barking of the hounds taking over from the noise of her feet slapping against the floorboards. They were so much louder than they'd been before. "They're almost here. Grab a weapon or two. You will need them. We're too late to run." There was a modicum of glee in her voice. Like she wanted to fight. I wondered if it had anything to do with her newly released fae ears.

My heart thudded in my chest. I looked over the pile of weapons on the table. I didn't know how to use any of them, except the hunting bow. Truthfully, I didn't want to use any, though that didn't seem to be an option. I picked up two smaller versions of the knife she had pulled from beneath the bed, tucking one into my boot and holding the other in my hand. I carried a knife when I hunted and had once gutted a young boar that had charged me. "Maybe we'd be better hiding beneath the cottage." Maybe I should have told Fergus where we usually hid.

She shook her head. "Not this time. We'll have a better chance of surviving if we're not cowering in that cramped space." Mother strapped a belt around her waist and slipped three knives into it, as well as another small knife into each boot. Then she picked up a sword and moved to stand beside the front door.

"Why now? Why is this happening now? We've lived in this same cottage for sixteen years, and the fae king never hunted you before." But as I spoke, I knew I was wrong. The king had hunted us. Father had died because of it. He'd lied that night. Told them Mother had died years ago. Had he sacrificed himself so the Wild Hunt wouldn't keep looking for Mother or me?

"Did you go to Faery with him? With ... your hunter?" She didn't look at me as she spoke, she just flexed her fingers around the hilt of the sword. There was an accusation in her words. Like by going to Faery, I'd drawn the king's attention.

"He's not my ..." I shook my head. She wasn't listening, anyway. "He took me there, against my will. But we weren't there for long. And I've been to Faery before—for the masquerade—and the hunters didn't come for us that time." If she thought I'd left a trail to our door by going to Faery, she was wrong. Fergus had been cautious. He wouldn't have come back here with me if he really thought we'd meet the king or the Wild Hunt. He had too much to lose.

She nodded. "You could have gone to Faery a thousand times on your own and no one would have known or cared. But the moment you went through the Crossing with Fergus Blackwood, it set off a tracking spell on one of you."

I swallowed, Mother's earlier words no longer sounded like the confusion of a fevered mind. "You know who he is?" Fergus' mask had stayed on his face the entire time. She shouldn't know.

"Our paths have crossed before."

"The night Father died." I wanted it to be a question, but it didn't come out that way.

She shook her head. "Before then."

I stared at her, my mouth falling open. Why hadn't Fergus told me? Why hadn't she?

Mother sighed, selecting yet another knife from the table and adding it to the arsenal around her waist. "Sorry, my darling. What we're about to face is my fault. I thought I'd done enough to keep us safe, but..."

"What did you do?" I whispered. I never imagined she could break any human laws, let alone do something bad enough that the Unseelie King would hunt her down.

"It's a story longer than the time we have." She smiled at me. I'd taken comfort from that smile every day of my life. "But after we fight them off, I'll tell you whatever you want to know."

The Hunt were almost here, and they never travelled with less than six hunters. Best case, they outnumbered us two to one—and that was only if Fergus fought against his own people, which didn't seem likely. There was no way I would ever hear that story, unless she planned on telling me in the afterlife.

"Hide, Bria." She nodded at the hatch that led beneath the cottage. "I'll sort this out."

I shook my head. I would not cower in the dark again while the Wild Hunt stole away another of my parents. I'd rather die.

Mother gave a nod as if she understood. Maybe she did. She'd been down there with me last time. She'd heard her husband die and could not help him.

My heart beat like thunder. The sound of the hounds barking was so loud, they must be mere moments away. I didn't want to die. Especially when I had no idea what any of this was about.

My hands were slick with sweat. I wiped them on my pants, then folded my hand around the knife again. This was the wrong thing to do. We needed to get to the horses or those hunters in their terrifying masks would drag us from the only home I'd ever known.

My mask. That was the answer.

"I have an idea." I pulled my mask from my pocket and held it to my face, hoping there was still magic in it. The mask attached to my skin like it belonged there, nowhere near as painful or as terrifying this time. I grabbed Mother's hand to drag her out the back door just as the front door broke open and a hunter burst in.

"Stop!" The hunter's voice was deep and echoing.

I pushed Mother outside but kept a grip of her wrist and turned to face him, enjoying the way his eyes widened when he saw my mask. "It's okay. I have her and she's not fighting. I'll take her with me." I wasn't sure if it was my imagination, but it seemed as if my voice had taken on that deep echo that the rest of the hunter's voices had.

A second hunter pushed through the doorway, closely followed by a third.

"How did you get here so fast?" one of them asked.

"Caught some good updrafts." Stars, what a lie. But those were the words Fergus used on our way here, so it must mean something to the hunters.

The first hunter's eyes narrowed. "Where's your stead?"

I pointed with my head out the back door toward the woods, trying not to flinch as hunters four, five and six tried to push through the door. "We should go. Before anyone has the chance to notice we're here and comes to her rescue." I was already backing out the door.

Mother pulled against my grip like she was my captive, and the first hunter's shoulders relaxed a fraction. Perhaps we'd convinced him.

"Help me!" Mother yelled.

I slapped a hand over her mouth and dragged her out the door. Calling for help might be taking things too far. Although ours was the last house before the woods, Selina's family were still neighbors. The last thing we needed was Selina or her mother coming over to check out the noise.

Shutting the door behind me, I whispered. "Run for the woods."

Mother was sprinting before I'd finished speaking. I followed behind, searching for Fergus and the horses among the trees. I couldn't see them.

Mother slowed when she reached the shadows of the woods. The night time woods looked blacker than they ever had. "You go first. I can't run if I'm looking over my shoulder to make sure you're all right."

I was selfishly okay with that. If one of us was going to be close to any chasing hunters, it might as well be her. I knew how horrible that made me sound, and I still couldn't make myself refuse her offer.

I sprinted through the woods, searching for Fergus, with Mother's footfalls close behind.

Wherever he was, he wasn't showing himself. I tripped on the rough path, jumping back to my feet. We just needed to make it to the second bend. After that, the trail split in four different directions. We could hide if they didn't see which trail we took.

More footfalls sounded at my back. I pumped my legs faster, my chest tight and my breathing heavy. I couldn't let them catch me. I would not be dragged to Faery again.

Behind me, Mother let out a grunt. I turned to find her scrambling to her feet, the first hunter behind her with his sword aloft. If only I'd grabbed my hunting bow.

Before I considered doing it, I threw the knife from my hand, aiming for his chest and wishing I knew how to use these weapons. It sank into the hunter's neck and he growled in pain. I stared for a moment, unable to believe I'd hit him.

He dropped his sword, his hands grasping the knife.

I glanced at Mother. "Are you hurt?"

She shook her head, drawing her sword and bringing it down on the hunter's neck. Blood sprayed everywhere. Over her, over me, over the forest floor. I gagged and backed away. Mother was a healer, not a killer. How was this even happening?

Mother's face was grim. "Grab his sword. Unless that horse you promised is nearby, we have to fight them." She pulled my knife from the hunter's neck and tossed it to me, handle first. "You'll need this, too."

Blood dribbled down the blade and over the handle to my fingers, sending a shiver up my spine. Not because of the blood. I'd seen plenty of that in my life. Usually, I was the one stopping the flow, not causing it. With hurried steps, I crossed to the side of the trail and slid the knife across a wide leaf on the nearest bush. When it was clean—or cleanish—I slipped it into my waistband. Then I ran back to the hunter on the ground and picked up his sword. By the time I'd done those three things, Mother was bringing her sword down on another hunter, and behind him, two more ran at us, just a few paces away.

The closest of them advanced on me. I threw my knife again, hoping for the same luck that landed it in the other hunter's neck. To my surprise, it hit just below the chest and he dropped to the ground like a stone. I threw my last knife at the second fae. He saw it coming and dodged it.

I wrapped my fingers around the sword hilt. I couldn't do anything with this weapon until he drew closer. Even then, I wasn't sure I trusted myself to use it. It didn't matter though because he didn't make it that far. Mother hurled a flat-bladed star at him before he could reach me. It hit the hunter's neck and blood was already spurting from his arteries by the time he hit the ground.

I stared at Mother in disbelief. The other fae— the one she'd been fighting—was lying in a bloody heap at her feet. That was four of them, dead or injured. If she could fight like this, why had we hidden before? Why hadn't she saved Father's life?

The final two came at her. She threw another of the flat bladed stars, but the first fae brushed it away without touching it, his magic doing the work for him. He advanced on Mother. She raised her sword, but compared to this hunter, her movements looked slow and sluggish.

I glanced at his face to find he was the only one not wearing a mask. He wasn't a hunter.

Mother was facing off with King Aengus.

He was clearly stronger than any of the hunter's had been, plus he still had a hunter working with him. Even after all our work to get out of this mess, Mother and I were still badly outnumbered.

I tightened my grip on my sword. I had to sneak up behind the king and the hunter while they were preoccupied with Mother. If I could bring myself to swing my weapon into one of their backs, Mother would have a better chance of getting away from the other. Even if the other was King Aengus.

I crept forward, watching them as I moved and quietly pleading that their attention not shift my way.

There was a blur of movement and Mother screamed. By the time I turned my attention from her attackers to her, she was on the ground. "No!" The word spilled from my mouth before I could stop it.

I ran toward her, but I was too slow. These last two fae moved so much faster than the rest. Before I could cross the short distance between us, the hunter had thrown Mother over his shoulder and was heading back up the trail toward our cottage. He followed along behind the king, whose long strides would have them at the edge of the woods in moments. Mother kicked and screamed, but the hunter's grip was strong.

"Stop!"

"Bria!" She paused her struggling, her eyes falling on me. "Run! You must go to Rhiannon."

Rhiannon? The Seelie Queen? Mother must have hit her head as she went down because that was the only way she'd ever suggest I visit Seelie.

I stalked after the hunter until I was close enough to touch him. Adjusting my grip on the handle of the sword, I lifted it high and slammed it into his side. My sword slid down his ribcage before finding purchase and slicing into his abdomen. His scream split the woods. He dropped Mother and clutched his side. I lunged for her, wrapping my fingers around her wrist. Our eyes met. We were okay.

The king turned at the screams. Alarm lit his eyes and he pounced, taking hold of Mother's other wrist. With a growl, he jerked her out of my grasp and dragged her from my reach.

The king was tall and slim. Looking at him, he shouldn't be strong enough to drag Mother away from me. But his age and his body shape hid his strength well. He'd taken Mother from me when I hadn't expected him to.

He held up one hand, his palm facing me, and an invisible force—his magic, I guessed—blasted me backward and into the trunk of a tree. The air whooshed from my lungs and I slid to the ground, gasping. I tried to sit up, to suck air into my lungs, but I couldn't move. All I could do was watch as a seventh fae— where had he come from?—ran toward me. The king didn't even spare me a second glance. He just threw Mother over his shoulder and stole her away.

Black edged my vision.

I was going to die.

That hunter in his grotesque mask running at me would make sure of it. I pulled my knees up, and pushed to my feet, trying to draw in that much needed breath of air.

Wind moved across my face followed by a blur of movement.

The hunter who had come after me a moment ago was suddenly lying at my feet with a sword through his heart.

Fergus stood beside me, his mask in hand. "Are you all right?"

I nodded, the smallest taste of beautiful air sneaking back into my lungs.

He touched my back with his fingertips and warmth flooded my body. My lungs expanded as if there had never been any reason for them not to.

"Mother." I struggled to get up, but he placed a hand on my shoulder.

He shook his head. "It's too late. She's gone."

"She can't be." I pushed him off and clambered up, panic making my voice shrill.

"She is. But we'll get her back. I promise." His eyes searched my face, and then my body, checking for injuries. Once he was certain I was okay, his focus shifted to the surrounding woods, and to the carnage we'd left behind. His eyes moved, from one body to the next. He let out a long sigh. "You killed some of my best men."

I followed his gaze, nausea rising from my gut. Bodies littered the ground. Some had died because of me. I put a hand over my mouth to keep from throwing up. I was a healer, not a killer. My eyes landed on the hunter with my knife in his chest. No, not anymore. I was a killer now too. "They attacked us." My voice wobbled. "I couldn't find you. Or the horses. We had to fight." My head was spinning. I'd killed one of them, but the rest of the deaths had been down to Mother. How was that even possible? I'd never once seen her raise a hand in anger. Trying to shift the blame, I said, "You killed one of them." If he cared about his men so much, why would he do that? He could have stayed hidden and let me die. "Why?"

He shook his head. "He wasn't mine. That one was a servant of my father's. The rest of them though..." He shook his head again.

"Where were you?" That was what I really needed to know. Had he run off when he realized the king was here, only to return once he thought it was safe? I needed to understand so I could work out what to do next.

"Trying to distract the king." He moved slightly, and I saw the sleeve of his shirt was cut open and blood dribbled from a long wound.

I looked from his arm to the mask in his hand. Not his usual skeleton, but a bear. He hadn't wanted the king to recognize him. "You're hurt."

He lifted one shoulder. "He saw me coming."

I took his arm and pulled the damaged shirt apart. The wound was long and deep. His black top hid how much blood he'd lost—his shirt sleeve was dripping, and there were red smears on the bushes behind him. I drew in a breath. "How are you standing up?" I glanced along the trail toward our cottage. "I can clean and stitch this. I just need to get my things from home."

Fergus shook his head. "It's only a sword wound."

"Only a sword wound? Have you even looked at it?" I suspected there was muscle damage as well.

"Careful, Bria. Someone might think you were worried for me." Before I could come up with a smart retort, he added, "I agree, it looks bad. But it wasn't made by magic so I can get someone to heal it. Once I get back to Faery."

"Why wait?" The wound was bad. There was a steady drip on the forest floor as blood ran from his body. "You should heal it now."

He shook his head. "I can't. I'm low on magic. I have to return to Faery."

Suddenly, everything came into sharp focus. "*We* have to return to Faery, you mean." I'd traded my life to see Mother a final time. I was pleased I'd done it, since Fergus had saved her life, but now Mother was captured. I needed to free her, and I wasn't sure that would be possible under the deal I'd made.

Fergus blew out a breath, a shaft of moonlight falling across his lips. "I will not force you to come to Faery, Bria. But you should come, anyway. You need somewhere safe to stay, and I can offer you that. The king doesn't like loose ends, and that's what you are at the moment."

I dragged my hands down my face finding the hard surface of the mask beneath them. He wouldn't force me to go. That should be good news, but it felt like the opposite. "I was wearing a mask. The king couldn't have recognized me." At least, if he was human, he couldn't. But he was the King of Unseelie. He was fighting with the Wild Hunt. Who knew what he did or did not know about me? I shook my head, my voice small. "No one in Iadrun knows the king is part of the Wild Hunt." Somehow, that made the Hunt even scarier.

Fergus' voice was soft. "He's not part of us. Not officially anyway."

I met his eyes. I wasn't falling for that. "And yet he was here, fighting with them, just a moment ago."

Fergus licked his lips. "The Wild Hunt is old. Older than the oldest fae. There are things about it none of us understand. And other things my father knows better than anyone." He looked down at his hands before continuing, his voice growing softer. "Father found a spell to link himself to the Hunt. Before him, the Wild Hunt never reported to anyone. Before him, the Hunt were heroes in Faery, our magic could bring bumper crops or make it rain or protect our borders. Before him, all fae had to be chosen to become one of us and many wanted that honor."

"The king was never chosen?"

He shook his head.

"But you were?" I'd always imagined anyone could join—perhaps after paying a tithe of some sort.

He nodded. "I got my call up when I was twelve, not long after Father began forcing the Wild Hunt to do his bidding." He shrugged. "I assumed Father had something to do with it, but after all this time, even when I meet with him each fortnight to receive our assignments as the leader of the Wild Hunt, I'm certain he doesn't know that when he is speaking with Xion Starguard, he's also talking to his son."

"And now, because of the king, you don't act like heroes in your realm, you instead terrorize ours."

He shook his head. "It's not what you think."

"Then what is it?"

He shook his head. "I ... can't tell you. Just know, you are safe from the king if you come with me."

Last week I'd have scoffed at the idea that I could be safe with a fae. Stars, a few hours ago I'd have scoffed. "You want me to hide from the Unseelie King in Unseelie?" Didn't seem like the smartest idea to me.

My question drew a weak smile from Fergus. "Not exactly."

I lifted my eyebrows, awaiting an explanation.

"I have a place that straddles both Seelie and Unseelie. The king doesn't know about it and I've warded it to make certain he won't ever find it. You'll be safe there."

I looked over the bodies scattered around the trail. Fae, every one of them. Including the one they'd taken prisoner. Probably including me. And now a powerful fae was offering me sanctuary in Faery. I couldn't stay here. The king would return. And if he found me, he'd kill me.

Then there was Fergus' offer.

Despite Mother teaching me since I was a child not to trust any fae, I trusted him. Perhaps that made me a fool.

Perhaps it made him one.

I nodded. "Thank you."

PART TWO

FAERY

TEN

FERGUS' *place*—the place he took me for my safety—was an island. Not the sort with craggy rocks, cold air, and high winds that I'd read about in books. Fergus' island—Lanwick Island—was like nothing I'd ever imagined. Actually, it was like something that should only have existed in one's imagination. Water the most brilliant shade of turquoise surrounded it, and Fergus assured me that if I dipped my feet in, the water would be as warm as bathwater. I hadn't yet been brave enough to try, though it was certainly hot enough here to tempt me.

White sand spilled from the water, leading up to bushes of the brightest green. Between the bushes grew trees that were only a long trunk until the very top where they sprouted into green fronds, and occasionally giant green fruit, too high to pick.

"They're called coconuts," said Fergus, following my gaze. "The most delicious fruit you'll ever taste. I'll bring you some with dinner."

At one end of the beach was a sprawling white building, two levels high in places, and large enough to fit most of the cottages from my village inside. Vast windows faced out toward the ocean and a balcony as wide as our living room and three times as long ran the length of the top level.

On this side of the building, set among the bushes and scattered all along the coast, were thatched-roofed cottages dotted as far as the eye could see. A small group of fae played a ball game on the beach, while others stood watching from the verandah of their cottages. I glanced at Fergus. "I thought you said I'd be safe here?"

"Relax. No one can find you here. And no one here will tell the king."

"Who are these people?" They didn't seem as interested in me as I was in them. One raised his hand to wave at Fergus. The rest seemed not to have seen us.

"The Wild Hunt. Their families."

I stiffened. He'd brought me to the very place the hunters lived. Perhaps coming with him was a mistake.

A wry smile crossed his face. "Oh, now you're scared? The moment I mention the Hunt you want to leave, yet traveling with Xion Starguard or the Crown Prince of Unseelie doesn't bother you?"

I let out my breath. "Point taken," I mumbled. If I was going to be scared, it should be of him. "The whole Hunt live here?" The island was large, the white sandy beach bending out of sight in each direction with a tall hill rising out of the tropical forest behind the mansion, and it was the last place I expected hunters to live. "This is what they do when they're not terrorizing Iadrun?"

Fergus looked at the group playing the ball game. "Everyone has a job here. Some work the crops, some fish, some tend to the horses. We've even got a few chickens and sheep around the other side of the island."

I nodded, trying not to look surprised. I wasn't sure why it had never occurred to me that the hunters had lives outside what they did at night.

We walked up the beach between two cottages to a hardened crushed shell track that crunched beneath my feet. Surrounded by lush tropical forest, the temperature back here was cooler than on the beach, but still hotter than it had ever been in Holbeck. We passed other fae, all of whom greeted Fergus by name, even a group of girls a year or two younger than me who giggled when he asked how their day had been.

"Looks like you've got some fans."

A grin spread across his face, and with his black cloak thrown over his arm and the sleeves of his shirt pushed up, he seemed relaxed and happy to be home. "What can I say? People love me."

The path led around the back of the mansion, but Fergus directed me onto a narrower side path which came out in front of it. Perhaps mansion was the wrong word. "Is this a palace?" I whispered. It was grand enough to be and even larger than it had seemed from the beach.

Fergus stifled a laugh. "No. It's just a ... home. Sometimes, anyway."

It looked nothing like a home. It was too big. The center portion was two levels with stone columns and a top floor balcony. Symmetrically running off to either side were single-story wings, each with a series of sliding glass doors along the front. All of it looked out over a large swimming pool that I couldn't drag my eyes from. The publican was the only person in Holbeck who owned a pool. I'd seen it once when Mother and I visited to treat his ill father, and compared to the sparkling water in the massive pool in front of me, the publican's pool looked like a bath.

"I'll take you to your chamber. Get some rest and we'll talk later." Fergus' voice broke into my thoughts.

I shook my head, dragging my eyes from the cool water. "I don't want to rest. I want to find Mother. And I want … you to help me." I swallowed, berating myself. I wouldn't get anywhere demanding things of the prince. "Please."

Fergus' smile was gentle. "Rest first. You've been up all night. Then we'll figure it out."

He led me into the central part of the building, which housed a lounging area with leather couches and coffee tables set up to look out at the ocean— the best view I'd ever seen. We walked along a corridor where he opened one of many doors and indicated I should enter before shutting it quietly and slipping away.

The chamber was bigger than the living area of my cottage, the curtains already drawn and the room dark. Stars, the bed was almost bigger than my living area. And Fergus was right. I was bone tired. I kicked off my boots and climbed onto the bed, laying my head on one of the many luxurious pillows. But I couldn't sleep. Every time I closed my eyes, I saw the king dragging Mother along the trail and away from me. As the sun set on the day, I gave up trying and threw open the curtains. An apple and some slices of dried meat sat on a tray on the dresser. My stomach rumbled, and I picked up the apple in one hand and shoved the meat into my pocket to eat later.

Then I turned and opened the huge sliding glass door that had been hidden by my curtains moments ago. I stepped out onto paving stones that led down to the swimming pool. Now that Fergus wasn't here, I could stare at it with the awe it deserved. I was truly at the home of a prince. Until now a pool was nothing but a distant wish, let alone staying in a home this size. Even the grass around the edge of this area was greener and lusher than anything I'd ever seen before.

Not bothering with my heavy boots—it was too warm for those here—I walked past the pool, past the brightly colored cushions scattered on the ground, past the tables and chairs, toward the beach, the sunset beckoning me.

Three steps led from Fergus' home down to the white sandy beach. I sat on the bottom step and buried my feet in the still warm sand, putting the apple down beside me. A gentle breeze played at my hair, but the evening was warm and pleasant. I watched the darkening sky, searching the endless blue of the ocean for another piece of land, but there was none. Fergus's island really was far from everything. It was also the most stunning place I'd ever seen. As the night grew darker; the waves hitting the shore sparkled. I didn't think I'd ever close my eyes to rest if I lived in a place like this, I'd always want to look at it.

"Don't you ever sleep?"

I turned to find Fergus leaning one shoulder against the nearest coconut palm. He had bathed and changed; his dark hair was damp against his shoulders, and he wore shorts and a bright green shirt, and looked as far from a prince as was possible. Far from the leader of the Wild Hunt, too.

I self-consciously straightened my hair with my fingers. I should have bathed. "Couldn't." My mind was too busy to sleep.

He stared at me without moving, and I wondered if he expected something from me. He was a prince—sometime during the hours I'd spent with him, he'd stopped being Prince Fergus in my mind and simply became Fergus. Perhaps there were certain protocols he expected when he wasn't either saving my life or attempting to kill me. "Excuse me if I don't curtsey to you this evening, your Highness."

Fergus' eyes swept over me, and I couldn't tell if he was irritated or amused. "When did you ever curtsey to me?"

Amused. He was definitely amused. I wasn't trying to be funny. "That I haven't has more to do with you pretending to be someone else for most of the time we've known each other. Besides, there's a first time for everything."

His eyes narrowed. "Clearly that first time isn't today." His tone was dry.

Clearly. I shuffled over and indicated to the space on the step beside me.

He closed the distance between us and stopped in front of me. "Did you sleep at all?"

I glanced up, surprised by his question. On closer inspection, although he was newly refreshed, he looked as tired as I felt. There were dark rings beneath his eyes and his skin was pale. "Very little. You?"

"I'm the leader of the Wild Hunt. I'm used to operating on little sleep. You, on the other hand, have no such excuse." He sat beside me, pushing his feet into the sand.

"Too much going on in my head." Before he had time to opt out of this conversation, and because I needed to voice the words that had been racing around my head all day, I added, "She mutilated me. She did it and then lied about it. She did it, then used magic to hide on herself the very thing she'd cut from me." My voice wavered. Saying it out loud made what Mother had done sound so much worse. I didn't want fae ears. I didn't want fae anything. But I'd never have chosen to be butchered just to hide them, either. I still couldn't believe Mother had lied all these years, telling me I was born this way, making me think I was human.

"Maybe she had a good reason. My father can be cruel. If she was running from him——"

I didn't want his sympathy. "If she was running from him, she would never have lived in the closest village to Faery." That was another thought which had been banging around in my head that I couldn't make sense of. Surely, if one was hiding from the Unseelie King, they would hide as far from Unseelie as possible.

Fergus lifted a shoulder in a way that said I might be right. "Or perhaps that was the very best place to live. The last place the king ever considered looking."

I shook my head, wanting to deny him, but really, I didn't know what to think. "What does he want from her?"

Fergus shrugged. "I don't know what my father wants with her. But you know what you have to do." He spoke softly, as if he didn't want to scare me.

I knew. But I didn't want to do it.

When I didn't voice the words, Fergus spoke them. "You have to go speak to Queen Rhiannon." The Queen of the Seelie Court.

"The woman who lets her people starve while she lives in luxury? Who kills those that wrong her in even the slightest way? Who loves watching her people tortured?" These were all things I'd heard from Mother, and they were all reasons to stay as far from Queen Rhiannon as possible. There was another, stronger, reason to go to her though, and by voicing my concerns, I hoped Fergus would dispute some or all of them. It would make walking into the Seelie Court that much easier.

"She can be cruel, but she's a queen." He shrugged as if being queen was reason enough.

There had to be a mistake. Mother had warned me for years against going into Seelie. It made no sense she'd change her mind now. "I really don't want to go to her court."

Fergus turned his head to look at me. "You went to my father's court. And you didn't seem half as nervous as this."

That was different. "I went to save Mother's life!"

"Could this also save her life?" His voice softened as he pointed out what was blatantly obvious.

Desperation laced my words. I'd seen how cruel King Aengus was, and his reputation had nothing on Queen Rhiannon's. "We don't know she meant *Queen* Rhiannon. It could be some other poor soul with the same name."

An amused tilt came to Fergus's lips. "How many other Rhiannon's do you know?"

"Well, none. But—" Perhaps it was a common name in Faery.

"Me, either. And I've met many people. I think it's safe to assume she was speaking of the Seelie Queen." Fergus lifted his eyebrows. "You're okay with rushing unprotected into the court of the Unseelie King to ask a favor, or staying at the private island of an Unseelie Prince, but you're not so keen to go to the one place in Faery your own mother suggested?"

The young girls from earlier walked along the water's edge. When they saw Fergus, they called his name and waved. "Evening, ladies."

"More candidates for royal bride?"

I couldn't decipher the look that crossed his face. "Most women dream of it."

I grinned. "So, you're saying most women don't need to be kidnapped to your island to spend time with you?"

A faint smile crossed his face, before instantly turning serious again. He shook his head. "Most women—and many men—want to spend time with a prince. Most hope it will lead to a better life, and better status." His voice turned hollow. "They aren't interested in knowing me."

"I'm sorry," I whispered.

He shrugged. "Don't be. I've long since learned that I'm not interested in knowing them, either."

I got it. Other than Selina, people looked at my deformity and instantly decided they knew all they needed to know about me. It was unfair and lonely. And a little deeper than I could go at the moment—there were too many other things happening inside my head. It was easier to joke with him. "You haven't been left alone on the dance floor often, then?" I let my face soften into a smile.

He blew out a breath. "Just the once. Can't say I enjoyed it overly." He tried to keep the grin from his face and failed. He was very handsome. Especially when he smiled.

I pressed my lips together, my grin threatening to widen. "Doesn't seem to have hurt you too badly. Perhaps it's something you should try more often." Everything I'd ever heard about Prince Fergus suggested he wasn't the sort of person I'd enjoy having a conversation with, yet here I was, struggling to keep my grin to myself.

He shook his head. "I think I'll pass." He turned his gaze back to the ocean, the sparkling waves brushing softly against the beach not too far from our feet. "Bria." He swallowed. "That night, after you ran out of the masquerade, I lied to Father and told him I'd bonded to someone."

He glanced my way before focusing again on the ocean. I didn't know why he seemed so nervous. He'd already told me he'd lied. "I did it because that night, with the mask over half your face and with the fake ears, I was certain you were from the Seelie Court."

"And?" The word stretched as I spoke it. There was more he wasn't saying. "Wait ... you can tell the difference between Seelie and Unseelie fae just by looking at them?" They all looked the same to me.

"Seelie fae have rounder faces and their ears are smaller. It's subtle, but it's there." Another long silence. "When I told Father we were bonded, I never expected we'd find you."

I lifted my eyebrows. Everyone in Iadrun knew the King wanted his son to be a strong and settled heir, with a wife and a child of his own. He didn't want to hand over his crown, but when the time came, he needed his son to be in the strongest position possible, with the strongest people around him to ensure the crown stayed within the Blackwood family. And the first person among those strong people would be a wife. Though the Prince didn't need to find his bonded soulmate, the marriage would go easier if he did. If the king thought the woman his son had bonded to was nearby, he would do everything possible to find her. "That seems a little naïve."

He shook his head, his lips turning down. "It wasn't. Seelie and Unseelie have been at war my entire life. We never mix. We would never lower ourselves to befriend one of them." There was such disgust in his voice that I didn't doubt he meant it. He threw me a wry smile. "They feel the same way about us. Because of that, Father would never consider one of the Seelie fae might sneak into his court. I knew he'd do everything possible to find you, but he didn't know you were Seelie, so he would never look for you there. I thought you'd be safe." He ran a hand down his face, tension pulling at the corners of his mouth.

"You expected you'd be free to remain doing all the awful things you do with the Wild Hunt for a little longer until he found me. Or gave up looking."

An emotion I couldn't decipher crossed his face, gone before I truly saw it. Had my words hurt him? I couldn't imagine it. "That was my plan. But it's not the point I'm trying to make. You look Seelie, Bria. Maybe you have a family connection and that is why your mother told you to go there. Maybe Queen Rhiannon will keep you safe from whatever Father wants from you and your mother." He licked his lips, his voice softening. "Perhaps she can introduce you to the rest of your fae family."

I stared at him. I didn't want a fae family. Mother was all the family I needed.

He shook his head, sounding more like himself. "Or maybe she'll do something else entirely, but there has to be a reason your mother told you go to her."

For years I'd feared the queen. Just thinking about walking into her court made my heart rate quicken. "Are you scared of her? The Seelie Queen?"

Fergus shook his head, something between a smile and a grimace crossing his face. "I have a healthy respect for her immense power from which I try to stay well away, but no, I'm not scared of her." He stared at me with pity. "I see her reputation proceeds her."

I nodded. "I'm terrified of her."

He ducked his head into my line of vision. "The only difference between her and my father is that she is a little more power hungry. You managed yourself fine around the king."

That wasn't entirely true, but I went with it. "Power hungry?"

A faint smile grew on Fergus' lips. "A very long time ago, Faery was one kingdom. The fae on the north side of the Azure river—the fae you know as the Seelie—were in control of all the lands. The fae in the south—the Unseelie—wanted to govern themselves. A war was fought and the Unseelie fae won. We established our own kingdom, and the Seelie fae have been trying to take it from us ever since. Rhiannon's made no secret of the fact she intends to make it happen while she's queen." He shrugged. "She won't be able to, but she likes us to know she wants to."

None of what he'd said had anything to do with me, except to remind me I had met King Aengus, and I'd lived to leave his kingdom. I could do the same with Queen Rhiannon, and I was done thinking about it. I changed the subject. "What did you mean back at my cottage when you said you should have remembered?"

He shook his head. "Your mother reminded me of another time I came to your home. It was a long time ago. Before the time I hurt her."

My heart stilled and my voice grew cold. "You killed my father that time." What sort of daughter was I? Sitting here having a conversation with one of my father's murderers and enjoying it. How dare he pretend to forget what he did to my family? That day had been the worst of my life. How dare I allow myself to forget what he was?

His voice was soft when he spoke again. "I remember very little about that night. Just that your father put up more of a fight than expected. I can't even recall what he looked like, though I should." He got to his feet and paced a few steps away, dragging both hands over his eyes and down his face.

Anger bloomed in my chest. He'd already told me how much he loved being part of the Wild Hunt—I'd seen the joy on his face myself as we rode to the cottage—yet he now expected me to believe he was upset over my father's death? No, he didn't get to do that. He didn't get to hurt Father, then ask me to feel sorry for him because he couldn't recall it. "You remember every person you kill or capture during your nightly raids, right?" My attempt to keep the sarcasm from my voice failed, and Fergus spun around as if he would bite back.

His jaw tightened and for a moment he was silent. When he spoke, it was without a trace of irritation. "You'd be surprised what I remember." His voice was soft, yet lethal.

I blew out a breath, my anger not so fast to dispel as his. "Just not the night you tortured and murdered my father."

He shook his head, pressing the heels of his hands to his temples. "Not that night. I should." His voice grew desperate. "I should remember it all. But your mother's comment showed me there's magic blocking my memory. I didn't remember any of it until she told me we knew each other. Since then, small things have been coming back, but none of the things I want to know. Like why we were there, or what was so unusual about that night that I wasn't allowed to recall it."

"How convenient." I didn't believe him for a second. It was a coward's excuse. A way not to have to own up to the atrocities he'd caused. It was very easy to forget what he was while spending time with him. Prince Fergus was easy to like. I had to remind myself he was also Xion Starguard, and that part of him wasn't pleasant at all. I stood up and climbed the steps, unable to look at him. He didn't even care what he'd done to my family. I was stupid to have come here with him.

As I opened my mouth to ask him to take me home, his voice floated softly up the stairs to my back. "I'm sorry."

My body stilled. Even as I wanted to keep walking I couldn't, waiting to hear what he would say.

"If it was me that killed your father, I'm sorry. If it wasn't, then I'm sorry I stood by and watched. I don't imagine my apology makes any difference, but please know it's sincere." There was a beat of silence and I imagined him shaking his head. "This isn't what we usually do in the Hunt. I don't understand any of it yet, but I'm going to. I'll break the spell on my mind, and when I do, the person who put it there will be sorry."

A shiver went up my spine as his tone hardened. My voice sounded small when I answered. "Well, when you do, let me know what you discover."

Later, after Fergus left, I returned to the steps and sat listening to the lull of the ocean with my feet in the sand. He was right about one thing. There was a reason Mother had told me to go to Queen Rhiannon. If I wanted to help her, and I did, then I had to go to Seelie.

Deep growling pulled me from my thoughts. I looked up to find Buttercup, Fergus' hound, on the beach in front of me, teeth bared and body vibrating with anger. I put my hand up, moving slowly to my feet.

Her growls increased in volume and the hound tensed like she was about to attack. She was so huge that one swipe of her paw would put me on the ground.

I glanced over my shoulder to my room in Fergus' mansion. It was too far to run; the hound would catch me before I got there. "Nice doggy." There was nothing nice about that animal.

I searched for something I could use as a weapon, moving just my eyes and keeping my hands out in front of me. There was nothing. Not even a stick on the beach. Unless I could pick up the apple I'd left here earlier and throw it at her, which would probably only make her angrier.

I put my hand into my pocket, my fingers closing around a chunk of the dried meat I'd found in my room. I really hoped this animal liked food.

I broke off a piece and threw it to her.

Her nostrils flickered and another deep growl rumbled from the back of her throat.

She dropped her head, sniffing until she found the food on the ground, and then gobbled it down. She fixed her black eyes on me again.

"You like that?" I broke another piece off, throwing it past her so she had to turn to find it.

The hound scampered after it, turning back a moment later and licking her lips, and not looking half as scary as she had a moment ago. I threw another piece even farther this time, and then spun on my heel and ran to my room, slamming the door closed behind me.

Strangely, sleep came easier after the chat with Fergus and the terror of facing his hound. I woke early in the afternoon, washed, and stepped outside, searching for Fergus.

I'd decided to go to Seelie, and I needed him to take me there. Or at least, get me off the island

and point me in the right direction. I didn't have to search far, because he and another fae were deep in conversation as they wandered past the pool, coming along the paving stones toward my chamber. Fergus carried a tray and was dressed the same as his friend in black pants, knee-high boots and a black shirt—similar to the attire Fergus had dressed me in.

Fergus smiled when he saw me and held out the covered platter. "Thought you might be hungry."

I lifted my eyebrows. I'd decided last night that I couldn't hold Father's death against Fergus. At least, I couldn't at the moment. Once I was off his island, I could go back to hating him, but for now, I needed his help. "Served by the Prince. I must be special."

Fergus' glance was mildly amused. "Not so much special, as I don't want to be responsible for your death because you haven't eaten. Plus, I promised I'd bring you coconut to taste." He glanced at his friend. "This is Jax Sunfall. My—"

"Impersonator?" He'd told me his friend Jax had pretended to be him at the masquerade. Right now, apart from the almost identical clothing, the two couldn't look more different. Jax was a little shorter than Fergus, and a few years older than him, with stunning emerald hair that fell into his eyes. His skin was dark, and his muscles bulged beneath his light shirt.

He stuck out his hand, his smile friendly. "I prefer the term lookalike." He turned to Fergus. "Is that a smile on your face, Ferg? I don't believe I've seen a genuine one of those from you in..." He pretended to count on his fingers. "... I'd say since you were a baby eighteen years ago. Typical that a pretty Seelie would make that happen."

The inference sent a jolt through me. I put up my hands. "I'm not Seelie." And no one had ever considered me pretty before. Jax mustn't know about my ears. I smoothed my hair over them to keep it that way.

Fergus spoke at the same time, his cheeks tinged magenta. "You are full of it, Jax. You know that's not true."

Jax's eyebrows lifted as he looked between us. "I think you both protest too much."

My stomach growled loud enough for them both to hear. I didn't get around to eating the apple last night, and I couldn't remember when I'd eaten before then.

Fergus seemed pleased to use it as an excuse to ignore Jax. He beckoned me out to the pool and placed the tray on one of the outdoor tables, then fell into the chair beside it, kicking one leg over the chair's arm. Jax followed his lead. Fergus looked at me. "Go ahead. Eat."

I stared at them a moment before sinking down onto the edge of the matching chair. I wasn't convinced eating was in my best interest. Mother had always warned me against eating anything in Faery. Hungry as I was, it wasn't advice I wanted to go against right now.

Fergus leaned forward, elbows resting on the table. "You know, strictly speaking, since you're fae, the food here in Faery should never affect you."

There were a few things in that sentence that needed clarification, not the least that he'd basically read my thoughts. "You want me to risk my life on *strictly speaking* and *should never?*"

He shrugged. "It would only risk your life if there was an actual risk involved."

Jax removed the lid from the platter. He took a grape, tossed it in the air and caught it in his mouth. "Eat. Or you'll fade away to nothing."

My stomach growled again. There was a chunk of bread sitting beside the grapes. Looking at it made my mouth water. And something white and fleshy that I assumed was the coconut. I looked between them both. "Assuming I am fae, I will need you to explain the *strictly speaking* part of that sentence." I wanted to eat, and I thought I could trust Fergus. He'd hardly have brought me to his island just to watch me starve to death.

Fergus broke off a piece of bread, smoothed some paste on it and took a bite. "Well." He stretched out the word as if he were thinking as he spoke. "You said you have no magic? Or magic so weak you have never felt it within you?"

We'd had this conversation. I'd used it as an excuse to argue why I couldn't be fae. "Don't you think I would have used it against you the night you burst into our cottage and injured my mother if I did?" That night seemed so long ago and the person who'd burst in so different from the person I currently sat with.

Jax tossed another grape in the air, catching it, and then speaking around it. "Without magic, if you were to eat enchanted food while in Faery, you would likely have the same reaction as any mortal."

"Meaning whatever spell is on the food will affect me?"

He grinned and nodded, his emerald hair falling into his eyes.

"Not making me feel any better." I stared at the bread, the grapes, the coconut and the cheese sitting beside it, my mouth watering.

"We're not trying to." Fergus lifted one shoulder. "This food isn't spelled. I have no reason to do that. It's up to you whether you believe me."

My stomach rumbled again. I had to eat. I trusted Fergus. Why was I even hesitating? I reached out and took a slice of the coconut, biting into it. The flavor exploded in my mouth, nutty and sweet. I grinned and took another mouthful.

"Good, right?" Fergus smiled.

I nodded, my mouth too full to speak.

Fergus and Jax watched as I ate foods I'd never eaten before as well as plenty I had. "I could get used to eating like this," I admitted, my eyes catching a slight movement in the bushes just over Fergus' shoulder. I broke off a piece of cheese and threw it toward the bushes.

Buttercup ducked out of her hiding place and gobbled it up, her tail swinging. She definitely wasn't as scary when she was eating.

Fergus looked over his shoulder just as Buttercup was licking her lips and staring at me with big eyes that made me want to give her another treat. "What are you doing here?"

"Anyone would think you never fed her." I threw her some more cheese.

"Lucky you're here to do it, then." He cast me a sidelong glance.

I wasn't sure if I was in trouble. I shrugged. "She's less terrifying when she's otherwise occupied."

Jax snorted. "Looks like Buttercup found your weak spot."

"She won't hurt you, if that's what you're worried about. Not now you're here." He whistled and Buttercup skulked over, her shaggy cinnamon-colored fur bouncing as she walked. She rolled onto the ground in front of him, eyes half closed while he gave her a vigorous rub down. "She's really very sweet."

Buttercup opened her eyes and walked over to me, tongue lolling. She didn't look like she was about to bite. I reached my hand out, and she nudged it with her nose, waiting for me to pat her. No, she wasn't scary at all like this. If I wasn't afraid of her anymore, then perhaps there were other things I shouldn't fear. I drew in a breath. "I've decided I have to go to Seelie. I need to know why Mother told me to go there. Can you take me?"

Fergus gave a soft smile. "I think you're doing the right thing." He glanced at Jax. "But I can't take you today."

"Oh. That's … okay." Of course he would have other things to do. He was a prince.

Before I could suggest waiting until tomorrow, or whenever Fergus was next free, he said, "Jax will take you."

I nodded, smiling to hide my disappointment. I hadn't realized how much I wanted to travel with Fergus again until he said he was busy.

"Jax can get you across the river at the border. After that, you'll be on your own. The Seelie guards will kill us if we're caught across there."

"Or worse," mumbled Jax.

I nodded again. I could get myself to the queen. They'd already been so generous, I needed nothing else from them. "Thank you. For giving me a place to stay. I appreciate it."

Fergus got to his feet. He inclined his head. "It was nice meeting you, Bria."

ELEVEN

THE SEELIE castle was in the far north of the fae lands, farther north even than Lanwick Island. Jax, his hair color now a fiery red, and Diamond— his horse—took me across the ocean, and once we reached Faery, we rode above the Azure river which split Seelie from Unseelie.

When the woods in Seelie looked deep and dark, we crossed the river and flew above them. Jax was silent. I could feel his nerves in the tightness of his body, and it made my own nerves build. Apart from knowing that we flew above the Seelie woods for much longer than I expected, I didn't take in the view, searching only for the Seelie castle.

The moment the first turret came into view, Jax brought Diamond down onto a trail in the thinning woods and pulled her to a stop. "This is as far as I can take you." There was an apology in his voice. He pointed up the trail. "Keep following this trail and once the woods end, you'll see where you need to go."

I slid to the ground. He'd already taken me farther than he should have. "Thank you, Jax."

He nodded and turned his horse. "Be careful, Bria." He left without giving me a chance to reply.

That was it. The Wild Hunt was out of my life, yet I didn't feel like celebrating. I wasn't sure what I felt, except perhaps disappointed.

The trail through the last of the woods was well worn and soon gave way to rolling green hills. The Seelie castle was closer than I expected, sitting among the hills and looking like something out of the children's book Selina loved so much. It was made of white stone, had high turrets and was surrounded by a moat of the bluest water I'd ever seen.

I followed the trail down to the castle. A guard in a grey uniform stood on either side of the bridge that crossed the moat, watching as people came and went. I checked my hair was covering my ears, pulled up the hood of my cloak and crossed the bridge behind a fae pushing a cart, hoping neither guard paid me any attention. They didn't.

Inside the castle walls was a busy and bustling town. The marketplace was to my left, where stall holders called at the top of their voices trying to sell their wares, but I wasn't interested in shopping. I was interested in the long line of fae snaking from the castle almost all the way to the gates.

They stood in silence—the opposite of the marketplace—and moved a few steps every few minutes toward the arched doors into the castle. Jax had warned me the queen would be holding court today. I joined the back of the line, put my head down and moved with them.

Around us, other fae passed by on horses or on foot, laughing or talking loudly and giving the castle a vibrant and bustling feel. Flowers grew from pots on windowsills, their color and fragrance reminding me of summer at the cottage and sending a sharp pang of homesickness through me. I straightened my shoulders. I was doing this so I could return home. Once I had Mother.

It took less time than I expected to enter the main building, the queue moving forward a few steps every couple of minutes. The vestibule we entered was high-ceilinged and narrow, just wide enough for the queue and almost as many fae guards lining each wall, their hands resting on their sheathed swords. The walls were white, and the room lit by something harsh and bright. At the front of the vestibule, two massive doors opened every few minutes to allow one person through, closing immediately after. No one came out.

I shifted nervously from foot to foot, my legs sore and tired from waiting. With each person who walked through that door, my chest grew tighter. This had seemed like a good idea from the relative safety of Fergus' island—the better option than staying with him. Now I was here, the enormity of what I was about to do hit me. The queen could end me before I said a word. If she didn't like the way I looked, the way I spoke, or what I wore, it wouldn't matter how much I pleaded, she wouldn't help and would likely kill me instead. I ran the words I wanted to say over and over in my mind.

When the doors finally opened for me, my heart was racing so hard I could barely breathe. I stepped through the tall golden double doors and set eyes on Queen Rhiannon for the first time. She sat on an ornate gold throne atop a dais at the far end of the large windowless room. Surrounded by guards all dressed in slate colored livery, she leaned toward a guard who spoke to her in a quiet voice. Two other guards stood shoulder to shoulder in front of me, waiting, I guessed, for the queen to allow me to speak. The gentle whisper of voices made me glance up. Above us were three levels of viewing platforms where fae dressed in their best finery stood looking down upon us. At me. Most were silent, their bodies angled forward as if trying to hear the queen's conversation. But a few whispered to the persons beside them, pointing at me or looking at the queen. I hadn't expected onlookers. I'd expected a private meeting with the Queen of Seelie. Totally stupid. There was never any chance she'd have had a private meeting with an unknown like me.

"Next!" The queen's voice echoed through the room, making me jump, a sight I was certain she enjoyed.

The guards stepped aside, leaving me to wipe my palms on my pants before beginning the long walk across the room. A deep red carpet led up to the dais, my boots sinking into the fibers with each step. Those who had been talking moments ago were now silent.

I kept my eyes down, looking up only when Queen Rhiannon barked, "Halt!" There was barely time to draw a breath before the queen said, "Speak, girl, or we'll call this meeting over."

Queen Rhiannon was beautiful. Her blonde hair was dead straight and fell to her waist. Brown eyes and high cheek bones gave her a regal look. As did the jeweled crown on her head, the many rings on her fingers and the burgundy dress she wore. By looks alone, I'd have guessed her age as perhaps ten years older than me, but she'd been ruling Seelie all my life and had to be closer to Mother's age than mine.

"My mother told me to come and see you." My voice came out small and unsure. I mentally kicked myself. That was not the image I'd hoped to portray. Not only that, my words weren't enough to hold Queen Rhiannon's attention. She looked at her advisor as she spoke to me. "Whatever she told you I could give you, she was wrong. Guards, take her away!" She clicked her fingers and two guards stepped up beside me, each taking an arm and turning me around.

"Wait!" I couldn't let them lead me away. Not yet. I twisted in the guard's hands until I was facing her. "Her name is Aoife Tremaine. She's been captured by the Unseelie King, and she said you could get her released." That wasn't exactly what she'd said, but I hoped it was what she meant.

One guard gave me a shove, his palm between my shoulder blades spinning me away from the queen. "Get out of here," he growled.

The queen's eyes turned my way. "Aoife, you say?" She still sounded bored, except for the smallest rise in the final syllable of Mother's name. "Does this Aoife have a middle name?"

I tried to turn so I could look at her as I spoke, but the guards held me tight. Fine. I'd direct my answer to the opposite wall and hope she heard. "Maire."

There was silence and the guard pushed me again. That was it, my meeting with the Seelie Queen over. Mother was wrong, she couldn't help us. Or wouldn't.

"Wait, bring her back." The queen still sounded bored, but a glimmer of hope blossomed in my heart.

Pushing me just as hard as they had before, the guards turned me to face her. One gave me another shove in her direction and I stumbled, falling onto my knees at the bottom of her dais.

Queen Rhiannon pushed to her feet, her actions slow and considered in the way of someone who doesn't care that an entire room is watching and waiting on her. She sauntered down the three steps, eyes fixed on me. I scrambled to my feet.

She turned to the guard on my left. "Pull back her hair."

"H-her hair?" The guard shuffled his feet.

I sighed. "She wants to see my ears." I spoke without looking at the guard, resignation washing over me. However well Mother knew the Seelie Queen, it already seemed clear that the queen knew what Mother had done to me. "Don't worry. I'll do it myself."

I undid the clip holding my hair at the back of my neck and lifted the strands off my ears, barely breathing. Fergus hadn't seemed bothered by the mutilation of my ears. Same with Jax. Selina was the only one in my life who had ever ignored my deformity that way. I already knew their reaction was not universal and braced myself for the queen's response.

Queen Rhiannon flinched away. She waved one hand at me as she retreated to her throne, one hand over her mouth. "Cover it up. No one in this room wants to see that." Disgust dripped from her voice.

I clipped my hair back, covering my ears, certain I'd shown the queen what she expected to see.

She sat with a sigh. "So, it's true, Briony Ridgewing. Your mother hated her birthright so much, she took a knife to her own child to hide what she was. What you are."

I swallowed, biting back tears. I loved Mother with every part of my body, but those words were a knife to my heart, a stark reminder of what she did without permission. Without even telling me why.

"And now, you come searching for the family you've ignored for sixteen years because you need something." Disgust returned to Queen Rhiannon's voice.

I shook my head. "N-no. It's not like that." My voice wobbled. "I didn't know about you."

The queen's shrill laughter rang around the room, accompanied by the rest of the crowd a moment later. "You didn't know about us? How is that possible? Everyone knows of the Seelie Court." Cold eyes fell on me.

I wanted to step away, but I forced my feet to remain planted. The queen was no different from Mrs. Plimmer. She was searching for a weakness, and if I showed any, I was certain I'd be out on my mutilated ear before I could object. "Of course I knew of the Seelie Court, but for sixteen years, I've been raised as human. For sixteen years, the only fae that ever came into our lives did so to torture or kill us." My palms were slick with sweat and a thin rivulet ran between my shoulder blades. This was for Mother. I might not agree with what she'd done to me, but I didn't want her imprisoned, or worse. I needed the queen to ask the king to release his Seelie prisoner. "Besides, it wasn't as if any of my Seelie family ever came searching for me."

The queen's eyes snagged on mine, and my heart flew into my throat. I'd gone too far. I'd angered her with my accusation.

She let out a laugh. It was harsh and forced, and it drew titters from the crowd above as they copied their queen. When the queen spoke again, the disgust was gone from her voice. "If I'd had any doubts whose daughter you were, that little outburst clinched it. Definitely Aoife's. What is it you need from me, child?" Her voice and face softened, and she sounded like a different woman.

I drew a deep breath. "A letter ... or something I can take to King Aengus stating that you wish him to release one of your people from his prison."

The queen's perfectly manicured eyebrows lifted. She bounced two fingers on her lips, watching me. Her voice was sweet when she spoke again. "Of course I will help you, child. If it's a letter you require, then a letter you shall receive. My guards will escort you back to the Unseelie border tomorrow. Tonight, you stay here. We must get to know each other."

I let out my breath, my shoulders relaxing for the first time since the king captured Mother. She'd been right. Rhiannon was the one who would get her out of this.

The queen continued speaking. "Your mother and I were once very close. Right until she disappeared all those years ago. Your fae family never searched for you because we believed you both dead." She smiled and clapped her hands together. "But what a treat to discover you safe and alive. I will do what I can for your mother, you have my word. In the meantime, you'll be my guest at dinner tonight. I have so many questions for you, as I'm sure you have for me." She waved a hand and one guard stepped forward. "Take Briony to a chamber in the guest wing and find her something decent to wear. By the time she returns, dinner will be served."

"Bria," I mumbled.

The queen turned to me, her eyes ablaze at my interruption. "Pardon me?"

I stepped back. "My name. It's just Bria."

Her eyes travelled over me. "But you were born Briony."

I lifted one shoulder. I'd never been anything but Bria.

She inhaled deeply, then smiled. "Very well. Take Bria to the guest wing."

There was no time to stop and think. Servants escorted me to the most luxurious bed chamber to bathe and change. This one room was larger than our entire house and didn't seem like it was used often as almost everything in it was pristine white. The high bed looked soft and welcoming, and even though my bed on Fergus' island had been comfortable, I couldn't wait to climb beneath the covers in this bed tonight.

I glanced out the window. I was higher than the castle walls and looking out at a deep blue glittering lake not far from the castle. I imagined it would be a glorious place to swim. Everything I'd seen in Seelie so far was stunning, and the queen was far nicer than the Unseelie King. If Mother knew Queen Rhiannon, I don't know why she hadn't allowed us to visit this place before.

I removed my pants, shirt and riding boots, folding them into a pile and placing them on a white chair, my bare feet sinking into the soft white rug that I was certain was softer than my bed at home.

The moment I finished bathing, a small fae servant who fluttered in on brilliant green wings brought me a dress to wear—yellow with a sweetheart neckline and a matching throw for my shoulders—and helped me into it. While I removed my hair clip—shoving it into the toe of my riding boots—and brushed out my hair, another servant brought in a pair of shoes and strapped them on my feet. Unhappy with my hairstyle, the first fae tutted beneath her breath before pulling it back into an elegant do that covered my ears. In what seemed like the quickest possible time, I was back downstairs, in a different room, sitting beside the queen for dinner.

This was no intimate meal, and I was beginning to wonder if Queen Rhiannon did anything small. The meal was served in a banquet hall almost as large as King Aengus' ballroom, with tables—and guests—as far as the eye could see. Trees with bright glossy leaves grew between the tables, the largest branches so tall they seemed to hold up the ceiling. But the room smelled glorious—it was as if we were outside.

The wall at the end of the room was floor to ceiling glass, looking out over acres of the most magical garden I'd ever seen before. Flowers and trees seemed illuminated from within. And beyond the garden lay a beautiful crystal clear lake reflecting all of Seelie within its depths.

The fae women and men were dressed as glamorously as I was, stunning dresses and tuxedos everywhere I looked. Most of them pretended not to watch me but did it when they thought I wouldn't notice. Like when I was answering the queen's questions.

"Where have you been living all this time?" The sixth question she'd asked in as many minutes. She sat beside me, a glass of what I could only assume was faery wine in one hand while she waited for her meal.

My heart raced. I didn't want to say the wrong thing and have her decide she wouldn't write that letter. "We have a small cottage at the edge of the woods, near the border with Faery."

She nodded. "So close, yet neither of us knew the other existed."

Not entirely true. I'd known about the Seelie Queen all my life. What I hadn't known was that she knew of Mother and me—that the Briony who received the king's invitation every year wasn't a prior resident, but me. Which also made me wonder if the king knew about me, too.

"When did you return to Faery?" She took a sip of her drink, her eyes going to the untouched glass in front of me.

"Almost a week ago." I was fairly sure this was a safe answer. If Jax hadn't brought me here on Diamond, it would have taken days to walk from the border.

Another nod. "And who brought you to Faery, child?"

I knew she would ask this and had an answer prepared. It wasn't even a lie. At least, this part of the story wasn't. "The Unseelie Prince brought me here on his horse."

Her eyebrows lifted and her fingers tightened around the stem of her glass. "You're friends with him?"

I shook my head, drawing in a deep breath to calm myself. "He captured me, dragged me from our cottage in Iadrun. I escaped." Still not really a lie, except that last part. Hopefully it didn't sound like one.

The queen gave a long blink and the grip on her glass relaxed. "How's your magic coming?"

I let out my breath. "Badly." Fergus expected me to have magic, too. Perhaps I wasn't as fae as everyone thought.

"We must get you a magic tutor. You've spent so long away from Faery, you must be suffering with stifled magic."

I didn't intend to be here long enough to require a magic tutor, but nodded anyway. I just needed her to stop speaking for a moment so I could ask when she would give me the letter.

A line of servants walked up to our table, each of them stopping at a different guest and depositing a plate of food in front of us. As one, they lifted the lids keeping our dinner warm, then turned and walked away.

The queen smiled at me. "You will love this. Faery food tastes so much better than human food. And the beef is to die for." She unfolded a napkin onto her lap and picked up her knife and fork.

Don't eat the food. It was something I'd known all my life, and Fergus himself had told me I wasn't safe eating fae food until I'd been in Faery a while longer. The advice made complete sense.

I busied myself with unfolding my napkin, adjusting the glassware in front of me and picking up my cutlery. Out of the corner of my eye, the queen was eating with such gusto, I could only hope she'd forget about me.

I pushed the food around my plate, trying to make it look like I'd eaten. The food smelled delicious and my stomach growled. I was glad the chatter of the guests hid it.

The queen dabbed her lips on her napkin. "What do you think? The food is delicious, is it not?"

I nodded, smiling at her.

But her eyes weren't on me. They were on my plate. "But, child. You have barely touched your meal." She looked me over. "You're already too thin. You must eat."

"I really couldn't eat another thing." I placed my knife and fork on the plate as if I were finished.

"Nonsense. And even if that's so, you must first try the beef."

I shook my head and patted my stomach. "Next time." Perhaps I was being stupid. I needed to be strong to help Mother escape, and the queen had been the perfect host. There was no reason not to eat. Even as I rationalized it, I still couldn't make myself put anything into my mouth.

The queen signaled to the servants to take our plates. I let out a breath, grateful I didn't need to pretend any more. Until the servants returned carrying deep bowls filled with dessert.

The queen smiled. "Now, your mother was a dessert person when I knew her. I'm sure you are too, right?"

I nodded before I had the chance to censure myself. On mine or Mother's birthday's, we ate dessert before we ate anything else. The plate deposited in front of me was filled to over-flowing with every dessert imaginable. Lemon cake, meringue, fruit salad. All my favorites. "You should have warned me about dessert." I smiled weakly at my host. "Then I could have left room."

"Pft. You ate nothing. Try the meringue." The queen took a large bite of her own. The rest of the guests, seeing the queen eat, made a start on their desserts.

I stared at my plate, hunger pangs twisting my stomach. I really wanted to eat that meringue. It would be okay, surely it would. I'd already been in Faery two days now, that had to be long enough for the food not to affect me. Besides, if Queen Rhiannon wanted to hurt me, there were faster ways, and she'd likely have done so already. I picked up my spoon and sliced into the meringue. It was crispy on the outside, light and fluffy in the center—the perfect combination. With a deep breath and my fingers crossed for good luck, I put it into my mouth.

It was the most delicious thing I'd ever tasted. A smile grew on my lips. The queen beamed back. "Good, isn't it?"

I nodded. Beside me, Queen Rhiannon looked light and see through, like she wasn't quite there. I blinked, trying to clear my vision. I wanted another mouthful of the meringue and I couldn't see it properly.

"Are you all right, child?" Her voice came from a distance.

I nodded, the world slipping sideways. "Fine." At least, I think I spoke. I was too busy trying to see through the haze surrounding me to be certain. I felt like I should panic, or run, but even as I thought it, I wondered why. There was nothing to worry about. Everything was perfectly fine.

"Bria? Child, are you okay? Perhaps you should lie down."

TWELVE

I OPENED my eyes to darkness. Not the kind where the moon was covered by clouds, the kind where there was no light of any sort. I sat up and bolts of fire shot through my head and my body was stiff and cold.

Slowly, the evening came back to me. I had eaten dessert. How had I been so stupid? The meringue was enchanted and now I was somewhere dark and freezing, unable to help Mother.

I shivered. The stone floor beneath me was icy, and my wrap was not thick enough to remove the chill.

"Hello?" My voice was thin, as if the darkness swallowed up sound as well as light.

Other than a distant scream, there was no answer.

I was such a fool. I'd told myself over and over not to eat the food. Fergus had warned me about it. And somehow, the queen had convinced me otherwise.

"Hello? Is anyone there?" I pushed myself to my feet, using the stone wall for balance. My head pounded. I swallowed to keep from throwing up.

A circuit of the room told me I was in a small cell, surrounded by three rough-hewn stone walls and one wall of bars—too close together to slip between—that burned like fire when I touched them. "Help me!" Someone had put me here. It stood to reason someone would also guard my escape. If I could speak to them, perhaps I could talk my way out of here. "Hello?"

"Shut. Up!"

The deep male voice came from my left. A guard? A prisoner? I wasn't sure.

I gripped the metal bars, trying to get closer to him, to hear what he had to say. Pain ripped through my hands. I pulled them away from the bars and stepped back with a hiss. They stung as if I'd fallen into a fire.

"Don't touch the bars. The iron injures us. They like to suppress our magic." He spoke fast, his voice flat, and I wasn't sure he was making sense.

I shook my burning hands. In Iadrun, many families believed it was possible to ward off the fae with iron. My parents thought it was hog-wash and refused to have even an iron bar in the cottage, just in case. With Mother being fae, I now understood their reasoning. And it would seem if I'd wanted to be certain of my heritage sooner, touching iron would have con-firmed it. "I have to get out of here. There's been a huge misunderstanding. Can you help me? Please." Silence stretched out. "Please." My voice sounded pitiful, and I was moments away from crying. No one knew where I was. "My name's Bria Tremaine, and I need to save my mother."

He breathed out a laugh. "Princess Briony Ridgewing, I think you mean."

I shook my head even though no one could see it. "Oh, no. I'm not a princess." *And a few days ago you were adamant you weren't fae*, a voice inside my head said.

"There's no misunderstanding. Your aunt has you exactly where she wants you. Be glad you're still breathing." His words slurred. Perhaps he wasn't groggy with sleep, but with that Faery wine the queen had been sipping upon.

Still, I felt the need to defend myself. "The queen is not my aunt. She was friends with my mother many years ago." That's what she'd said.

A hiccup turned to rolling laughter. "Deny all you like, little princess, but if it walks like a duck..."

There was no cruelty in the voice. I almost wished there had been. It would have made it easier to hate him. Instead, I hated the words he spoke. "What does that mean?"

More shuffling and the voice grew closer. "I was sitting in my cell when they dragged you down here. I saw you. Even by torchlight, you're the spitting image of Aoife Ridgewing, our rightful queen. Then there are those ears. No one in the Seelie Court would ever forget those ears."

By reflex, I put my hands on my ears. The other prisoner couldn't see them, but that didn't stop me from being embarrassed by them. I sank down onto the floor, the iciness of the stone biting into my body.

"Everyone thinks you're dead, little princess. How is it you're not? And why did your mother kill herself? Why did she leave her tyrant sister to rule us?"

Mother was supposed to be queen? I shook my head. He was wrong. Mother was loyal. And compassionate. That's why she'd become a healer, because she hated to see people hurt. She would never have run from her duty. She'd never have let someone as cruel as Queen Rhiannon take her place if it meant people would get hurt.

The voice cleared his throat. "Enjoy the time you have left, little princess, because the only way the queen is letting you out of this cell is in a box. And even then, she might not. She's not overly partial to challenges to her throne."

"I don't want to challenge her throne." I blurted the words before I'd considered them. But it didn't matter how much I thought about it, I meant it. I didn't want to be queen. I wanted to return to my old life in Iadrun and bring Mother with me. I didn't want any part of this fae world.

The voice sighed, and shuffling came from his direction, as if he was settling down to rest. "You are challenging it, little princess. Just by living."

I lost all track of time in that cell. With no light to mark the passing of the day, I had no idea how long I'd been here. Guards dragged my fellow prisoner from his cell soon after that single conversation. His screams as he left filled my ears long after silence fell.

Guards came and went, but I couldn't tell how often. Sometimes it seemed as if they'd been there moments before, other times it felt like days between visits. They came in pairs, carrying a reed torch—it was the only time I ever saw any light—food and water, which they pushed silently between the bars. No matter how hard I pleaded with them to let me out, they never responded.

Once, they brought a new prisoner with them, dumping him into the cell beside mine and leaving me in the darkness with only the groans of my new neighbor and the distant screams of other prisoners to keep me company.

The only lighter moments during the following weeks came from my fellow prisoner. He never spoke, but sometimes he'd sing, his deep and melancholic melody rising and falling to block out any noise from other prisoners. Even if his music had been bad, I'd have loved it just because of that. But his songs were the most beautiful sounds I'd ever heard.

"Where did you learn to sing like that?" I always asked as his voice faded away. No one sung in Iadrun. No one played music of any sort, not since the Wild Hunt had broken every instrument in the realm when I was a baby. Mother often spoke of the woman who owned Selina's house before Selina's parents, and how she used to sing every day. The Unseelie King overheard her and barged into her home, picked her up by her ankles and rode high into the sky. When his horse couldn't fly any higher, he dropped her to her death. Given how much Mother wanted to keep out of King Aengus' way, I could no longer believe it was he who'd done such a thing—he would surely have noticed Mother living next door. Some villagers in Holbeck said it was the Wild Hunt who'd come for the woman—before Fergus' involvement. Whoever it was, the effect was immediate. No one dared sing anymore, unless it was beneath their breath. I was lucky not to have suffered the same fate as our old neighbor for singing the day the Hunt took Tobias.

I thought singing wasn't allowed in Faery, either.

The man in the next cell never answered and no amount of cajoling could convince him to start again until he was ready, but at least I didn't feel so alone here when he sang. And I had something to look forward to, even if I never knew when he might next start.

I leaned against the cold stone wall, watching the flickering torch light of the incoming guards growing brighter as the moments drew out, steeling my nerve. I couldn't stay down here indefinitely, and my only weapons—if I could call them such—were words. Today I planned to embrace what the first prisoner next door had told me. I would tell the guards I was their princess and that keeping me here was treason. I had no idea what counted for treason in Seelie, but my only other escape plan—telling the guards I was good friends with the Unseelie Prince and could get them better work than service to the queen in her dungeons—seemed somewhat flimsy.

The first guard appeared, torch in one hand, two bowls of food balanced in the other.

I stepped up to the bars, my movement catching his eyes. "You have to let me out. I'm your princess."

The guard's eyes rounded for a moment, perhaps surprised I'd spoken. "You are nothing of the sort." Shifting his grip on his torch, he bent and shoved my bowl between the bars, eyes defiant as he stared at me. The bowl hit a bump in the stone and tipped on its side, thick globs of gruel sliding onto the floor. I stared at the willfully inept guard, refusing to do what I desired and lick the food straight from the stone. It was what they wanted to see, and I still had enough pride to refuse.

The guard smirked at me. I turned my head, pretending not to care, but a splashing sound made me turn back. "Whoops." The second guard put his fingers over his lips, while his other hand poured a steady stream of water from my mug onto the floor. "I spilled it. So clumsy of me."

My throat was already dry from the small amount of water they gave me each day. A mild sense of panic shot through me at the realization I'd have nothing to drink until they returned. But I'd known bullies all my life, some worse than these guards. I wouldn't show them how much they hurt me. "No harm done since you will get me a new one." I gave him a tight smile.

The guard's laughter was slow and mocking, and once the second guard joined in, they both bent in the middle like I'd told the funniest joke in Iadrun.

The bars of the cell next to mine rattled so hard I jumped. Both guards' laughter immediately cut off. The one who spilled the water took a step back.

The voice that came from the cell next door was deep and menacing. And far too familiar. "Give her my water."

The first guard smirked into the other cell. "You mean this water?" He held the other mug high. Then he upended it all over the floor, his eyes locked on the owner of the voice that sounded very much like Prince Fergus Blackwood.

The cell bars rattled so hard it sounded as if they might rip from their hinges. Still the guard smirked. "Keep going, *prince*. Burn up your hands a little more."

I closed my eyes, imagining what Fergus' hands must look like after gripping the iron, knowing how painful mine had been after a light touch.

When Fergus spoke again, it was through clenched teeth. "Get. Her. Some. Water."

"Or what?" The guard looked down his nose and I wanted to slap the arrogance from his face. "You're not exactly in a place to bargain."

"I might surprise you." Fergus' voice was a low rumble.

The guard's expression didn't change, but he took a step back and turned to the other guard. "Let's go. I've had enough of being stuck down here with these two." He started to leave and fell on his face. The torch flew from his hand, hitting the floor and plunging my cell and the corridor outside it into darkness.

"Tarryn. You all right?" The other guard's voice bounced off the stone walls.

"Pick up the torch and light it." Tarryn's voice was breathy. I hoped the fall had winded him.

"Can't find it." There was a swooshing sound and I could imagine the guard on hands and knees, searching for the dropped light. I hoped that floor was covered in rat droppings. Mushy rat droppings from the water they'd spilled out there.

"Never mind." A note of terror crept into Tarryn's voice. His fear made my heart drop into my stomach. "Let's get out of—" There was another crash, this one accompanied by cursing.

"Tarryn. Are you all right?"

"Fine. I tripped is all. Let's go." There was a thud, and a murmured conversation. Then their footsteps disappeared up the distant staircase. They were gone, and we were back to dark silence.

I waited for Fergus to speak. He must realize I knew he was here. He remained quiet, leaving me to open the conversation. "Fergus? What in the stars? Why didn't you tell me it was you in there? And ... why are you here?"

He was quiet for so long, I didn't expect him to speak. When he did, his voice was thin and lethargic. "I came looking for you."

My mouth dropped open. "What! Why?"

"Doesn't matter." He didn't sound like himself. He certainly didn't sound to have the strength he'd shown those guards moments ago.

"Can you get us out of here?" Probably not, since he hadn't tried in all the time he'd been here.

"No." A deep sigh came from the cell beside me. "I can't use my magic down here. The iron in the walls of the cells renders my magic useless. The queen knows I'm no threat. Actually, she probably now knows I still have just enough magic to tie her guard's laces together and trip him up."

"You did that?" I hadn't seen the laces tied together, didn't know what had caused the guard to fall, but thinking about it made me smile. "He deserved it."

"Perhaps. But we both pay the price of having no water today." We sat in silence for a few minutes before he spoke again. "Bria?"

"Yes." Something about the way he said my name put me on edge.

"The day Jax brought you here, I went to Unseelie. I spoke to my father. He denied any knowledge of your Mother, so I did some investigating. I believe she's in a cell, much like these, beneath the Unseelie castle."

"You believe?" A heavy weight crushed my chest. I'd hoped she had escaped. Or that it had been a misunderstanding, and she was back home already. I hadn't wanted to think about where else she might be.

"I couldn't get near the dungeons. But I talked to some people I trust. And they confirmed there is a woman who fits her description down there." He swallowed loudly. "I'm sorry."

I leaned my head on my hands. Mother was captured in Unseelie, and I was captured here. Neither of us could help the other. "Why didn't you tell me sooner?" *Why didn't you tell me the moment you arrived in that cell?*

There was another long silence. When he spoke, his voice was weak. "The queen ... she wants to make sure I ... can't escape." The gaps between his words grew longer, his voice quieter. "Apart from the iron in the walls, she's suppressed my magic in other ways. It makes me feel ... tired. I heard your voice, but I ... could never answer. Was always too ... tired."

That made little sense. "But you could sing?"

"N-no. I didn't sing."

"Yes, Fergus, you did. Often. And it was beautiful."

"S-sorry. I didn't realize." His words slurred together.

"What changed? Today, I mean. For you to yell at the guards."

The silence drew out, and I thought he'd drifted off to sleep. "Heard your voice. Saw them taunt you. Had to help. Couldn't ... stop ... myself."

He slept after that for what seemed like the longest time. The next time I heard him moving in his cell, I said, "Fergus? Are you awake?"

"Mm-hmm." He didn't sound very awake, but that was too bad. I'd come up with a plan during the hours he was sleeping, and I needed his help to put it into action. "Can you show me how to use magic?" If I could learn it, if I really had my own magic, then maybe I could get us out of here.

Silence followed, and I suddenly wondered if he might decline to help. Instead, a scratching came from his cell and light flared. Long shadows filled my cell. "Whoa. Is that magic?" Of course it was. What else would it be? "Teach me how to do that."

He chuckled quietly, and it sounded delightful. It was a relief to hear him laugh. "Not magic. But I used magic to drag the guard's torch and flint into my cell."

I laughed. "You sound a little better today. Are you?" His voice was firmer, and he seemed more coherent. If he was getting stronger, perhaps he could beat the spell on him. Perhaps he could use his magic to get us out.

"A little. For a while, at least." I took his words for what they meant. He would help me while he felt okay, but it might not be for long. "It's easier to learn magic when it's light. And normally, learning isn't difficult. You just imagine it, and it happens. Down here, you must concentrate. A lot." Because of the iron in the walls.

It was okay, I was prepared for this to be difficult. "I just think something, and magic will make it happen?"

"More or less. But start small. Maybe try moving your food bowl without touching it."

I tried. It remained where it lay. "I can't do it."

"You're overthinking it. Talk to me as you try. Sometimes that helps."

I glared at the wall. Concentrate but don't overthink. Fine, if he wanted a conversation, he'd get one. I drew in a breath and asked a cowardly question. Cowardly because I wanted to know more about the Hunt rather than his role in it. I just couldn't bring myself to ask. "What would happen if your father found out about your double life?"

There was silence in the other cell that could have been him considering an answer, but I knew he'd thought about this. He knew exactly what would happen. "If he didn't kill me on the spot for lying to him all these years, he'd strip me of my name and title and send me to the Army of Souls."

"The Army of Souls?"

"They fight against the Seelie army at our border. They are the worst fae in the Unseelie kingdom. They have no morals. I'd rather be dead than go there." He was silent a moment. "Father uses the Wild Hunt to restock the slaves that service that army."

I blinked. That was the question I'd been too scared to ask. "You steal humans to put them in an army too horrid for even you to be part of?"

"I do. And you should never forget that about me."

"But—"

"I need to rest."

That was the end of the conversation. He didn't speak to me again until the guards had come down with food and water two more times, and I tried to put what he'd said to the back of my mind. I went back to attempting magic without talking.

Magic wasn't easy at all. Thinking about the bowl moving didn't suddenly make it move. Envisioning it didn't help. Having Fergus talk through how he did it while I followed along didn't work. My bowl remained planted firmly on the stone floor. I even tried while he was sleeping, but nothing helped.

When I swore the following day, still not able to do what he deemed simple, he bribed me with music. As I worked, Fergus sang.

"Isn't music banned in Faery?" I looked up from my food bowl as if I could see Fergus through the wall. I wished I could. He seemed stronger than yesterday, and the day before, but still not himself. I wished I could see if he was all right.

"It is. But what are they going to do? There's not much worse than this, right?"

Except death. I stared at my bowl, willing it to move. "I guess not."

"Did you ever hear the tale why music is not allowed?"

I looked toward Fergus' cell again. That was the first time he'd offered any conversation since he arrived. Usually, it was me talking and him answering. "No."

There was some shuffling as he made himself comfortable. His voice grew deep as he began his story. "Long ago, the most beautiful young woman the two kingdoms had ever known lived in Faery. She was kind and caring. All the boys wanted to marry her, all the girls wanted to be just like her."

I hesitated in my work, already interested in his story. "Did she live in Seelie or Unseelie?"

There was a brief pause. "You know, I don't know. And I never thought to ask. Let's say Unseelie. Anyway, this young woman spent hours working with the sick, or teaching, or spending time with the frail, doing anything anyone wanted from her. She worked with a smile and always sang. Just hearing her voice could make a bad day good. Until the day she disappeared."

"That seems to happen a lot in Faery," I said dryly. "Or at least a lot in any stories I've heard of Faery."

Fergus didn't bite, continuing as if I hadn't interrupted. "Fae everywhere searched the land and never found a trace."

I frowned. "What does that have to do with music?"

His voice was growing weaker. He'd need to rest soon, but he answered anyway. "She was so beloved by the king and he was so heartbroken when she disappeared that he outlawed all music, especially singing, so as not to be reminded of her."

I lifted my eyebrows. "Seriously? That's the reason?" I laughed. Fae had banned music in their lands and ours, all because the king was sad? He should try living in Iadrun after the Wild Hunt had been there, then he'd know what sad was.

"You don't think it's good enough?" His voice was soft.

"I think it's the height of arrogance." It was a pathetic reason to outlaw something so beautiful.

"Fergus?" I called days later as I was still attempting to move my bowl and getting nowhere.

"Hmm." He still spoke very little down here. Each word a massive effort.

"Why did you come here? To Seelie." The question kept bothering me, jumping into my mind each time I tried to fall asleep and demanding an answer. He'd told me it was dangerous for him or Jax to be caught in Seelie. I didn't understand why he'd risked coming here.

There was shuffling and a grunt from his cell, and his voice moved closer than it had been the whole time he'd been here, like he was leaning on the wall that separated us. "Despite all indications being that you are the dead Seelie princess and therefore my enemy, and against my better judgement, I find I quite like your company."

"Seems like a good reason to spend your days locked beneath a castle." Against my better judgement and to my complete surprise, I enjoyed his company, too.

He gave a quiet chuckle. "Not my best thought out plan, I concede." He let out a deep sigh. "There are things you don't know, and I have no doubt that once you learn them, you will hate me and never speak to me again." I imagined him resting his head back against the cell wall.

Seemed a little over dramatic. "Did you forget you're the only person I can possibly speak to at the moment?"

"Even so..."

I sighed. Loudly. My curiosity was now piqued. "I'm not sure what you want me to say, Fergus. That there's no need to tell me whatever it is you're keeping to yourself? Because now we've

started this conversation, I really want to know."
Shifting my bowl was momentarily forgotten.

Fergus' voice dropped lower, and I moved to
the edge of my cell, right next to his, to hear. "I
pushed you to come here. I was trying to get you
to do it from the moment I brought you to
Lanwick."

"You didn't want me to stay there?" A moment ago, he'd told me he enjoyed my company.
That admission had made me unexpectedly
happy. Now he was saying he wanted me off his
island? "Why didn't you just ask me to leave?"
Better yet, why invite me there in the first place?
My heart sank to my toes. He'd blindsided me
with his words. "It's better if you hate me." His
voice was quiet.

"I don't hate you, Fergus. Not anymore." Not
since he saved my life the day the king took
Mother. "I'm just … confused."

"If you knew me better, you'd understand. I'm
a coward. I didn't want to cast you out and leave
you to find your way alone in Faery. But if you
left of your own accord *and* you had somewhere to
go, my conscience was clear." His voice had grown
so emotionless and flat it didn't even sound like
him.

I felt like my chest was caving in. Perhaps we
were never quite friends, but we'd been more than

acquaintances. I didn't understand how I'd read him so wrong. "If you hate me that much, why are you here?" The prison was unusually quiet as I awaited his answer.

The silence was long, and I thought he'd fallen asleep until he continued. "I was with Father for three days after you left, still trying to find out why he'd taken your mother and where he might have hidden her, when one of his spies rode in, directly from Seelie. She'd ridden for two days solid and was so exhausted she almost fainted in front of us. Before that could happen and before Father could send me away, she blurted out her message. The dead princess had returned to Seelie. And Rhiannon had locked her in her dungeon, where she'd stay until they could arrange a public execution." His voice dropped even lower. "I knew without a doubt the moment she said it, that you were the princess Rhiannon had captured. But I swear I didn't know who you were until then, Bria. I'd never have made you come here if I thought you were the lost princess."

I shook my head, my heart still hurting from his admission. "Why not? With me dead, aren't your problems solved? You can keep your father searching for the woman you're pretend-bonded to, and no one will be any wiser."

"I didn't want you dead, Bria. I never wanted that. I just wanted you … gone. Hidden away somewhere Father couldn't find you."

"Out of sight, out of mind," I whispered.

I heard him swallow. "That's what I thought. When I discovered you were the princess, I knew you weren't safe here. I came to rescue you, but a guard caught me trying to break into the prison."

His reasoning for all his actions made no sense. "Why are you so against having to marry? Once you do, you'll eventually become king. As king, don't you get to make the rules? Couldn't you just decide you want to be king *and* Xion?" If he married—someone other than me—and eventually received the crown, he could start making the rules and enjoying his life. He'd no longer have to pretend to be bonded. All his decisions would be his own. If I were him, I'd want that crown as soon as possible. Which probably meant it wasn't so much marriage he objected to, but marrying me.

"You've seen my father. Do you see any differences between our personalities? Actually, don't answer. I already know you don't. You can't think of a worse fate than being fae." It was the most force he'd spoken with since he arrived.

It was no secret I didn't want to accept my fae heritage, but he was wrong about the rest. I saw the differences between the king and his son.

Fergus wasn't cruel. He wasn't unfeeling. He wasn't ruthless. Xion Starguard, on the other hand, was all those things, his personality much closer to that of the king. And Xion was part of Fergus. "But I've seen you in the Wild Hunt—"

"Ah, yes. The Wild Hunt. That tells you all you need to know about me, right?" His voice vibrated with rage and darkness.

I'd managed to keep hold of my emotions, but a hint of anger rose in my voice in response. It wasn't an unreasonable assumption. "Shouldn't it?" Just because he hid those parts of himself until he was Xion didn't mean they didn't exist.

"No! You should..." His voice petered out.

I waited, but the silence stretched on. "I should what?"

He laughed. It was cold and hard. "I hardly think you will do anything I suggest. I'm a cruel and hard-hearted fae, after all."

What was driving this anger? I'd never said these things to him. Not directly, at least, though I'd thought something similar in the past. "Not always," I whispered.

His voice was just as soft when he spoke again. "And yet you still expect the worst of me."

His admonishment was on target. He'd hurt Mother, but he'd fixed her as well. He'd carried Father from our home, but he hadn't been the one who'd killed him. He'd saved my life in the forest in Iadrun. Fergus was still Xion Starguard, and his reputation proceeded him, but he wasn't Xion right now. And he hadn't been for most of the time I'd known him. "I'm sorry."

He sighed, returning to my original question. "I don't have the stomach for what's required of me as king."

"Anyone want food?" Tarryn banged a mug against the stone wall, holding a torch in his other hand. The sudden racket made me jump. With Fergus' torch burning and our strained conversation, I hadn't noticed the guards heading our way. Today he had with him two guards instead of one. One held our bowls while the extra guard held a torch in each hand.

My heart rate kicked up. Something was different. I'd kept my imagination in check about what would become of me, but with Fergus mentioning execution, my imagination ramped up. Were they here for me? To kill me? To hurt me? For some other hideous reason I couldn't even imagine?

"Princess." Queen Rhiannon's voice bounced off the stone walls as she picked her way down the staircase behind the guard carrying the torches. She held her dress up off the floor, showing off her delicate black ankle boots. "You must be hungry."

I kept my eyes on the ground. I would not engage. She'd tricked me once. I wouldn't allow it to happen again.

"Thirsty?"

Stars, yes. I didn't move.

"Oh, Princess." She strolled toward my cell, her boots tapping on the stone. "I *know* you're thirsty. Do you know how I know? Because my guards give you just enough water to survive. Never enough to quench your thirst."

With her words, my throat grew drier than it ever had.

"But today, I'm in a generous mood and I've brought something special with me. Two mugs filled to the brim with ice cold water. Just for you."

I lifted my head, certain she must be joking. But no. Her dress was no longer in her hands. Instead she held two mugs, water sloshing onto the ground each time she took a step. I licked my lips, my tongue barely wet enough to make a difference. "What do you want in exchange?" I bit down on my question, wishing I could have ignored her, but it was an effort not reach through the bars and rip the mug from her hand.

"Bria." Fergus' low voice contained a warning. *Believe nothing she tells you. Trust nothing she offers.*

"Give up your right to the Seelie throne." Queen Rhiannon held one mug of water out toward my cell.

I didn't want the Seelie throne, but surely giving it up was worth more than two mugs of water, no matter how thirsty I was. "You'll set me free if I agree?"

The queen's eyes narrowed, and she puffed out her chest. "Did I say anything about setting you free? My offer was for extra water." Her voice grew loud and shrill. With a disgusted glance down my body, she lifted one mug into the air and upended it.

As the water hit the ground, a drop bounced onto my leg. I scooped it onto my finger and put it in my mouth. It tasted so good, but it wasn't enough. Perhaps I'd made the wrong decision. I needed water. I'd die without it. I reached my hand between the bars, careful not to touch them. "Please."

"You agree to give up your right to the Seelie throne?"

Wait, no. That had been the agreement for the extra water. Not for my usual ration. I opened my mouth to object but before I could, the queen tipped the other mug over the ground. Then she slapped both mine and Fergus' bowls of food out of the guard's hand where they fell onto the floor.

I stared at the stale bread and slop lying out of reach. There'd be no food or water for either of us until they returned. I turned away, walking to the back of the cell. It was more of a reaction than I wanted to give, but better than dissolving into tears which is what I felt like doing.

The queen laughed. Tarryn did the same.

I shattered.

I whirled around and ran at the cell bars. With each step, Mother's voice echoed in my head spouting words I'd heeded every day of my life. *She wants a reaction, then she wants to use that reaction against you. Don't respond, Bria. You're better than that.* But I wasn't better. I was angry, and I was sick of taking everyone else's crap like they shouldn't have to own the way they acted. I was also beside myself with hunger and thirst.

Heat washed over me, the warmth starting in my chest and radiating out to my hands. I hadn't been warm in all the time I'd spent down here. Before I could enjoy the feeling, the cell lit up with pink light. The queen's eyes rounded and my palms itched.

A loud crack sounded from high above. It seemed to go on forever.

With a deafening crash, hundreds of rocks fell from somewhere high above and the pink light flickered out. But not before the guards were hit then buried beneath the falling rocks.

THIRTEEN

ONE MOMENT the guards all stood in front of me, heads thrown back in laughter, the next they were gone, entombed beneath a pile of rubble that fell for so long, I wasn't sure it would ever stop. Though I wished it weren't true, I was sure the queen had saved herself. Her form flickered away just as the first stones fell.

When the noise quietened and the rocks stopped moving, a thin layer of dust coated my body. None of the rocks had fallen on me. Or near me.

I turned in a slow circle.

I was no longer trapped in darkness. The rocks had come down from high above, leaving a jagged hole to the outside world through which light filtered. Around my feet, I could walk two paces in every direction before I'd have to climb the rockfall to move. When I stood in just the right place, I could see the grassy side of a hill, and, for the first time in a long time, I could see the sky. Even murky gray, as it was today, it was beautiful.

Better yet, if I climbed up the pile of fallen rocks, I could reach that hole in the ceiling and escape this cell to freedom.

But I wasn't going without Fergus.

I rubbed my itching palms together while a slate colored cloud drifted by. The wall between our cells was now an enormous pile of rubble.

"Bria!" All around, the prison walls groaned like they might collapse at any moment, but the muffled sound of Fergus' voice floated over the noise.

I scrambled up the rubble that was once the wall between our cells, dodging an iron rod that jutted from the rocks. "Fergus? Are you all right?" Hundreds of rocks had come down into his cell before spilling out past the iron bars and into the corridor where the guards had stood. I climbed carefully, searching for his black mop of hair among the rockfall.

"Fergus!" The only response was the creaking of the walls. I didn't know if I'd imagined him calling to me, or if he was too hurt to call out again. *Please don't let him be dead.* He was the closest thing I had to a friend in this wretched place. I didn't want him to die.

"Bria?" Fergus' muffled and weak voice came from somewhere below my feet.

I let out a breath. He was alive. "Where are you?" I dropped onto my knees. A rock tumbling from somewhere high echoed in the distance and I tensed, waiting for the walls to collapse again.

"Beneath the rock pile. Beneath … where you are now. Can you dig me out … please?"

Some rocks beneath my feet were huge, which meant Fergus was probably badly crushed beneath them. All the healing training I'd ever undertaken kicked in. I had to get him out of there. Then I could assess his injuries. Then we'd find a way to leave this place together.

Balancing on my hands and knees, I pulled away rock after rock, throwing them as far as I could—the small ones, anyway. The large ones, I dug around until I could push them down the pile. My nails tore and my hands grew bruised and bloody, but I wasn't stopping. There was so much creaking and groaning around me, I was starting to wonder if either of us would be alive by the end of the day.

Using my legs, I pushed a large rock until it tumbled away, and I found myself staring into Fergus' brown eyes.

He lay on his back, arms locked and stretched into the air above him. He was shirtless—the dim light making dips and hollows of his perfectly formed chest and abs—and he seemed unhurt, if somewhat dirty. In fact, it seemed as if, although buried beneath the rockfall, none of the rocks had touched him, either. I held out my hand to pull him to his feet. "Are you okay?" Because he looked better than he had any right to look.

With a nod, he took my offered hand and pulled himself to sit up. "My foot." He ground the words out, and I followed his gaze.

The rest of him may have been untouched, but his left foot was trapped beneath a huge rock. A rock larger than I could lift.

"I only had enough magic to shield when the roof caved in. And apparently, I couldn't even do that particularly well." He leaned forward and pulled two smaller rocks from beneath his foot. His movements were slow and labored.

I did the same, getting rid of any rocks I could shift. "Shield?"

Fergus' hands shook as he worked. "I used my magic to stop the rocks hitting me."

I pulled and pushed at the rock on his foot, trying to get it to move. "I can't do it. Can't you use your magic now?" Since there was a giant hole in the ceiling and the walls were gone, perhaps the iron that blocked his magic was gone.

He shook his head and twisted at the waist until his back was facing me.

Piercing his skin and running parallel to each of his shoulder blades was an iron rod, each about a hand's length wide, capped with flayed barbs on either end. His back was caked in dirt and dry blood, and more blood oozed from the places the iron penetrated his skin.

"What is that?" I whispered. I reached out to touch it, stopping short. The barbs looked sharp enough to cut my finger. I couldn't imagine how lying on it felt.

"A suppressor. This is how Rhiannon stops me using my magic. The iron dampens it down and stops me accessing most of it." Every word was an effort.

"I thought it was the iron in the walls that did that." I couldn't take my eyes off his back. "Or a spell."

"I'm a prince, Bria. It takes more than iron walls to stop my magic."

I stared at the two objects with disgust. "She did this to stop you escaping?" Now I understood why he'd seemed so quiet and lethargic.

He nodded. "I need you to take them out."

I'd been thinking the same thing. "How?"

"I can't reach them. That's why she puts them through the skin at the shoulder blades—so they are impossible to remove alone. I need you to pull one end off, then slide the rod out. Same on both sides." He clenched his jaw. I could only imagine how much pain he was in. Two lumps of iron lodged inside his body must be excruciating. Yet he hadn't once complained, not in the entire time he'd been down here.

"Which end?" I eyed the barbs with displeasure. This would hurt. But it was just like any other healing procedure I'd ever undertaken. I would do it because he needed my help.

He shook his head. "I don't know. One end is welded in place. The other will come off if you pull it. And it will hurt. Both of us."

I nodded and inched forward. I'd already figured that much. "What if I covered it with material from my dress? Would that make it hurt less?"

He shook his head. "The iron will still burn through."

On closer inspection, his shoulder blades—beneath the blood—were covered in scars; long, thin marks that crisscrossed his back, some old, some more recent. There were also four very noticeable puckered scars the same width as the iron bar. I ran a finger over one of them. "This isn't the first time she's done this to you, is it?"

He shook his head.

"But you came looking for me anyway, knowing what would happen if she caught you?" I didn't understand him. This was the sort of thing you did for someone you cared for, not someone you wanted to be rid of.

Fergus turned and looked at me, hesitating before he spoke. "I didn't mean what I said before. I didn't want to make you to leave the island." He shook his head. "I was trying to make you angry. I was trying to bring your magic out." He looked up at the hole from the rockfall. "I knew you could do something like this. I should also have known if Rhiannon ever showed her face, she'd goad you enough to make it happen."

I smiled—he didn't hate me—then followed his gaze, weak sunlight now filtering through the clouds. "I did this?" I shook my head. No chance.

"Are you warm? Does your skin feel tingly?"

I nodded, rubbing my palms. The warmth had diminished, but my hands had tingled since the rocks fell. "N-no." I couldn't have done this. "You said I had to think about what I wanted to happen. I wasn't thinking about bringing the roof down. I wasn't thinking about anything at all."

My words came out so fast they were almost on top of each other.

Fergus' eyebrows rose. A question and a statement at once. He didn't believe me.

I hated and loved in equal measures that he was right. There was no one else in the world who would have picked up on that lie. "Except hurting the queen and her guards," I mumbled.

A half-grin played on his lips. The worry in my gut eased to see him smile. "If there was any doubt about you being the princess, that's gone now."

I cast my eyes over the mess I'd made. The staircase the guards had come and left from was completely gone, covered by rocks. Fergus' cell was the same. "It is?" Because I had plenty of doubts. And even more questions.

"With magic strong enough to do that, you can only have royal blood."

Another thing to add to my growing list of Things I Don't Know About Myself.

Fergus turned away, and I was again looking at the suppressor in his back. "Ready?"

I nodded, though I wasn't ready at all. I didn't want to hurt him. With a deep breath, I took hold of the barbs at both ends. The metal sank into my skin and I held back a moan. It wasn't just the bite of the barbs that hurt. A bone-aching pain shot through my entire body. It was impossible to think of anything but how much every part of me hurt.

"Bria." Fergus' voice floated through the pain. "Bria. Look at me."

I locked my eyes on his as red-hot coals filled my body, pushing down into my fingers and toes.

He looked over his shoulder, his voice gentle. "Concentrate on pulling the suppressor apart. You may have to twist it. Once you've done that, let the iron go."

Right.

Pull it apart.

I could do that. I gripped the iron bar tighter and pulled.

A thousand hot pokers stabbed every part of my body. They wedged beneath my skin, under my nails, sank into my bones.

"Bria! Let it go!"

My hand jumped and my body jerked. And my head cleared. My palms felt as if I'd raked them through a hundred shards of glass, but I was back in Fergus' cell, not the place of pain I'd been moments ago.

"Are you okay?" Fergus twisted around.

"I'm fine. Did I get them out?" I glanced at my hands. Ribbons of blood dribbled from them and onto the rocks beneath me.

He shook his head, angling his back away.

I moved around him. I wanted to see what he was hiding. Both suppressors were still lodged in his back, but on the left side, the side I'd been working on, blood poured from the two places the suppressor pierced his skin. I'd done that as I tried to work the pieces apart. If it hurt me to be touching that thing for just a few moments, I couldn't understand how Fergus was sitting upright, let alone talking. "I'll try again." I moved to touch his back, but he jumped away. "I mean, if you want me to."

He shook his head and spoke through his teeth. "You need to leave."

So did he. By now, Rhiannon's guards surely knew what had happened. They'd be on their way to check it out. "We'll leave together. As soon as you're free."

"I'm not getting free, Bria. I'd almost come to that conclusion before you found me, anyway. But you can. And you should. Get out of here before the queen's guards arrive."

I shook my head, too stubborn to leave. He'd gotten into this mess to help me, I wasn't walking away from him. Pulling at the rock again and hoping to distract him from the pain, I started back into our conversation from earlier. "What are the things I don't understand?" What was he keeping from me?

He shook his head. "Don't ask me this."

I shook mine, unsure what I was asking of him. "Please."

"There are things that you're better off not knowing." His voice softened. "Go, Bria. You're safer if you leave me behind."

It was easy to forget he was the leader of the Wild Hunt. Even if that meant something different from what I'd always thought, it probably would be better if I walked away from him. But I wasn't doing it. He'd come here for me. I wouldn't leave him behind. If I couldn't remove the iron, I'd damn well move the rock. I bent and started pulling at it again. When it didn't budge, I turned and pushed it. Nothing changed. It didn't move a fraction.

Fergus sighed and reclined back onto his elbows. He looked casual. Relaxed, even. But only when I ignored the tightness around his eyes and lips. And when I forgot about the blood running down his back. "You can't do it, Bria."

I glared at him. "I can. And I will."

When Fergus blew a breath out his nose and shook his head, I tried harder. My blood heated until I felt warm all over, my body tingling. I felt strong. With a final shove, the rock flew from Fergus's foot, shooting across the cell to hit another rock with so much force it shattered into a hundred pieces.

I grinned. Magic. I'd moved the rock using magic!

Fergus climbed to his feet, groaning as he got up. "You're a lot like my sister, you know. If anyone tells her she can't do something, she takes it as a challenge."

I glowered. That was exactly what had just happened. He'd talked me into using magic I didn't yet know how to control by telling me I couldn't do it. I lifted my chin. "It seems to be a problem only around you."

He threw me a wry smile. "That's lucky for me. Good job with your magic."

Without waiting to think better of it, I took his arm and threw it over my shoulder, wrapping my arm around his waist. The pile of rocks we needed to climb to reach the hole in the roof was steep. It would be a challenge to get him up there with an injured foot and iron rods in his back. But I had nothing to heal him with and we needed to get out of here, so he would just have to deal with it. Which he did.

Every different shaped rock was in that pile that rested against the back of the cells, rising to the hole in the ceiling. Some moved the moment one of us put a foot on them and sent us sliding

back a few steps—bringing other rocks with us—
until we regained our balance. Each time that
happened, I crossed my fingers and hoped we dis-
lodged nothing from above with our clumsiness—
or didn't break a leg as we fell. It was a relief to
find occasional rocks wedged tightly into the pile
that were stable enough for us to stop and catch
our breath upon, but they were few and far between.

The higher we climbed, the tauter Fergus' face
became. He held his breath every time he took a
step.

I needed to distract him again. "You never talk
much about your family." Except to say he hated
his father.

He gave a humorless laugh. "Most people know
all about the dysfunctional Blackwood family.
Most people offer their detailed opinion without
me telling them a thing."

The pain in his voice made me soften mine.
"I'm not most people." I gave his arm a squeeze.

"So I'm learning."

Something in his tone—something I didn't understand—made my cheeks heat. I put my head
down and continued picking my way over the
fallen rocks, trying not to jar his foot.

"You are standing next to the world's biggest
disappointment. Father wanted an heir who could

use magic before he could walk. He wanted his son to be as powerful, as unforgiving and as cruel as himself. He takes his frustration at my lack of all those things, and many others, out on me with a cane."

"The scars on your back?"

"The ones Rhiannon didn't cause are from Father, but not from his cane. When he decided the cane wasn't getting the results he expected, he punished me with lashes of his magic, usually until I passed out."

"Usually?"

He let out a breathy laugh. "Once, I was so angry that he was hurting me again that I threw up a shield and somehow turned his magic back on him." There was no satisfaction in his voice, but I found his story satisfied me.

"You hurt him?"

"Barely. If you look closely, you'll see a scar on his right cheek that I caused that day. I hurt his pride, but even that wasn't enough to make him stop. Now, he suppresses my magic before he lashes me. So, excuse me if I find little joy in speaking of him."

What about your sister? I wanted to ask. I couldn't voice the words. I couldn't imagine a father hurting his child that way. Or a child having to put up with it when he was an adult himself. "That's why you live at Lanwick?"

"The king still insists I spend some nights in my chamber at the castle. But whenever I can, I'm at the island."

I nodded, climbing in silence for a moment. "Why do you think the queen put us in cells beside each other?" I'd been wondering as we climbed. If I'd blasted a hole in the ceiling and not known Fergus was here because he was in some far off cell, I'd have left him behind when I escaped and Rhiannon would only lose one of us.

He grunted as he climbed. "To torture me, I guess. My path has crossed with Rhiannon several times before and she disagrees with my ... decision-making process. I think she hoped that seeing you down here, seeing the guards harass or hurt you, would be enough to bend me to her will."

His answer only created more questions than it gave answers. "But why? Why does she care what you think?"

He gritted his teeth. "That is a story I'd rather not get into right now. Just know I'm grateful your magic made an appearance when it did."

We were more than halfway up the rock pile, but the farther we went, the heavier he leaned on me. My knees buckled with each step. I would not make it to the top while supporting him. Plus, I was sure I could hear voices coming from outside, probably more of the queen's guards. We were almost out of time. "If you could use your magic, could we escape the guards?"

"With my eyes closed and hands behind my back." He grunted as he spoke, my rough steps making us both uncomfortable.

"And could your magic get us out of here?" Because Fergus' magic was starting to seem like our only option if we didn't want to end up back where we'd started the day. "Out of Seelie?"

"Of course." The trace of a grin formed on his lips. "I am a prince, after all."

We climbed a little farther to reach a large stable-feeling rock, and I made him sit down. Those suppressors were coming out of his back and they were coming out now.

With closed eyes and panting breath, he said. "Is this as far as we're going?"

"For now." I shook out my shoulders, aching from dragging him up here. "Lean forward."

He stared at me as if he had no intention of doing as I asked.

I crouched next to him, uncomfortably close on the small rock. "I'm removing those suppressors, then you will use your magic to get us both out of here."

He grinned. It was weak, but it was there. "What are you waiting for?" He bent at the waist, giving me full access to the suppressors.

I stared at the iron a moment, mentally walking through what I had to do. I wasn't failing this time, not when failure meant more time in the queen's prison, and possibly my very own set of suppressors. Without warning him, I raised my hands, gripped the barbed ends and pulled.

Pain ripped through me the moment I touched them. I didn't blink. Didn't breathe. I just focused on pulling the pieces apart. I pulled and twisted as the pain raged inside me until the first one came free. I dropped the pieces and moved onto the second suppressor, barely stopping for a breath. My hands burned and my fingers felt hot and fat, but not too fat to move. The moment Fergus was free, I dropped the offensive item and watched as it tumbled down the rock pile.

The pain subsided instantly, and the world came back into focus, and I found Fergus staring at me, his frown concerned. "I'm fine." I nodded.

Voices, louder than before, came from outside our escape hole. Fergus let out a long, low whistle. "We need to go. The queen's guards are close." His voice was already stronger than it had been.

I helped him to his feet, and we dragged ourselves up the final few rocks and climbed out into day light. We were outside the castle walls—outside the moat—at the bottom of one of the rolling hills that surrounded it. Only the top turrets of the castle were visible from where we stood, and in the other direction, the tops of the trees from the woods Jax had deposited me in.

At the top of the hill, not fifty paces away, an army of Seelie guards were assembling.

"Escapees!" someone shouted.

There was movement from above as the guards drew their weapons.

I stepped back, colliding with Fergus. He gripped my hand and gave me a small smile. He pointed his other hand at the guards and there was a flash of blue light—his magic, I guessed—and the group of guards all dropped to the ground.

Fergus whistled again, blue magic coming from his lips as he did so, and Obsidian galloped down from the sky, barely stopping while Fergus climbed on his back, then caught my hand and pulled me on behind.

A barrage of arrows followed us from a second group of guards running from the castle. Fergus gave quiet instructions and Obsidian galloped us into the sky.

FOURTEEN

IT TOOK all my strength to keep Fergus seated on Obsidian as we rode in the sky back to Lanwick Island. I wrapped my arms around him from behind and silently wished Obsidian would move faster than the break-neck speed he was already going. Fergus' head lolled, jolting upright every few minutes. I talked to him, asking him questions to keep him awake, which he managed to answer. Even so, the moment Obsidian's hooves touched the sandy white beach in front of his home, his body slackened and he tilted to the side, dragging us down onto the sand.

"Fergus!" Jax called. The pounding of his steps echoed in my ears as he ran toward us and I pulled myself from half beneath Fergus.

I leaned over him. His eyes were closed, but they moved beneath his eyelids and a fine layer of sweat shone on his skin. Jax stopped beside me, brushing his hair—pale pink today—from his eyes. "What's wrong with him?" I asked.

Jax ran his gaze over his friend and he cursed. Then he bent and hoisted Fergus to sitting. With a quick glance at me, he said, "We need to get him inside. Grab his other arm and help me get him up."

I took Fergus' arm and with Jax, got him on his feet. Fergus was a dead weight and my knees almost buckled. "What's happened to him?" I asked again. He'd seemed fine at the Seelie prison, but once we climbed on Obsidian's back, it was as if all his energy disappeared.

"Hurry," growled Jax, as we dragged Fergus up the steps in front of the pool.

I was lagging. Jax was quicker, carrying Fergus' weight more easily than I could. We moved a little faster once we reached the concrete tiles beside the pool, but I was nowhere near as strong as Jax. Plus, I'd barely eaten since I left this place. "Can't you magic him to his rooms?"

Jax's laugh was harsh. "You've been spending too much time in the prince's company."

"Meaning?" Sweat dripped down my back. I'd forgotten how humid this place was.

"I don't have enough magic to get Fergus to his rooms. No one here does." He swiped his hair away from his face.

"But you can fix whatever's wrong with him?" I hadn't been worried about Fergus. I'd thought there were plenty of fae here who could heal him. Until I heard the urgency in Jax's tone.

Jax pressed his lips together, not bothering to answer. Using his shoulder, he opened the door into the lounge room.

A chill went through me. Someone must know how to help Fergus.

We dragged him through the lounge and up a flight of stairs to what must be Fergus' rooms— they occupied the entire level—before depositing him on his stomach onto the four-poster bed. Jax drew in his breath as he stared at Fergus' back. Sand stuck to blood and sweat, covering half his back. Where there was no sand, his back was black with dried blood. The places where the suppressors had been looked inflamed, though it was difficult to tell while the wound was dirty. Jax stared down at him, his hands in his hair, his face desolate.

"Is there anyone who can help him?" I pushed. Because standing around looking at him would not make him better.

The door to Fergus' chamber burst open and a girl ran in. She was tall and leggy, with a tiny waist and cropped auburn hair. Her eyes fell on Fergus and she stopped short. "He's back. I thought I felt his presence. What happened to him?"

Jax shrugged and drew a hand through his magenta hair. "Rhiannon, I'm guessing." He looked at me for confirmation.

I nodded.

The girl drew her lips together.

I had no time for their dramatics. I took Jax's elbow and turned him to face me. He seemed in shock. If he couldn't organize the island healer to come to Fergus, then I would do it. "Where is the healer? Tell me and I'll get him. Or her."

Jax shook his head, watching the way Fergus' shoulder blades rose and fell with each shallow breath. Fergus groaned and Jax winced. "The healer can't help him. He's a prince. For wounds this bad, he needs someone with stronger magic than him. He needs..."

"The king," I finished. He needed one of the royal family. "Then let's take him to Unseelie. On Obsidian." Or maybe Jax could use his own horse.

Jax's eyes didn't leave his friend. "He's like this because he's out of magic. The Wild Hunt magic, the magic that allows the horses to fly, is tied to him as leader. No one's going anywhere on the horses unless he recovers." He glanced at me. "You're lucky you two made it home."

"His magic makes you all fly? Maybe you should make the rest of the Hunt stop. Won't that make him better?" There had to be some way to help him.

Jax shook his head. "Not exactly. A kernel of his magic makes the rest of the Hunt strong enough to do all we need to. His magic gets us started so we can do the rest. But there's no kernel there now, and no one's going anywhere. Unless you're talking about taking a rowboat back to the mainland."

I shook my head. "I don't understand. All he did was send a blast of magic at some guards. Then he called Obsidian and we flew her here. How can he be out of magic?" I'd seen Fergus do far more than that and still have plenty left over.

"How long after you..." He glanced at Fergus' shoulder blades and almost choked on the words. "... removed the suppressors, did he use his magic and call for Obsidian?"

"Straight away."

Jax closed his eyes and drew in a breath. "The suppressors that Rhiannon uses stop Fergus accessing most of his magic. There are two permanent drains on his magic—the wards on this island and the Wild Hunt."

The girl came over to stand next to Jax, running a reassuring hand from his shoulder to elbow. "We have things in place to stop these spells using his magic should Fergus find himself ... in trouble. The wards were no longer his problem because we had fae working in groups of twenty to keep them up."

"And," added Jax, "the Wild Hunt only affects his magic if we go out. So, we've been out only one time since he went missing. And that was to try to locate him." He shook his head. "But the minute the suppressors are released, the ward spells find him and take the magic they need. The Hunt spells, too. Usually, it's fine. But if he uses his magic on other things, too..." Like attacking guards or flying his horse.

The girl shook her head and cursed. "Fergus knows he needs to rest for at least an hour after the suppressors come off."

I swallowed. He might have known, but he hadn't told me. "The queen's guards were coming. He had no choice."

Fergus groaned.

Jax's face hardened. "There was a choice. Fergus chose to die."

"D-die?" No. He hadn't chosen that. He'd chosen to escape. "Where's the rowboat?" I'd take him to the king myself. If that's what he needed to live, then I'd do it.

Two more fae burst into the chamber, their gasps filling the air when they saw Fergus.

Jax shook his head. "There's no time. It would take you hours to row to the mainland. Then hours to get to the castle. Fergus might last two more, if he's lucky."

The new fae pushed past me to sit beside Fergus on his bed. One picked up his hand, tears on her cheeks. She spoke, but I couldn't hear over the rushing in my ears. Two hours? Why had he told me he could get us out of there? He should have said he couldn't and we could have searched for another way.

"Who can help him, then?" I stared between Jax, the girl, and Fergus' wounded back.

Jax shook his head. "The king. The Princess. No one that is on the island at present."

I looked around the chamber, as if that would show me the answer. It was opulent and princely. The four-poster bed backed onto a black wall, a bedside table and lamp on either side of it. A fluffy gray rug covered the wooden floor, and an entire wall of windows opened onto a huge balcony looking out over the pool, across the beach and out to the ocean.

I saw myself reflected in the glass. My hair was dirty and matted—I didn't even have my hair clip any longer to tie it back. The dress I'd worn to the queen's dinner was ripped and gray, but it served as a reminder. "What about me? I'm a..." I'd never said the words before. "Princess."

Jax eyed me warily. Not because he didn't believe me—Fergus must have told him who he thought I was before he left—but for some other reason. "In name perhaps, but as I recall, you have no magic, let alone magic strong enough to heal a prince."

Fergus' body shuddered, gooseflesh forming on his skin even though it was too warm in his chamber. We had to do something to save him. If I was the only one here who might be able to do it, then I would try. I lifted my chin, my voice firm in an attempt to make him believe. "I have magic now. It's the reason we escaped." I didn't mention that I had used it only one time since the ceiling of our cells caved in. Or that I had no clue how to make my magic help Fergus. I hoped it was an intuitive thing. Like how I'd wanted the guards in the cells to go away, and the ceiling had caved in, making it happen.

Jax watched Fergus a moment, and then, with a glance at the girl, gave a slow nod, before taking a step away from the bed. "Very well. We have nothing to lose. Let's go." He clapped his hands and indicated to the doorway. The girl and the two other fae walked out without another word. Jax shut the door behind them and stood watching from the back of the room.

Had I really just begged to save Fergus with my magic? Magic I didn't have the faintest idea how to use?

I stood to one side of the bed, sucked in a deep breath and clasped my injured hands together. I just had to think about what I wanted. That was all. I could do this. I was a princess, and I was powerful. Fergus had said so.

I closed my eyes and imagined his magic refilling within him. I imagined the wounds healing on his back, his ankle getting better. It all happened in my mind's eye. And this time, I felt the magic form as warmth crept into my palms, brushing up my arms to my shoulders.

Opening my eyes, I looked at Fergus. Magic centered inside me. I unclasped my hands.

A magenta flash shot from them and across the chamber. Jax jumped to one side, and it just missed him as it surged into that black wall he had been leaning against. At the same moment, my ears popped with rising pressure and the windows—the entire wall of windows— sucked into the chamber and shattered, the glass falling like rain around the room.

Pieces, big and small, lodged in Fergus' back.

I stepped toward Fergus, but Jax, with blood dripping from cuts caused by falling glass, beat me to him. He glared at me, yelled words I didn't hear and pointed at the door.

It took a moment to realize he was yelling at me. Pointing for me to leave.

I stared at the mess I'd caused. At Fergus, now cut and bleeding on his bed. The glass shards lying across the floor. The hole in the wall. How stupid was I? To think I could suddenly use magic just because I had it.

I turned on my heel and ran.

I didn't know where I was going, just that I had to get away from that room. I sprinted down the stairs and outside, running along the crushed shell path Fergus had walked me along the first day he brought me here. Some residents strolled toward me. Their wide-eyed stares told me I looked a fright. I veered off and into the lush woods that grew off the path, coming to a stop when I couldn't breathe anymore.

Prince Fergus Blackwood was about to die. All because he'd helped me escape the Seelie Queen.

Worse, I'd almost killed him and his best friend using magic I had no business using.

As I bent over, catching my breath, my eyes snagged on a pygmy root at my feet. I might not be able to save Fergus with magic, but I was a healer. I could make him comfortable. Maybe I could even prolong his life enough for someone to come here and help him. Like his sister.

I pulled out handfuls of pygmy root, careful not to touch the poisonous flowers on the top of the stems and ignoring the pain in the wounds on my hands as I did so. After hunting around the area for a few minutes, I turned up two blooms of ash flower which would help his fever, though it was marginal if two blooms would be enough. I also picked a handful of round green berries from a small-leafed plant and shoved them in my pocket.

I ran back into Fergus' home and into my chamber, grabbing up towels and a basin, then sprinted up the stairs to Fergus' room.

Jax glared as I let myself in and stopped just inside the door. "I'm sorry." Fergus' chamber was quiet with only Jax in here, and I pitched my voice to match. "It was foolish of me to attempt that when I don't know how to use my magic yet." The broken glass was cleaned up and gone, the windows replaced. Magic, I guessed. Though that didn't seem to extend to removing the jagged pieces from Fergus' back, something Jax was half-heartedly doing with a small pair of tweezers.

Jax's eyes slid from me back to Fergus. He remained silent.

I took a step toward him. "I ... ah ... I'm a much better healer than a princess." I swallowed. This was so much harder than it had been in my head. I wouldn't want me in here if I were Jax, yet I was desperate to convince him otherwise. "I can make him comfortable. Take away the pain, maybe even break the fever."

His eyes remained on Fergus' back and I took his silence for agreement. I went to the other side of the bed and placed my pile of towels and basin on the end, along with my selection of herbs. Sitting opposite Jax, with Fergus between us, I nodded at the tweezers in Jax's hand. "I can do that. If you want me to."

Jax stared at the tweezers like he'd forgotten they were there. He handed them to me along with the small bowl he was dropping the glass shards into, watching as if he'd tackle me should I attempt to use my magic again. He needn't worry. That would not be happening any time soon.

My hands were stiff and sore from removing the suppressor from Fergus' back. Somehow, I bent my fingers around the tweezers and pulled out a piece of glass. Jax had done a good job of removing much of the rest of the glass. "I take it you can't do this by magic, either?"

He shook his head. "I'm not strong enough."

"And the king or princess are really the only people who can save him?"

He nodded, his gaze moving to the newly glazed windows. "That's why we use mortal weapons to fight each other." His voice was quiet. I wasn't even sure he knew he was speaking. "So we don't die."

I dropped a piece of glass into the bowl. It tinkled against the other pieces.

"Can I do anything?" Jax asked.

I nodded to the basin on the end of the bed. "Can you fill that with water please? Once I've removed the glass, we'll roll him over and give him some medicine. Then we'll roll him back and I'll clean him up." Calmness washed over me. This was the sort of help I was used to giving people.

Jax took the basin without a word. The water ran in the bathroom and a moment later, he placed the basin next to me on the bed. "You know human medicine won't work." He sat heavily on the other side.

I caught the basin before it toppled over, placing it on the bedside table. "Because he's a prince?"

"Because he's fae." There was an edge to Jax's voice, like he thought I should know what he meant.

I glanced at him. "What do you mean?" Human medicine worked on me. Mother had given me ash flower once when a cut on my hand had become infected causing a fever. I'd given pygmy root to her plenty of times for her headaches.

"Why would we need human medicine? For almost everything, we can use magic." He dropped his head into his hands.

I watched the gentle shaking of his shoulders for a moment, then gave Fergus' back another once over. I'd removed all the glass. Where the suppressors had been, one side was inflamed, the other was fine, and his skin was hot and dry. He needed the herbs and a cold compress. If I mixed the pygmy root with the ash flower, he'd only have to swallow once to get the benefit of both.

With Jax's help, I rolled Fergus over, placing pillows beneath his head and lower back so he wasn't lying on his wounds. His eyelids fluttered. I pulled off the petals from the ash flower and broke off a small piece of pygmy root, holding them in one hand. "Fergus? I need you to swallow this. Can you do that?"

He nodded, and I placed them in his mouth.

Once they were gone, we rolled him back over. I cleaned his back and placed wet towels on his back for his fever and a compress on his forehead. He shivered, but his skin was hot. Too hot. I placed a towel on his forehead and cast a sidelong look at Jax. He'd moved from the bed to sit in a chair. His head was resting on the chair back and he watched every move I made. He seemed so certain Fergus would die. I hoped he was wrong.

I took one berry from my pocket, holding it up to the light coming through the window. Jax jumped to his feet and was around the bed in an instant. He smacked the berry from my hand. It bounced across the wooden floor, coming to a stop at the bathroom door. "You can't give him that! It's poison."

I stared at the nightbalm berry lying on the floor. It was poisonous. Even the youngest of children were taught never to touch those little green berries. That one lying on the floor could kill Fergus, Jax and myself were we all to eat a piece.

Fergus groaned. I took the towel from his back, rinsed it with cool water and replaced it. He let out a deep sigh.

When I was eleven, not long after Father died, Mother and I were walking through the woods after a visit to a sick elderly man one town over. She'd heard a noise and pulled me off the trail where we found a woman lying on the ground, the skin on her back so badly burnt, there seemed to be none left. I hadn't been able to watch, so Mother had sat me behind a tree while she did what she could for the woman. Only, I hadn't been able to resist not watching, either, and I'd poked my head around the tree.

The woman told Mother she'd been tied to a post in her village for days with no one giving her food or water.

I'd expected Mother to put bandages on the woman, but she hadn't. Instead, she held a nightbalm berry in her hand and gently squeezed it until the center popped out onto her palm, a skinless version of the round green berry. She pressed on it with her finger, then dipped that same finger in the juice that escaped before placing a drop on the woman's lips.

It had seemed that as I watched, the woman recovered. The burns turned from open, weeping sores to red welts. In minutes—or so it had seemed—she was upright and on her way. As she left, waving a grateful goodbye, I caught a glance of her ears. Pointed.

When I asked Mother if the woman was fae, she denied it, said the woman was the same as the two of us. When I asked if she'd healed the woman with nightbalm, she told me I must need an early night because I was seeing things.

I'd taken what she said as true and had never thought of that day since. Not until I saw the nightbalm growing in the woods and recalled the deep burns on her back. Burns I was now certain had been caused by iron.

"I think it will help him," I said to Jax.

He shook his head. "You know it won't. You're a healer. You've seen what happens when a child eats one."

I had. Instant vomiting. The berry ate away at the insides until there was nothing left. Until they died. "I have a theory."

Jax shook his head. "Now is not the time for theories."

"Perhaps it's exactly the right time," I breathed, pulling another berry from my pocket. I pressed it between my fingers the way Mother had all those years ago, squeezing until it shed its skin. I held the skin up to Jax. "I think this is the poisonous part. And this—" I lifted my other hand. "—is the part that will help him. I saw Mother use it once. I'm sure she used it on a fae."

Jax shook his head, resolute.

"He will die anyway, right?"

Jax wouldn't meet my eyes.

"Isn't it worth a try?" Stars, I hoped I was right, because no matter what I said, nothing was worth the horrific death that would come from nightbalm poisoning. But, I reminded myself, this was more than a hunch. I was almost certain it would work. If I wasn't, I wouldn't be trying it. "Shouldn't we do everything we can to save him?"

Jax crossed the chamber and opened a window, stopping to inhale the ocean scent. His shoulders drooped. "Okay. You can do it." He kept his back to me.

I drew in my breath, unsure if I was pleased or disappointed by his reaction. If this didn't work, it was all on me. "I can do this alone. If you prefer."

He turned to stare at Fergus. "I'd like to stay."

I wanted him to stay. I didn't want to kill Fergus, and I certainly didn't want to be in here alone when I did it. But I said, "It might not be pleasant."

He nodded. "I know."

I took the last berry from my pocket and squeezed it to reveal its center. Taking a deep breath, I placed a drop of juice on his lips, then took his hand and waited.

Nothing happened. A sheen of sweat remained on Fergus' skin.

I glanced at Jax.

"Did you even give him any?" He took an uncertain step forward.

With one hand still in Fergus', I peeled the towel from his back, leaning closer to stare at his wounds. "Is it my imagination, or do those wounds seem less angry?"

Jax moved toward his friend and both of us stared at Fergus' back. "Better. I think."

I thought so, too. But perhaps it was wishful thinking.

Fergus squeezed my hand, his lips moving. I bent to hear what he said.

"You tried to kill me," he whispered.

I shook my head. "I ... thought it would work. I mean ... I was almost certain." I glanced at Jax. Was I in trouble?

"You broke ... my windows."

I let out my breath and touched his shoulders and back with my fingertips. His fever was gone. I looked at Jax. "It's working." To Fergus, I said, "They were dirty. Now you have a nice clean set of windows." I peeled the compress from his head.

His lips turned up into a weak smile and his eyes fluttered shut. There was no more groaning. "He will be fine," I whispered to Jax.

Jax wrapped me in a hug and lifted me off my feet with a whoop. "He will be fine!"

FIFTEEN

"I OWE YOU an apology."

I jumped at the sound of Fergus' voice. It had only been a few hours since he'd taken the night-balm, but his recovery had been fast. Within the hour, the weeping wounds on his back healed, but he'd spent that time, and then some, sleeping. Jax said he needed to sleep to recover his magic. I'd left about then, giving them both some time alone. In the time since, I'd bathed and changed into a knee-length summer dress with thin straps I'd found in the cupboard in my room, and had seated myself on the steps that led down to the beach. I watched the waves roll in, enjoying my last few hours on the island. Tomorrow I was leaving. I hadn't told Fergus yet, but I hoped he'd allow me to take Raven to Unseelie to rescue Mother.

In the time since I'd last seen him, Fergus had also bathed and changed into a pair of shorts and a navy blue shirt. He still looked tired, but a lot better than when I'd seen him last.

I shuffled over for him to sit on the step, keeping my hands cupped in my lap. I had taken little notice of them while I worked on Fergus, but there wasn't a place on my palms that wasn't cut or burnt. In some places, whole chunks of skin were missing. "What for?"

He crouched in front of me and took my hands, cupping them between his. I winced at the pressure. Now that I wasn't working on adrenalin, it appeared the slightest touch lit fire beneath my skin.

"For not doing this sooner." As Fergus spoke, the fire in my hands dimmed and disappeared, and I had no doubt that when I next looked, the wounds would be like the ones on Fergus' back, just placid red scars.

With the pain gone, I was suddenly aware of how close we were. Our knees touched and our hands were between our chests. I couldn't meet his eyes. "You were ... busy." He'd been in no state to heal anyone.

"I had this dream," he leaned forward as he spoke, his voice soft. "I dreamed that someone blew in all my windows, trying to stab me with the glass. Then they tried to poison me with night-balm. I wonder why I dreamed such things."

He was too close. I shook my head. "No idea. Overactive imagination, perhaps?" I filled my voice with mock innocence.

"Could be. It just seemed so real." He grinned and released my hands. "They should feel better now."

I glanced down to find them healed, as I expected. "They do. Thank you."

"No. Thank you. Jax would be planning my funeral rite were it not for you."

So, Jax had told him what happened. I lifted one shoulder. "I'd have done the same for anyone."

Fergus' eyebrows rose.

"Minus the glass explosion of course." I looked at my hands to hide my smile. "That's what I do … did. I was a healer in Iadrun, and I was good at it. I always thought it would be the only thing I ever did." I didn't know if I'd get the chance to be a healer again. It would depend on whether I could rescue Mother. And whether this princess thing came with added responsibilities.

Fergus lifted his hands. "You need not sell it to me. I know firsthand how good you are at your work."

I blew out a laugh. "You have to say that."

He shook his head and turned down his lips, eyes dancing. He placed his hand on his chest. "Prince, remember. I'm sure the job description confirms I don't have to say or do anything I don't want to. Which reminds me. I came out here to apologize." He indicated to the beach. "Can we walk? After so long away, I need to bury my toes in the sand."

I nodded, and he stood, held out a hand and pulled me to my feet.

The evening was hot, and I'd long since removed my shoes. Apart from the last time I was here, I'd never been on a beach. Last time, there was no chance to enjoy it. The sand beneath my feet felt glorious, rough and smooth at the same time. It was still warm from the heat of the day, and it moved and molded beneath the soles of my feet.

Fergus watched the ground as he spoke. "What you did with the nightbalm, there are only a few who can access the sort of magic required to do that. And even then, they can only—"

I shook my head. He had it all wrong. "It wasn't magic. I healed you with human medicine." I would never use magic on him—or anyone. Not after almost killing him.

"There is no human on earth who could access the part of the nightbalm berry that can heal fae.

Only someone with powerful magic can do it. Royal magic. I've only ever seen it done once." He smiled. "But I'm glad you knew how to do it."

I shook my head, though it was becoming harder to deny. "It wasn't magic." My voice was small. "I tried to use my magic, and the result was a hole in your bedroom wall and almost a new scar for Jax." My mind was working. I'd only seen it done one other time. Close to the Crossing. By the woman everyone thought should be the Seelie Queen. My mother.

Fergus tried not to smile. And failed. "Yes, well, it would seem that the rest of your magic may not be as ... honed. But you can fix that with practice."

I shook my head, everything that had happened these past few weeks catching up with me. "I don't want to fix it. I don't want magic. I just want to go to Unseelie, rescue Mother, and get as far from this place as possible." I glanced at Fergus as I heard how that sounded. "No offence."

He shook his head. "None taken."

We wandered with slow steps along the beach, my thoughts sticking on Mother. "I have to rescue her."

Fergus nodded. "I know. But I need to tell you something first."

"Okay." Whatever he was about to say, I was suddenly certain it was the reason for the beach walk.

"I remembered some things while the night-balm was in my body, things I hadn't thought of for years. Like the day I came to your cottage ... before." He glanced my way.

"The day that was blocked in your memory?" The day Father died.

His mansion was far behind us and the few beach cottages on this side of his home were spaced well apart. Between them, a long field sloped up to the bottom of the large hill behind Fergus' home. Horses—so many horses—grazed on brilliant green grass at the back of the field. Raven was there. So was Obsidian.

Fergus indicated with his hand and we walked up to a grassy knoll where the beach met the field, where a bench seat was angled perfectly to take in both the grazing horses and the beach. He waited until I sat, then sat beside me. "This view is the best on the island at this time of night."

I couldn't deny it. The sky was turning shades of magenta and orange, reflecting on the water, which was just beginning to sparkle. I couldn't focus on the view. I wanted to hear what he'd recalled to make his face so grim. "So what did you remember? And who did it?"

"Father did it, though I'm still not sure why." He ran a hand down his face. "That day, the first day I came to your cottage, it was my first job with the Wild Hunt. We were to bring in a man, alive or dead, Father didn't care." He licked his lips. "The man was Myles Ridgewing. Also known as Myles Tremaine. And he was the husband of the dead Seelie Queen."

"Father," I whispered.

He nodded. "The night we first met—the night I hurt your mother—I felt this ... pull toward your cottage. I wish I could have ignored it, especially knowing the things I now know about you. Had I, you would not be in the position you now find yourself. But I couldn't stop myself from entering your cottage, especially after I caught sight of you running up the path toward it." He shook his head. "When we went back there together, Aoife told me she knew my secret. No one outside the Wild Hunt knew my secret, apart from you, and you'd had no chance to tell her."

"I promised to keep it, and I meant it." I still would. There was nothing in the world that would convince me to part with it.

"I know you did." He met my eyes with a small smile. "Your mother's words were laced with magic—a spell. It's been eating at me since, allowing me to recall the smallest details but nothing of substance. Mixed with the nightbalm magic though, all my memories came back. I remembered your cottage. I remembered why I'd gone there all those years ago. For almost seventeen years, everyone in Faery thought you and Aoife dead. Everyone, it seems, except Father. Had we found you and Aoife that night, we had different instructions on how to deal with you. Different to how we handled your father."

"What instructions?" My hands were shaking. Just talking about that night took me right back there. Mother and I had been so close to being found.

"The two of you were to return to Unseelie. Alive."

"Why? What does he want with us?" My voice sounded small. I didn't understand why the Unseelie King would hunt us this way. We were from the Seelie Court, enemies of the king, sure, but was that good enough reason for him to hunt us down?

Fergus shook his head. "I don't know. Never knew. I only know you need to be careful around him."

I was sure of that, too, but it didn't help. None of this told me what was going on or how I could save Mother. I got to my feet, tired of sitting still, and headed down to the water's edge. Fergus followed without speaking.

We wandered on in silence, the last of the sun on my back and the water warm at my feet. My thoughts shifted to Rhiannon. My aunt. Mother's sister. A woman who loved the power her title brought. A title that shouldn't belong to her. "Why didn't Rhiannon use magic suppressors on me?" Had she, I'd still be in Seelie.

Fergus took in my profile for a long moment before answering. "She didn't think she needed to. You didn't have magic when you two met, though I believe she thought you had weak magic. You were no threat to her. And her love of theatrics meant she preferred to make an example of you and publicly execute you rather than doing it behind closed doors. I imagine that's where you were headed had you not brought the prison down around her." He kicked through a wave that rode up over our feet. "You must have been very young when you left Faery. Definitely under five. Probably much younger."

I cast him a sidelong glance. The setting sun lit up half his face, momentarily removing the tension and exhaustion. "I guess so. Otherwise, surely I'd remember something about this place."

He shrugged. "There are spells that can stop that happening, but you're not spelled." I waited for him to expand on his statement. Instead, he spoke of something completely different. "Do you know all fae children are born without magic?"

That was something I'd never heard before. No magic made fae children vulnerable.

As if he read my thoughts, he said, "They're also assigned guards—four for each child—who stay with them every moment until their magic comes in."

"That's a lot of guards."

He shook his head, his eyes darkening with sadness. "Not really. There are very few children born in Faery. I guess it balances out our immortality. Those rare children are treasured."

"By assigning guards to them?" Didn't seem like a very loving environment to grow up in.

"They only have guards until their magic comes through. It usually happens just before their fifth birthday. Unless you're royal, then it comes earlier, usually by the time a child is one. Most often, it comes in gently; soft and serene. One day a child has no magic, the next their guards are replaced by magic tutors because they have new talents."

I knew why he was telling me this. "That's what happened to me in the prison. My magic came through." But it hadn't come soft or serene.

He nodded. "I imagine if Rhiannon knew you'd never received your magic, rather than assuming it was weak and restrained by your time in Iadrun, she'd never have left you unsuppressed. It's unheard of for a fae to have no magic until they're … how old are you, sixteen?"

I nodded, feeling like a failure. I was at least twelve years late receiving my magic. Longer if I really was a princess.

He gave my shoulder a nudge. "Don't feel bad. We'd still be in Seelie if your magic hadn't made an appearance when it did."

That made me feel even worse. "My body is doing things I can't control. Guards are dead because of me. I almost killed Jax. I don't want to go around killing people because I don't know how any of this works."

"Then it's your lucky day. I happen to be an expert in all things magic." He laced his fingers together, pushing his hands out in front of him. His eyes danced and I could feel him trying to make me smile.

"Good thing you owe me a favor."

His eyebrows rose. "I do?"

"I'd say so." I nodded. "For saving your life."

He smiled. "Of course. How could I forget? We'll start your lessons tomorrow."

I tried to smile back, but I couldn't. Twice now, bad things had happened when I tried to use magic. I wasn't sure I wanted to risk a third time.

As if he could read my mind, he said, "You used your magic perfectly when you knew what you were doing with the nightbalm. And you won't get a surge of magic like that again. It only happens when there's an abundance."

I nodded, understanding why he'd told me all this. "Which I had because I left Faery before it came through."

He nodded. "For you, yes. For others, for people that have a lot of magic, that build up can happen if they don't use their magic often enough."

"You've seen it happen before?" There was something in his tone that told me I was right, and that the last time had been traumatic.

"I have. That story doesn't have such a happy ending as yours." The words sounded like he meant it as a joke, but his tone was heavy.

I turned to face him, something about those words and the bleakness on his face telling me who he was talking about. "It happened to you. Did you kill someone?" My cheeks reddened. He was the fae leader of the Wild Hunt—something I seemed to have forgotten since coming to Faery— as if killing someone would bother him. To hide my embarrassment at my stupid question, I asked another. "Or does killing not matter to you?" I bit down on my tongue as soon as the words escaped my lips. And bit down harder when I saw the flash of pain cross his face.

Immediately his eyes hardened. With nostrils flaring and pressed lips, he turned away and started up the beach. He didn't even deign to answer my cruel comment.

"Fergus. Wait! I'm sorry."

His face was so hard when he turned back that he didn't even look like the person I knew. "Don't be. And don't worry. It's not you I'm angry at, it's me." He marched up the beach toward his home, his hands squeezed into tight balls.

I watched him go, the look on his face before his eyes hardened etched into my mind. I hadn't just hurt him with my comments, I'd disappointed him, too. My question was brutal, asked to cover my embarrassment. I wanted to go after him. I should go after him. But that brief conversation had reminded me of something I'd been avoiding.

The Wild Hunt. It was everything I hated about Faery.

Fergus wasn't just part of it. He *was* it.

He made it so easy to forget about his alter ego, his other life. Because here in Faery, he wasn't the terrifying mask of a man who stole away the things I loved. Here in Faery he was caring and kind. A friend, perhaps even an ally.

But he was also the hunter. Wasn't he?

I'd ignored that part of him before, given him a free pass because he seemed so decent, but at some point, I had to acknowledge it. I needed to understand how he reconciled the evil of the Hunt with the good person I knew. And then I needed to decide where that placed him within my life.

I watched the steps up to the mansion—the place he'd disappeared—until the waves covered my ankles and splashed up the backs of my legs, until the day dimmed and night fell. I watched as whoops and yells came from behind Fergus' home and four of the Wild Hunt took to the air—none of them Fergus—noisy silhouettes against the darkening sky. I watched until the barks of their hounds died away to nothing, caught between apologizing to Fergus and returning to my room without a word to anyone. But I couldn't slink away and hide. I needed to ask Fergus about the Wild Hunt, and soon, but I hadn't meant to ask him tonight, and never in that manner. I needed to apologize, and I needed him to hear me.

As I walked up the steps and between the bright colored chairs, tables and cushions set out around the pool, strains of haunting music floated toward me. It came from a pianoforte—I knew because, back when I went to school, a teacher had an old recording of one from before the fae destroyed all our instruments. One afternoon when I was about fourteen and not long before I gave up school entirely, I'd raced back into my classroom intending to get the pencil I'd left behind. I found my teacher leaning back in his chair, eyes closed, listening to the recording. Most people would have turned it off and denied ever listening to it, but Mr Hobbs must have seen something on my face. He turned the music down low to make certain no one else could hear it, then beckoned me over. I sat on the floor beside him until my backside grew numb, listening to the way the music rose and fell, to the tale the notes weaved. It was glorious.

This music was nothing like what I'd heard that day. This was mournful, angry and intricate. I moved toward the sound, skirting around the edge of the pool, past my room and along the length of the building until I saw him.

Sat beneath a wide veranda, his back to me, Fergus was playing the pianoforte. His fingers flowed across the keys while his hands varied between movements that were rough and sharp, to smooth and gentle. I felt like I was watching something incredibly private, but my feet wouldn't let me walk away. As I listened, the hair on my forearms rose and tears pricked my eyes. The only other sound I'd ever heard which had brought tears to my eyes were Father's screams as the Wild Hunt forced the life from him. But the tears that blurred my vision tonight didn't make me want to hide or hurt someone. I just wanted to listen. I was sure I'd never again hear anything half as beautiful as this. It made me feel safe and strong, two things I hadn't felt in a long time, feelings I'd never expected to come from music.

I don't know how long he played. The night grew deeper, the moon bathing the house in gentle, warm light. While he played, I listened, not moving and barely breathing.

Finally, his fingers slowed, and the music ceased. He sat looking down at the keys, his shoulders rising and falling as if he were catching his breath. I couldn't catch mine, either.

I turned to leave. I should have gone sooner, but there was nothing in the world that could have dragged me away while that music played.

"Going already? Without so much as a round of applause." Fergus' voice lacked the venom I was certain he wanted to lace through those words. Instead, he sounded tired.

I turned back to find him still staring at the pianoforte. I swallowed the urge to apologize.

"That was the most beautiful thing I've ever heard."

A deep breath shook his body. "That … wasn't beautiful."

I took a hesitant step toward him. "It was angry. And soulful. And it made me want to cry. It was stunning."

He turned, the moonlight showing off a line of tears on each cheek. He brushed them away with one hand. "Thank you," he whispered.

I moved closer still. "Do you want to talk about it?" That music had been about more than a few ill-spoken words between the two of us, I was certain of that.

His eyes narrowed. "About how I'm a killer and always have been? No thanks. It's not news to me. It shouldn't be news to you, either."

I held my palms out, hoping to calm him. I didn't want to argue. Especially not after hearing his beautiful music. "I should never have said that. I'm sorry. It was unfair."

"It wasn't unfair. It was entirely accurate." He sighed and ran a hand down his face, the self-loathing so sharp on his features I wanted to run up and hug it away. "I'm so used to people knowing everything about me—knowing things I wish they didn't. I forget you don't." He shuffled over on his stool, making room for me to sit.

There was barely room for two, but I wasn't ready to be alone, and I didn't think he was either, so I sat. Our legs touched from thigh to knee, but neither of us moved away. Every part of me wanted to ask what he was talking about. To beg him to tell me all those things I didn't know. But I hadn't forgotten my manners enough to ask. When he was ready to tell me, he would. And right now, he didn't seem inclined. But there were other things I wasn't too polite to ask about. "If you worked out I was a Seelie princess, what else do you know about me?" Because I had vast gaps in my knowledge and he was the one person I could ask.

He sucked in a deep breath and loosed a long sigh. "Very little. Everything that happened in Seelie with your mother, happened when I was a small child. No one in the Unseelie Court has spoken of Aoife since."

"Until now," I prodded.

"I don't think I can tell you what you want to hear, Bria. All I know is that your mother created a problem in our court. When she and her baby daughter died during the child's first year, there wasn't a single tear shed for her."

"Do you think she faked our deaths?" Whatever Mother was running from, it must have been bad.

"It's looking that way. Your mother must really have not wanted to be queen."

It made no sense. The person I knew would never walk out on her duty, especially if it meant leaving someone like Rhiannon in control. As a healer, I'd seen her go many nights in a row without rest to make sure her patients were comfortable.

We could go round in circles trying to guess what we didn't know. I opted for a change in subject. "Don't you get in trouble for creating music in Unseelie?"

He gave a harsh laugh. "I already told you, the rules around music are the same in Faery as they are in Iadrun. If anyone I didn't trust heard me, I imagine the king would enjoy the punishment he'd get to hand out."

I glanced at his profile, trying to decide if that meant he trusted me, or just that he knew I couldn't get off the island to tell anyone.

"I use music as an outlet for my magic."

I wasn't sure what he meant. "You created those beautiful sounds with your magic?"

He shook his head, a faint smile gracing his lips. "No. It was all me. And today it was an outlet for … my anger at myself. But usually I play when I haven't been … out with Obsidian…" Meaning when he didn't ride with the Wild Hunt. "If I have an abundance of magic, because I'm not using enough, playing, or singing, calms the magic in my veins, stops me overreacting or taking out my anger in ways I might regret."

I shook my head, stuck again on thoughts of him with the Wild Hunt. "I don't understand how you keep the two sides of your personality so separate."

He frowned. "You think I don't act like a prince?"

"This has nothing to do with being a prince. This is about Fergus Blackwood versus Xion Starguard." Two sides of the coin. Black versus white. Different in every way.

Understanding crossed his face, and he lifted a shoulder. "You learned when you were young never to trust me."

"I learned never to trust Xion. Yet when I'm with Fergus, I see very little reason to do that." And the one time I'd seen him as Xion since I found out who he really was, he had saved my life.

He stood and strode away, stopping when he reached the edge of the pool to look out at the ocean. "When I'm around, people die."

I thought about the guards I'd killed in Rhiannon's prison. Of my magic shooting toward Jax's face. Perhaps the same could be said of me.

He shook his head and I could just make out the hard line of his jaw. "Don't say it. Those guards aren't the same. You didn't love them."

My mouth dropped open. "You killed someone you loved? On purpose?"

"What does it matter if it was on purpose or not? Either way, they're still dead." He tried to keep his voice hard, but it broke on the final syllable.

My heart ached. I may not have killed Father, but I knew how it felt to lose someone you loved. I stood and walked over to him. "It matters a lot." I slipped my hand into his. Physical contact always helped me when I was feeling the way Fergus was. I hoped it was the same for him.

For a moment, his fingers tightened around mine. That slight movement making my heart lurch. Then he pulled from my grip. "Don't. Or there might be another name to add to that list."

I stared at my empty hand for a moment, then shook my head. "I think you'd have to lose control for another name to go on that list, and I've never seen you out of control."

"Spend some time with me in the Unseelie Court and you might just see it. Better yet, come with me when I'm with the Wild Hunt."

I shook my head. "You don't lose control with the Hunt. You're the exact opposite of that."

He blew out a breath, and some of his tension, looking down at me. "You're right. I don't lose control with the Hunt. I do exactly what is expected of me." His voice was still hard.

I gave him a weak smile and bit down on my tongue. There were so many things I wanted to know, but after the way I'd phrased my question earlier, I couldn't voice them.

"Go on," he said, the faintest of smiles on his lips. "Ask me. Whatever it is you want to know, just ... ask. I promise I won't storm away again."

Fine. If he was answering questions, I would ask. "What happens when you become Xion Starguard? Where does Fergus go?" I asked softly. Because I saw none of one in the other.

His shoulders stiffened. "Nothing happens. I put on a mask is all."

I shook my head. Xion and Fergus couldn't be more different. There had to be more to it. "And suddenly you enjoy stealing people away to Faery, killing them if you deem it necessary?"

"I'm under my father's command." His voice was strained.

"Your father demands you steal defenseless children? He demands you drag away adults, leaving their families to starve? And you have no say in it?" I wanted him to nod and tell me I was right, that he couldn't do anything but what his father commanded. I wanted to blame someone else for the horrible things Fergus did, because I liked him. Really liked him. And it was easier to feel that way when I ignored Xion. Or when there was someone else to blame for the way Xion Starguard acted.

"Father demands it. I guess I could refuse if I wanted to. I just never saw the point." His voice had gone distant, and he turned his back to me. Like he knew I would judge him, and he knew what my judgement would be.

He was probably right. "You never saw the point? You have a sister, right? How would you like it if the people of Iadrun trapped her next time she visited our lands, then tortured her to death?"

"My sister would never go to Iadrun, so your example is unlikely." He turned to face me but refused to meet my eyes.

A spark of anger ignited in my chest. Why wouldn't he look at the Wild Hunt from a different point of view? "Use your imagination, Fergus. I dare you."

He sighed, his voice softening. "I don't need to imagine. I already know how devastated I'd be should anything happen to her." He ran his hand down his face.

"How could you take Tobias? He was just a tiny baby." The question I'd been too scared to ask since the moment I found out who Xion Starguard really was finally crossed my lips. I didn't understand how he expected a child that young to survive without his parents long enough to make it to the Army of Souls. It hurt my heart to think what Selina's much-loved baby brother might become. All because of a person I was beginning to like. When he didn't answer straight away, I turned to leave. His silence was all the response I needed.

"Bria." He laced his fingers around my wrist, holding just tight enough to stop me walking away. "Wait."

I shook my head. "I should never have asked." I pulled my hand away and began to walk.

"Tobias was sick." He paused, perhaps waiting for me to turn around. When I didn't, he added, "You know it's true."

My steps faltered. The coughing sickness had found Tobias in his first week of life. Mother and I had tried everything to make him better. We thought we'd succeeded. The wetness of his cough had decreased, and he no longer fought for air each time a fit overtook him. But most babies that contracted the sickness died. Often just as we thought they were recovering. "I fail to see how that makes you look any better." Because that was what I wanted. Fergus to come out of this looking like he was good. How stupid was I?

"I'm not trying to make myself look better. Believe me, I know what you see when you look at me. I see the same thing every time I look in the mirror."

"Then tell me how you live with it. Tell me how you get out of bed every day knowing that you might have to go out and steal away someone's baby. Or someone's father. Tell me what you say to yourself to make it all right. Because it makes no sense to me." I was positive this would be the end of the conversation. Each time I'd asked him about the Hunt in the past, he'd tell me a little then refuse to speak anymore. We were probably at the point in this conversation where he would shut it down.

He closed his eyes. "It's complicated."

"Luckily, I'm good at understanding complex things." My voice was so hard, it didn't even sound like my own.

He was silent and I could see him considering whether or not to tell me. He took a breath so deep his shoulders lifted. "I have a quota to fill, Bria. A number of humans set by the king to replace those slaves that die each month in his army. If I don't provide what he requires, I receive six lashes of his magic to my body for every human missing. As do each of my men."

"The marks on your back?" I'd seen them when I removed the suppressors.

He nodded once.

I turned to him. "But you could stop him. You're strong enough to shield your men."

"Perhaps. But even if I could do it—and I'm not convinced I can—there is no one else in this kingdom strong enough to shield against Father's magic."

Understanding tumbled over me. "Doing so would show him who Xion is," I mumbled.

"You've only seen the worst parts of the Wild Hunt. Here in Faery, there are some nights of the year when seeing the Wild Hunt ride in front of the moon is considered a blessing, nights when we ride around Unseelie just for people to see us and think good luck has visited them. Together, our elemental magic is strong and if my father allowed it, we could keep crops yielding year round, keep prey in the woods for hunting, fish in the ocean. Every one of us hopes one day the king will let us do this again. We could make life in Unseelie so much better." Hope lit his eyes.

"But you can't because you have a quota to fill."

"Eternally." He nodded. "The Wild Hunt has been good for me. Good to me. Filling Father's quota is the only way to keep him from hurting them. If I could shield them from pain any other way, I'd do it."

It all made sense, but it didn't make Fergus into the person he'd become in my head. He was still a conscienceless killer, and I'd allowed myself to forget it. "So you ignore what you're doing to humans because you're saving the Wild Hunt— your friends—from lashings." All he'd done was shift the pain elsewhere and ignore those humans he was hurting. The humans who didn't heal as easily or live as long as his fae brothers did.

Fergus looked out across the pool. "So long as I bring the right number of living, breathing humans through the Crossing and into Faery each month and most of them end up serving in the Army of Souls, no one checks anything else. The Hunt finds murderers, child molesters, and people who are violent to their partners, and I bring them across the border for the border guard to mark another tick on his checklist." He spoke angrily and hit his chest. "*I* do it, Bria. I do it so my people don't have to feel the guilt of putting your people in an environment they aren't meant to survive." His voice shook, but his chin dipped to his chest as anger and guilt warred over which emotion he felt stronger. "Sometimes they don't come easily. Sometimes we hurt them before taking them. Occasionally we hurt them so badly they die—but that is never our intended outcome."

I stared at him. If he hadn't taken Tobias, I'd almost have forgiven him after that explanation. He was taking away only the worst of our society.

Except he wasn't. "Tobias wasn't any of those things. He hadn't even had the chance to prove himself yet, so you can't even say he was going to be like that." My voice rose in pitch as I fought off tears. Protecting his own people might have helped Fergus, but it devastated me.

"No." His voice grew soft, and he repeated what he'd said earlier. "But he was sick." He took a step toward me, his hand out like he was going to run it down my arm for comfort, but he stopped short. "The child was always going to die the night we visited, whether or not we took him. He was an easy check mark on my quota list. One I didn't have to feel guilty about because no one in Faery hurt him and he didn't have to go to the army."

"He was just a baby," I repeated, tears running down my face. Tobias really was dead. In my heart I'd known it was true, but it still hurt to hear it.

"Once I got him to Faery, I tried to save him but even my magic couldn't help, so I removed my mask, took away his pain and held him in my arms while he drew his last breath. I buried him as close

to his family home as I could on the Faery side of
the border. I'm sorry, Bria. It doesn't make it any
better, but I don't know what else to do. The Wild
Hunt is trapped in the spell Father created, perpetually finding servants for the fae in his army.
If we weren't bound to his will, I believe one of
our roles—what we were created for—would be
easing the path of the ill to their final destination."

I sank to the ground at the edge of the pool,
crossing my legs. Tobias was dead. It would
devastate Selina. Death was what she'd hoped for
after the Hunt took him, but a large part of me
had hoped he'd come back one day, just walk up
to their cottage and resume his life with them.
That would never happen. "I have to tell Selina."

"She knows," he whispered.

"You told her?" Someone had. Selina had told
me as much the last time I saw her, though I
hadn't believed her.

He nodded, dropping to sit beside me.

"Why did you refuse to tell me any of this
sooner?"

He looked at me through sad eyes. "I know I'm
a murderer and a kidnapper and I can live with it.
But every time you look at me, I can see you
searching for the good in me, and it made me
forget what I am." He clenched his teeth, his voice
shaking with anger. "And I liked it. I liked that

for once, I was someone other than the person everyone has always known me to be, in your eyes anyway." He shook his head. "You're doing it now. In your mind, you're justifying all the horrible things I do in Iadrun."

I pressed my lips together. He was right. I *was* justifying. He was taking away the worst people in Iadrun, therefore he was helping us. He was making the sick feel better before they died.

"You can't do that Bria. You should always remember when I'm with the Wild Hunt, I'm everything you hate." He swallowed. "Sometimes I'm that person even when I'm not with the Hunt. Even if spending time with you allowed me to forget for a while."

He was wrong. "You've never been that person since I've known you."

"I can assure you, it's never far from the surface."

I shook my head. It wasn't true. He wasn't the monster I thought of Xion as. When he went to Iadrun, he did what he had to in order to keep the important people in his life safe. "Fergus, this is stupid—"

"It's not! The only stupid thing was spending time with you and allowing myself to forget the things I've done to the people you love. And hoping you'd forget, too." He stood and walked a few steps away, folding his arms over his chest.

I got up and followed, walking up behind him and placing my hand on his arm. "I won't ever forget. But I can forgive you. And I do."

He shook his head, his voice thick. "Don't."

I kept my hand resting on his arm. "If there was a different way to do what you have to do, would you have taken it?"

He nodded.

"Then that's all I need to know about you."

He turned, looking down at me with eyes so intense it was as if he were seeing into my soul. "I've done nothing good enough to end up with someone like you in my life, but I'm glad you're here."

"Me, too," I whispered. And I was. But I was still worried about him. "The Hunt, it doesn't seem to make you very happy."

His smile was weak. "I love the Hunt—the feeling of freedom, riding as fast as the wind, knowing no one can touch me when I'm riding with them. I enjoy making a person's last hours easier, I just wish I didn't have to drag them this side of the border to do it. What I dislike is the hold Father has over the Hunt, the quota he makes us fill, and the punishment we must suffer if we fail. Even if he doesn't know it, he always seems to wind his way into my life and change it for the worse." He sighed. "I have to meet with him in the morning."

He didn't need to say the words for me to know he wasn't looking forward to it. "Are you meeting with him as Fergus? Or Xion?"

"Xion. Jax pretended to be Xion while I was trapped in Seelie, but Father was growing suspicious. I need to smooth things over." He shrugged. "Maybe I'll show up as myself after. Maybe not."

It said a lot about his father that he was more worried about seeing Xion than his own son. "Sounds like you're lucky to have Jax around. Good job someone didn't kill him with her rogue magic earlier."

"I'm sure he's as grateful about that as I am." A wry smile settled on his face. It was good to see him let go of his anger. "His magic is weak in other ways, but he's a strong shifter. Helps that Father has no idea what he's capable of."

"Because it leaves you free to do whatever you want to? Like, say, at a masquerade?"

Fergus' lips twitched.

"You know, I'd never have danced with you that night had I known you were the Unseelie Prince." I'd have fought with everything I had to get away from him. I'd had no intention of ever being part of Faery. Still didn't, but perhaps when

I resumed my life in Iadrun I'd have some friends on this side of the border.

"I know." He let his gaze wander across the horizon. "What about now? Now you know more about me than almost anyone in the world, would you still turn down a dance with me?"

I looked around. There was room enough for dancing beside the pool if we moved the furniture around. I wasn't sure if he meant to dance with me right now or sometime later.

He took my silence for worry. "Why do you think Mother gifted me this island? It's so far from everywhere that no one will hear the music. You need not be concerned. Remind me to take you to a Wild Hunt party one day. We have music like you've never heard, played so loud it feels like the beat matches your own heart."

"You do?" He made such music sound amazing.

Fergus nodded and his face lit as he spoke of the Hunt. He looked so happy.

Perhaps I could take a break and be happy, too. "Then, yes. I would dance with you, Fergus Blackwood."

Fergus flourished a hand, holding it high for me to take. "What, no *your Highness*?"

I huffed. "When have I ever called you that?"

One of his shoulders rose and his eyes danced. "There's always a first time."

"And a last." I dropped into a low curtsey, locking eyes with him. I hoped he was watching, because I was never curtseying to him again. "Your Highness, I'd be honored to dance with you."

Fergus' his eyes rested on me a moment longer than necessary, and my heart jumped. He let out a low whistle, and Obsidian and Raven trotted up the beach and stopped in front of the steps.

I looked between him and the horses. "I don't understand."

Fergus grinned. "You don't have to. Just get on." He nodded to Raven.

Dancing beside the pool or riding Raven, it wasn't much of a choice. I'd never felt as free as I had the last time I rode her. "I'm not dressed for riding."

Fergus shrugged. "There is clean riding gear in your room if you want to change."

"I won't be long." I ran to my room and dressed before sprinting back out to where Fergus and the horses waited. With a giggle, I climbed on Raven's back and had only just gathered her reins in my hands when she took three galloping steps along the beach and rose over the island.

While I'd been speaking with Fergus, clouds had rolled in. Raven climbed up through them until we came out the other side. They looked like a cushion beneath her feet, the moon lighting them up like daylight.

Raven slowed, and Fergus rode up beside us. Wind blew his hair back from his face and he seemed refreshed. It suited him. He kicked a leg over Obsidian's head, turning to sit upon her as if she were a park bench. With a grin, he slid off.

"Fergus!" His name spilled from my mouth before I had the chance to stop it.

He grinned up at me, standing on the clouds as if he stood on solid ground. He held his hand out.

I shook my head. "No way am I getting off this horse. I don't know how to control my magic to stop me from falling." Based on my earlier attempt, I doubted I would ever have that sort of control.

"Relax. I'll keep you safe. And if the worst should happen—which it won't..." He suddenly dropped away, sinking through the clouds and disappearing.

"Fergus!" I screamed, digging my heels into Raven, begging her to go after him. She refused to move. Frantic, I searched for a gap in the clouds through which to spy Fergus. Until the bastard came prancing up beside me on the back of Obsidian. I hadn't even noticed Fergus' horse go after him.

He slid off his horse again and held out his hand. "As I was saying, should the worst happen,

Raven and Obsidian will have your back. Now I believe you promised me a dance."

I shook my head, my hands clenched tight around Raven's reins. "Not up here. I said I'd dance with you down there. Beside the pool."

"I don't believe we ever discussed a venue. Besides, you haven't lived until you've danced among the clouds." His hand remained steady, outstretched just above my knee.

I wanted to take it. Every part of my heart wished to take his hand and let him guide me around this private dance floor the way he'd done at the masquerade. But every part of my head told me not to be a fool. It was too dangerous.

"I'd never let you fall," he said, his voice so soft I might have dreamed it.

Before I could talk myself out of it, I took his hand and slid from the horse. The cloud beneath my feet was more than air, firm but spongy. Not like standing on the ground. I gripped Fergus' hands tight, sure I'd fall if I went too far outside his arc of magic.

"Look at me." He pulled on my hands, trying to direct my eyes up.

Taking a deep breath, I did as he asked, lifting my chin to meet his eyes. His gaze made my heart race. I didn't think I'd ever get used to how handsome he was. I frowned. "Why do you look ...

hazy?" Faint blue light surrounded him. He hadn't looked that way before.

Two lines formed between his eyebrows. "Hazy?"

"It looks like I'm seeing you through a veil. A light blue veil."

His eyebrows rose. "You can see that? Let me try using a little less magic. Now, how do I look?"

"Arrogant, conceited, full of yourself." And also handsome, regal and gorgeous, but those last thoughts I kept to myself.

"I aim to please." His lips pursed as he tried not to laugh. "What I meant to say was, is the blue veil gone?"

Almost. It was still there if I looked hard enough. "What was that?"

"Me gathering my magic ready to use it. I was about to cast a spell to keep you warm. Most fae don't see magic as it gathers. Most often we just see the condensed version like ... like the blast of magic that almost hit Jax."

I nodded. I'd certainly seen that. It had been a burst of light, but what I'd just seen was different. "I never noticed it like that before now." I'd never seen magic at all until my magic came through in the prison.

"I believe the correct response is, *I'm indebted to you, Prince Fergus, for thinking of my comfort while we're up here.*"

I'd never seen Fergus like this. Playful. Happy. I'd seen flashes, but never so much at one time. Seeing him this way made me smile. "You'll need to offer me more than a magic jacket if you want me in your debt."

His mouth dropped open in mock despair. "I loaned you a horse. Does that count for nothing? A *flying* horse."

I shook my head. "I'm afraid not." Opting for a change of subject, I added, "Why did I see your magic?"

Fergus pulled gently on my hand until I took a step away from the horse. "Because you'd never accessed your own magic until recently. You'll see it so often now that eventually you won't even notice it."

"It's pretty." It was the most beautiful shade, and I wished to see it again.

"That it is. Now, are you ready for that dance?" He gave my hand a squeeze.

I nodded. At least I couldn't see how high I was if I looked down—the clouds made sure of that.

I gripped Fergus' hands tight, every muscle in my body stiff as I waited for him to pry one hand from mine so he could place it on my back. But he didn't do it. Instead, the blue haze appeared again, and a moment later music played as if we had our own private orchestra. He moved me around our invisible dance floor using the connection between our hands, pushing and pulling to direct me where he wanted me to go. He was a strong lead and there was no chance for me to make the wrong movement. Or perhaps I did, and Fergus adjusted his own steps to match.

The music rose, loud at the crescendo, and Fergus twirled me around and around until the world blurred and I was laughing so hard, I could barely stand. My hair came loose from its binding, strands floating across my face, but I was too busy to do anything about it. I didn't even think to care until the music stopped. For a moment Fergus and I looked at each other as we caught our breath, then his gaze moved from my eyes.

To my ears.

I pulled my hands from his, self-consciously pulling my hair down. For a moment, in his arms, I'd believed I was a princess. Dancing with a prince. Way to bring me crashing down.

He caught my hand. "Don't."

I pulled away, trying to arrange my hair as it had been, my eyes on the clouds billowing beneath our feet.

He caught my chin in his fingers and lifted it until I met his eyes. "You don't have to hide them around me."

"I do if I want you to think of me as someone you enjoy dancing with. If I want you to think of me as just another girl." My cheeks reddened at my admission. The words had slipped out before I had time to stop them. I was acting crazy around him and I didn't know why.

His fingers still rested beneath my chin. "I couldn't ever think of you as just another girl."

My heart fell. There were no surprises there, but it hurt to hear it. I couldn't meet his eyes.

He ducked into my line of vision. "Bria, you are so much more than *just another girl* and you never need to hide your ears—or anything—from me. I think they're beautiful."

That was the princely charm I'd heard so much about. Fergus Blackwood had always had plenty of opportunities to recite pretty words and watch the recipient's knees go weak. It wouldn't work with me. I didn't care that he was a prince. I didn't expect him to shower me with gifts, I just wanted his friendship. And I could see through his words as easily as if they were a pane of glass. I pulled from his grasp and snorted. "Here's a tip, Prince Fergus. If you want to sweet talk a girl, it's better to use lies she will believe." I started back toward the horses knowing I was relying on his magic to keep me up here, but not caring to be in his grasp any longer.

As I reached the place the horses waited, a picnic rug appeared, and on it, an array of sandwiches, fruit, cake and drinks. I stared a moment before turning back to Fergus.

"I was hoping you … wouldn't want to leave just yet. That you'd consider staying up here with me a little longer." He lifted an eyebrow. "You might even have fun."

My shoulders slumped. "You don't have to spend time with me." Perhaps he felt like he owed me this because I'd saved his life.

He placed his hand on his chest, the way I'd seen him do before. "Prince, remember. I don't have to do anything I don't want to."

He waited, watching for the smile I tried to keep off my face. He had a point.

"But, just in case no one has ever told you, Bria Tremaine, your ears aren't something to be ashamed of. Stars, they aren't even something to worry over. There are so many other parts of you that are so much more interesting, that I never even notice your ears. I notice how much you care for your friends. How loyal you are. Your bravery. And the way you press your lips together when you're trying not to smile. I wouldn't have brought you up here if I didn't want to spend time with you. So, please stay." He pouted. "Let the poor prince have some fun … it's been so long."

I pressed my lips in exactly the manner he'd described. He was right, I would have fun with him. And maybe I deserved that, for one night before I went to rescue Mother. I lowered myself onto one edge of the blanket, while Fergus spread himself out on the other side, lying back with his hands behind his head.

Silence reigned and I tried not to watch him, but my eyes kept creeping back. Each time, I'd find him watching me, but I couldn't hold his gaze. I picked up a sandwich and began to nibble.

He picked up his own sandwich. "I lived in Iadrun for a time. When I was a child."

I looked up to find him watching me. Still. "You did?"

"Just for a month or two. But it was the best time of my life. It was the last time I felt truly loved. And I have such strong memories of laughing with Mother, and the feel of her hair blowing against my face as she held me, of her looking at me like I was the most important thing in the world. I keep telling myself that it can only be a dream because I was so young when we went there. I keep telling myself there's no possible way I could recall it the way I do, like it happened yesterday. I tell myself those things to make it easier to take humans—maybe the same humans who made my stay so pleasant—into Father's army."

I didn't envy him. He was in an impossible situation. "Do you wish you'd never joined the

Wild Hunt? That when the magic chose you, you'd refused?"

He looked up at the stars a moment before he answered and, in that moment, I knew what he'd say. I could see it as if it were inked on his face. "I love the Wild Hunt more than I love almost anything else in this world. And I'd do anything for those people I ride with every night."

I loved Mother that same way and I'd do anything to get her back. "I'm going to Unseelie tomorrow. To rescue Mother." It's where I should have gone originally, instead of relying on Rhiannon to help. "Would you mind if I took Raven?"

"What's your plan?" If he was surprised at me wanting to go to Unseelie, he didn't show it. "I'm sure you have one."

I shrugged. "Sneak into the prison and break her out. Then run." Probably for the rest of our lives. But at least we'd be together.

Fergus nodded. "You're welcome to Raven anytime you want her. Would you consider letting me come too? We could leave now."

SIXTEEN

OBSIDIAN and Raven flew us through the night sky to Unseelie. As we left our picnic spot, Fergus whistled, and Buttercup came bounding along beside us. We only came down from the sky after we were through the castle gates. Fergus hid the horses with a glamour, and we left them grazing at the back of the stables where, he assured me, his trusted stable hand, Milo, would take care of them.

Fergus put his hand on the small of my back, directing me along a loose stone path toward the castle. The wind was cold, snow was in the air, and it was a shock after the humidity of the island.

"Where is the prison?" I'd never seen the Unseelie castle from the outside, and the dark stone building was huge. Four separate turret-like wings set in a square around the main building were attached to the main castle by floating walkways which could only have been held in place by magic.

"Beneath the main castle."

It was fully dark, but the castle was illuminated. Balls of light in every color were dotted along the walkway from the stables to the castle. The same balls of color were strung from each of the many turrets, and light shone out from every window. Other, smaller buildings surrounded the castle inside the walls. According to Fergus, some buildings were homes to faithful servants and others were storage houses.

With his hand in mine, Fergus directed me off the path and into the darkness. He didn't want anyone else to know he was here, and the lit pathway seemed to be a main thoroughfare with fae and humans rushing to and from the castle. We put our heads down and walked toward the nearest wing, where Fergus' rooms were. Fergus wanted to change into *more suitable Unseelie attire*, whatever that was—probably anything but the black pants, shirt and riding boots he was currently wearing— after which, we'd search for Mother.

He let us in through a locked door with a flick of his hand, a blue haze wafting around him just before the door swung open. We climbed many narrow and winding flights of stone stairs to reach his rooms. A section at the top looked different from the rest, like the staircase and walls had been repaired more recently than any other part. My heart hammered the whole way. I told myself it was that way because I was finally close to Mother after all this time, and that it had nothing to do with Fergus' close proximity.

Fergus' rooms were bigger than our entire cottage. The bed chamber contained a huge four-poster bed at one end and two double seater black couches at the other. Between them was a small glass table with two chairs, and a bowl of fruit sitting in the center. Large windows looked over the brightly lit path below. Buttercup made a lap of the chamber, sniffing the couches, before jumping up on the bed, turning in three circles and curling up to sleep.

When Fergus emerged from his dressing room, he was wearing the same black evening wear I'd first seen him in, minus the mask. He held a pale pink tie in one hand and an ice-blue tie in the other. "Which one?

I nodded to the blue tie. It reminded me of the color of his magic.

He threw it around his neck and knotted it, just as there was a knock at his door. He walked over and opened it a crack, speaking quietly to whoever was on the other side, before pushing the door soundlessly shut. When he turned back, his face was grim.

"Who was that?"

He swallowed. "Milo. The stable hand."

I jumped to my feet. "Are the horses all right?"

"Fine." His nod was distracted.

I walked over to him. "What's wrong?"

"I asked Milo when we were in the stables if Father had any unusual prisoners at the moment." He glanced my way with a little shrug. "He's good at shrinking into the shadows. Hardly anyone knows he's around, so Milo often knows things he shouldn't."

"And...?" It was bad news, I could tell that much by Fergus' face. "Is Mother ... dead?"

He shook his head. "No. I mean, I don't think so. But she's not in the prison. Milo checked."

"Oh." I didn't know what to say. It was good he didn't think she was dead, but we'd come here planning to break her out of the prison. If she wasn't there, we had no plan.

He moved toward the window, a frown creasing his forehead.

"What do we do now? Search the castle? Check if she's hidden somewhere else?" I moved to stand beside him at the window, following his gaze.

Below, on the pathway, groups of people dressed in their best outfits flowed toward the castle. "What's going on down there?"

Fergus shook his head, his frown deepening. "Winter Solstice Eve," he murmured.

"You're joking, right?" It had felt cold enough when we arrived, but surely he was wrong about the date.

Fergus opened his mouth to answer, but another knock at the door made him still.

"Prince Fergus?" A male voice called from the corridor.

Fergus moved to stand between me and the door, a finger on his lips.

"Prince Fergus! I know you're in there. Laidlaw informed me you were seen exiting the stables."

Fergus cursed beneath his breath before speaking in a bright voice, pitched toward his door. "Of course I'm here, Chester. Wouldn't miss it. Just running a smidge late. I'll be down as soon as I've bathed."

A disgruntled and very loud sigh came from the other side of the door. Fergus didn't relax until retreating footsteps marked Chester's departure.

He swore again.

"What's the matter?"

Fergus put his hand in his hair and his body hummed with tension. "Tonight is the eve of the Winter Solstice."

He'd said that already, but I'd assumed he was wrong. I couldn't have been in Faery that long. That would mean we'd spent five weeks in the prison in Seelie. "It can't be. It didn't seem cool enough for Winter Solstice on your island."

Fergus' face turned a pale shade of white. "Trust me. It is. Lanwick Island has its own microclimate, and it's far hotter there than here on the mainland." He ground his knuckles into his temples, speaking to himself. "There's no way out of it. I'd hoped there might be, but..." He met my eyes. "I have to go. Royal duties. Stay here. I'll be back as soon as I can."

"You're going to leave me in your chamber?" I shook my head. That was not happening.

"Well, it's that, or you find your way back to the stables without anyone capturing you thinking you're a spy from Seelie, unglamour Raven and ride back to the island."

I sat down at the table. He knew I didn't have a good enough handle on my magic to unglamour anything. "What's going on?"

"Unseelie Court business. I can't get out of it now, they know I'm here." He sighed and sank down onto the edge of his bed.

Perhaps this was a good thing. I could sneak around the castle while he was gone. Search some empty rooms for Mother and once I had her, run back to Iadrun. I had to do something. There was no chance I was sitting around in this room waiting for Fergus to finish his *Unseelie Court business.*

Fergus met my gaze with serious eyes. "Don't," he whispered. "Whatever you're thinking you might do, don't. Do not wander around this castle without an escort or you'll end up some place worse than here." Like the prison beneath the castle.

There was shuffling outside his door. Fergus jumped to his feet, his sudden movement making me stand. He again stepped in front of me. "Do not move." He spoke through gritted teeth.

The door to his rooms flew open, banging against the stone wall behind it. Whoever it was hadn't even bothered to knock. Fergus folded his arms in front of his chest and squared his shoulders. If he was trying to hide me, he was doing a superb job. I couldn't see a thing past his body. Even on tip toes.

Two arms wrapped around his neck. "Ferg! You're back and you're alive. I was so worried. Was it awful? Did Queen Rhiannon hurt you?"

Another set of feet ran into the chamber, and I was greeted with Jax's back as he stood shoulder to shoulder with Fergus. He was so wide—had so many muscles over his arms and chest—there was no chance I could see past to whoever he'd brought with him. What was he doing here, anyway?

Fergus cast Jax a questioning stare as he extracted himself from the female's grasp. "Willow. Don't you ever knock?" He spoke like he was bored, but the stiff line of his shoulders and his rushed instructions to me said he was anything but. At least I now knew who the mystery woman was. Princess Willow was Fergus' sister. "And Jax, didn't you go out with the Hunt tonight?"

Jax shook his head, his midnight blue hair rippling. "We just went for a quick ride. It's been a long time." Five weeks since many of them had been on their horses. "Saw you leaving. Thought you might come here. You didn't expect me to miss your naming ceremony, did you?"

Fergus sighed. "I'd hoped *I* might miss it."

I moved a little, trying to glimpse Willow, but Fergus moved blocking my view. She walked across the room and he turned with her, pushing me behind him with one hand. The bed squeaked as she sat down. "You didn't answer my questions." When Fergus remained silent, she huffed. "Fine. Will you at least tell me you're all right?"

"Sorry, Ferg. I tried to keep her out." Jax shook his head again.

I tried to peek around Fergus' arm. I wanted to see his sister. And I wanted to know why they were hiding me from her.

Fergus sighed. "I'm fine, Willow. It's good to see you, little sister." There was a smile in Fergus' voice, though his shoulders remained tense.

"I'm so glad you could make your own party. Jax said you'd escaped from Seelie, but he was sure you hadn't come back here." There was an accusation in her voice, and I wasn't sure if it was aimed at Jax or Fergus. "Have you seen Father's latest whore?" Willow's questions came one after the other with barely a breath between.

Fergus gave a stiff shake of his head. His shoulders lifted like he was taking a breath to speak, but Willow was faster.

"Don't worry. You soon will. She's coming tonight. At least this one's not the same age as you."

"Thank the stars. Can you leave, please? I need to get ready." He indicated toward the door.

There was a shuffling movement from the bed. "Ferg? Why are you standing like that?"

"Like what?" He dropped his arms to his sides. If he was trying to appear casual, even from behind, it was a fail.

The bed moved again, then there were footsteps on the wooden floor. Willow's voice was suspicious. "Both of you. You look like you're hiding something."

Fergus shook his head. "Not hiding anything. Just need to get ready."

"No hiding. Just hanging out with my friend while he gets ready." Jax dropped his hands to his sides.

I raised my eyebrows. They both needed to work on their lies if they didn't want to raise suspicion.

More footsteps. Closer footsteps. "You look fine to me."

Fergus and Jax shuffled backward. I did too, so they didn't trample me.

"Interesting, Ferg." said Willow. "In all your eighteen years, I never noticed you had four legs." She stood on her toes and looked around Fergus. Right at me.

"Ahh."

Fergus grabbed her arm and dragged her across the room to the door. "Ahh, nothing."

"Ouch! You're hurting me!" Willow pulled to get free, her long blonde hair splaying out as she twisted to look back at me.

It didn't look like he was hurting her. His grip on her arm didn't seem very tight at all. "If you'd bothered to knock, I wouldn't need to hurt you." He spoke through gritted teeth.

She pulled free with a wicked grin and snorted. "If I'd knocked, you would have had time to hide your date." Her eyes swung my way. "Ooh. This one's pretty."

Fergus sighed and marched over to the door, his voice softening. "Please, Will. Can you just leave?" He shot Jax a imploring glance.

Jax jumped forward, placing an arm over Willow's shoulders. "Come on, Willow. Let's get some food before the big party."

Willow pulled from his grasp. "Oh, is this *her?*" Her eyes rounded. "I'm not going until I've had an introduction."

"No. She's just a ... friend." Fergus rubbed the bridge of his nose.

I walked toward her with my hand out to shake hers. Both Fergus and Jax were acting weird. I recognized those high cheek bones and mischievous smile. Fergus' sister was the fae girl I'd talked to while we waited to enter Faery the night of the masquerade. She looked younger than she had that night, perhaps about fifteen. "I'm Bria. Fergus' *friend.*" I wasn't sure why I emphasized the word friend. It was what we were. And sometimes not even that.

She shook my hand. "Willow. Ferg's sister. Nice to meet you, Bria." She looked me over, then turned back to her brother. "You can't be thinking of taking her tonight looking like that. Father will lose it." She narrowed her eyes. "Wait. Are you trying to upset him, because that's not a good idea. If you're going to take her, at least have her dress appropriately." Willow was wearing a pale green strapless gown with wide skirts and her blonde hair was pulled elaborately from her face. The difference between her attire and my black riding gear was stark.

Jax wandered over to one of the black couches and sat, kicking his legs out in front of him, a half-smile on his face. He looked like he knew what was coming and would enjoy watching it.

Fergus sighed again. "She's not coming tonight. I wasn't even planning on attending, but Chester found out I was home."

Willow shrugged, walking over to the table, choosing an apple from the fruit bowl and taking a bite. "That's what you get for strolling around the grounds before coming to visit your darling sister after being gone for weeks. Plenty of people will talk for a little coin." She turned back to me, her eyes bright and excited. "I have the perfect dress for you. It's cobalt and the color will match your eyes. And I can style your hair." She reached out and pulled a few of the dark brown strands back from my face before I could stop her.

Fergus wasn't so slow. He was across the chamber in a moment, batting her hand away. But it was too late. Willow had already seen my ears and was staring at me open-mouthed. "What happened to you?"

I touched my ears self-consciously. "My mother cut them off, then hid me in Iadrun." Might as well own it.

"Why?" Willow whispered, her mouth hanging open.

"Willow," Fergus reprimanded.

I glanced at him. "It's okay." To Willow, I said, "I don't know. But I was wearing fake ears the night we met."

Willow's jaw stiffened and her voice grew tight. "You must be mistaken. We've never met."

"We did. At the—"

As I spoke, her eyes rounded, as did her mouth. She looked from Fergus to Jax. "She's the lost Seelie Princess? And you've brought her into our Court? If you want to rile Father, there are other, less dramatic ways than marrying a Seelie." Willow shook her head, her mouth still hanging open.

"I'm not—" Fergus started.

"Marrying? No. No way. That's not why I'm here." I turned to Fergus. "I've come for Mother. Nothing else." There was a plea in my words because Willow had reminded me of something I hadn't wasted a thought on in weeks. The reason Fergus brought me to Faery in the first place was because the person who fitted the shoe—me—was bonded to the Crown Prince. Weeks ago, he'd promised that was a lie, and I believed him. I did. But now, with Willow talking about marriage, I needed confirmation.

Fergus touched my arm. "Nothing's changed. We'll find your mother and get her out of here. I promise."

Willow stared at Fergus' hand on my arm. "Your mother's not here." She spat the words at me, her face hard. In mere seconds she'd gone from carefree teen bouncing off the walls, to a hardened and hateful looking fae.

"What does Father's newest consort look like?" Fergus withdrew his hand, his words quiet and deliberate.

Willow shrugged, dropping some of her hatred as she answered her brother. "Blonde hair, blue eyes, slim." She blinked twice, then stumbled back to sit on the edge of the bed. She shook her head. "That's your mother? She's the lost Seelie Queen? Does Father know? He can't. He'd never allow her here." She shook her head as she spoke, as if she could talk herself out of the truth of her own words.

Fergus shrugged. "Father knows something about her. What it is, I have no clue." He turned to me. "I apologize for my sister's language earlier, but I believe it is your mother down in the ballroom with Father. I'll head down there to get her back."

Willow stood up. "Fergus! You can't *get her back*. That's treason. Father will—"

Fergus cut Willow off, glaring at her. "I don't care what he does to me. Trapping that woman here against her will is wrong, and you know it." He pointed at me. "Bria has been in hiding her entire life. Her magic only came through yesterday, and she's sixteen."

Willow's eyes widened. Great. Now she thought I was even more of a freak.

Fergus continued before anyone could speak. "Bria doesn't want to be in Faery. She wants to be far from here with her mother. And for once, I want to help, rather than sitting back and allowing Father to do whatever he wants. I want to help her get away from here."

"Fergus," I said, my voice soft. His offer of help, knowing what his father would do to him, brought tears to my eyes. "You don't have to. I don't know your father well, but even I know you should care what he'll do if you're caught." I would rather do this alone than subject him to his father's wrath.

Fergus' eyebrows rose as his gaze fell on me. "Let's hope I don't get caught, then."

I grabbed his arm, keeping my voice firm. "You're not leaving me up here while you take all the risk. I'm coming, too. I'll wear the dress Willow offered and I'll be able to confirm if it is Mother down there or not." Fergus had seen her more than once. He could probably confirm it too, but this was about my mother. I wasn't sitting this out.

Fergus paled and shook his head. "You can't."

I threw Willow and Jax a *please help me* glance. They didn't want Fergus in trouble with the king any more than I did. Surely there was less chance if I was there, too.

Willow shook her head. "What he said."

"Sorry, Bria." Jax pressed his lips together.

I looked between the three of them, trying to figure out why they were so resolute about me staying up here. "What exactly is going on down there tonight?"

Fergus swallowed. "It's my naming ceremony." He took in my blank stare, gave a long blink and added, "It's the last chance for the Unseelie heir to commit to his future queen."

"A wedding?"

Willow shrugged. "More of a public commitment ceremony. And a chance for Father to gift Fergus with a family heirloom."

"Pfft." Fergus shook his head. "He's giving me a sword. Of all the things I need, it's not one of those." That was true. As Xion, he always had a sword strapped to his waist.

Willow sighed. "Play nice, Fergus. Father is doing his best."

A rough laugh came from Fergus' lips. "His best? My so-called heirloom isn't even something from our family. It was given to him by a friend!"

"Well…" Willow's smile was weak. "It's better than nothing."

The ancestry of the sword didn't interest me, but something else did. "Do you have someone to commit to?" I smiled as I spoke, hoping to hide how much I already disliked her.

Fergus shook his head, letting loose a deep breath. "The search for the woman from the masquerade should have delayed my naming ceremony. Once she was finally found, the king would have granted me a year to get to know her. But…" He shrugged. "Other things happened, and I never got to ask for the extra time." Other things like both of us spending weeks imprisoned in Seelie.

Willow cleared her throat. Fergus turned to her. "If you have something to say, Will, just say it."

"Father expects to either meet the woman you're bonded with tonight or invoke the Choosing."

Jax climbed to his feet, not looking quite so carefree. "Sorry, Ferg. The king pushed so hard for answers, I had to give him something."

Willow took a step toward Fergus. "He knows Xion ditched the rest of the Hunt with a girl. He believes Xion brought that girl straight to you. Haven't you and Jax talked yet?" She looked Jax's way. "Haven't you told him that Father's been questioning you for weeks?"

Fergus shook his head. "There hasn't exactly been a lot of time, especially since I expected he would be out with the Hunt all night tonight. We were planning to speak in the morning. I had no intention of coming here tonight."

I was totally lost in this conversation. "What does Jax have to do with this?"

Jax and Willow gave Fergus a pointed glance. Fergus shrugged. "Bria knows about Xion. And about Jax's ability to look like others. Just say whatever it is you want to say."

Jax grimaced. "Your father called for Xion several times while you were gone. He was overly suspicious, and I thought he would guess he wasn't talking to the real Xion Starguard. Or the real Fergus Blackwood, because I pretended to be Fergus as well. So I told him..." Jax looked at the floor and scratched the back of his head.

My heart fell. I knew what Jax had told the king without him saying it. "You told him that Fergus found the woman he bonded with." And if I went down to that ballroom with him tonight, we were as good as telling the king the two of us would marry.

Jax nodded.

I didn't want to be mistaken for anyone's bonded mate. "Why would you do that?"

Jax ran a hand across his face, a snap in his voice. "I was trying to find a way to get you and Fergus out of Seelie while dealing with the king's demands, while pretending to be Fergus and Xion. I just needed him off my back for a few days to give me time to think."

Willow scooted around the table to stand beside Jax. "He was planning to come back to Unseelie today to tell the king that Ferg was in the Seelie prison. But he didn't come." She stared at Fergus, then at me. "And since you're here instead, I assume he rescued you. So perhaps a little gratitude is in order."

"Jax didn't rescue us. Bria got us out of there." Fergus flashed a tight smile at his sister. "She's the only reason I'm standing here right now. Saved my life twice in one day."

Willow leaned forward, her hands clenched into fists, and hissed, "She's also Seelie." She didn't look at me, but she also didn't hide the disgust on her face. Disgust over something beyond my control.

The same disgust I'd seen all my life from almost everyone I met. Everyone but Fergus and Jax. "Maybe I am Seelie. But unlike the rest of the world, I don't choose my friends because of the things they can give me. I choose them because of who they are. Your brother and I are friends. Seelie or not, I chose to save his life. I'd do it again in a heartbeat. And I believe he'd do the same for me."

Willow took a step back, shaking her head. She looked at her brother. "Is that true?"

Fergus nodded. I wasn't sure if she was asking if we were friends or if he would save my life. But since he'd already saved me once, perhaps that was a given.

She turned her attention to Jax. "You're okay spending time with a Seelie?"

"Fergus would be dead if it weren't for Bria." Jax shook his head. "So, yeah. I'm okay with Bria sticking around." He looked directly at Willow. "I mean it, Will. You wouldn't have a brother now without her."

"Okay." Willow strolled over to stare out the window. After a few moments, she drew in a deep breath. When she turned back to us, her face softened. "If you trust her, then I do, too." She smiled at me, friendlier than before. "Now, how are we going to help your mother escape?"

I wanted to make sure I understood the problem. "If I go down to that ceremony tonight on Fergus' arm, we are telling the Court that we intend to marry?

All three of them nodded.

Fergus said, "You don't need to come with me. I can get your mother out."

Jax raised an eyebrow. "The king really wants to talk to you. I'm not sure how you think you will extract the lost queen from under his nose without speaking with him. Without telling him you do not have someone to name as your partner tonight."

Willow's eyes narrowed as she looked at Fergus. "If Bria says she doesn't want to sit up here and wait while you search for her mother, then you should listen. You'd never leave me behind if I wanted to go with you."

Fergus spoke carefully. "Because I know you won't leave me alone until I give in."

I opened my mouth to speak, but Willow was quicker, stealing the words from my mouth. "I don't think she will either."

She was right. I wouldn't. "What time will the king expect this public commitment to happen?"

Jax shrugged. "Who knows with the king?"

Fergus' smile was tight. "Any time he wants it to happen."

Okay, so once we were down in the ballroom, we'd have to work on getting Mother out fast, before the ceremony began. "If I can't go with Fergus tonight, then perhaps I should go as Jax's partner. I'll confirm the woman with the king is my mother, then we'll smuggle her out of there when—"

"When she goes to the bathroom!" Willow pointed at me, her voice rising in excitement.

Fergus nodded. "That might actually work. And if all else fails, Willow can distract Father while Jax and I drag the lost queen out of there.

I wasn't sure if it was a sound plan, but it was a plan. And I didn't have to do it alone, for which I was undeniably grateful.

Willow turned to Fergus. "You'll wear Father's anger if you pull this off, big brother."

"I know," said Fergus. "But every lash of his magic if he captures me will be worth it."

Willow's dress fit me perfectly and she some-how piled most of my hair into an elegant twist on top of my head, while keeping enough down to cover my ears, humming as she worked. We were in her chamber, just the two of us. I opened my mouth a few times to ask why she pretended we'd never met, but every time, I lost my nerve and bit down on the words I wanted to say. Suddenly, I wasn't sure any of this was a good idea. "Won't everyone be able to tell I'm Seelie?"

Willow fussed with my makeup. "They will if they look closely." She turned her head so we were both staring into the mirror, preening her blonde hair a moment before speaking. "Your face is a little rounder here." She touched her cheeks. "And here." She touched her chin. "And your ears should be smaller than ours at the tips. But that one's not an issue." Her long and pointed ears were displayed proudly over her updo, while mine were safely hidden behind my hair.

I swallowed. "Not reassuring." Nerves made my heart pitter-patter inside my chest. Maybe I'd see Mother tonight. Maybe I'd help her escape. Or maybe I'd finish the evening in a different prison cell to the one I'd just escaped from.

She grinned, her smile mischievous. "It is. No one will take that much notice. No one thinks my brother is stupid enough to invite an enemy into our home." She pointed to a full-length mirror. "You look good, right?"

I stood and turned side to side in the mirror. I looked nothing like me. Nothing like the me I re-called seeing in the broken mirror in our cottage in Holbeck, anyway. I was thinner than I'd ever been—too thin, Mother would say. I hadn't exactly had three meals a day since coming to Faery. The blue dress pinched in at my waist, making it appear even smaller than it had grown. With my brown hair piled up on my head and threaded with tiny blue flowers, the face that stared back seemed older, my eyes wiser. But those things could have marked me as any girl from across the border in Iadrun. It was what Willow had done with my makeup that had me staring in open-mouthed disbelief. With liquids, powders and brushes of all shapes and sizes, she'd accentuated my high cheekbones and full lips. The result was that—if I ignored my hidden ears—I was staring back at the face of a fae girl from Seelie. And that girl didn't repulse me. She actually looked pretty good, even if I wasn't used to seeing this part of my heritage. "Thank you, Willow. I couldn't have done this myself."

She beamed.

There was a knock at the door and before Willow could answer, Fergus poked his head around the edge. "Are you almost—" His eyes caught on me and he pushed the door slowly open, Jax walking in behind him. Fergus' eyes wandered across my face, down my body and back up, while his mouth hung open in surprise. Everywhere his eyes lingered, my body tingled, almost as if he were touching me with more than just a glance. "You look ... wow. Bria, you look exquisite. I wish it were you on my arm as I head into the ballroom."

My breath caught and my heart somersaulted. No one had ever called me exquisite before. "You do, too." My cheeks reddened. Exquisite wasn't the right way to compliment a guy. Still, he looked good. His black hair was plaited down the center of his scalp and his eyes sparkled with anticipation. I would have liked to walk into the ballroom with him, too. Not because he was the Prince. But because I felt like everything would work out how it should if he were near.

Except, tonight it wouldn't. Walking into the ballroom with Fergus was as good as announcing our relationship to the entire Kingdom of Unseelie. A relationship that didn't exist. Better that I go in on Jax's arm. Through the same entrance as the other guests who didn't have rooms in the castle.

Fergus' lips twitched. "I'm humbled I meet your approval, lady. I do aim to look exquisite each day as I leave my chamber."

Oh, so that was how we were playing it? Some light banter to keep the nerves at bay? I could do that. "Ah, well. You shouldn't feel too disappointed."

His eyebrows rose, the smile he was trying to keep away, growing. "Disappointed? What reason do I have to feel such a thing?"

I shrugged, trying hard to keep my smile away. "That you only manage it once a year, of course. At least it gives you something to strive for each day." Stars, what a lie. Fergus was the best looking fae in the entire kingdom. Everyone knew it.

Jax clapped Fergus on the back and Willow laughed loudly. Fergus opened his mouth in mock shock. He placed his hand on his chest. "I'm a prince, remember. I believe the rules of prince-friendship state that you must always tell the prince how good he looks, at any point of the day."

I walked over and took Jax's arm, ready to leave Willow's chamber. Looking back over my shoulder, I said, "I believe I just did."

Jax and I climbed down the staircase I'd used to come into Fergus' chamber. With my hand on his arm, we strolled up the path as if we had not a care in the world, behind a large group who were talking in excited tones. At the ballroom entrance, Jax handed over an invitation while my heart pounded inside my chest. Mother was on the other side of the huge arched doors, and I hadn't seen her in weeks. All that stood between us now, was the footman in his long-tailed blue jacket, holding Jax's invitation.

I needn't have worried. The footman cast a quick eye over the card Jax gave him before opening the double doors and letting us inside.

Jax nodded and waved to people as we walked in, everything about him looking comfortable in the ballroom of the Unseelie King.

Whereas, I felt the least comfortable I'd ever been. I cast my eyes around the room. "It looks different from last time I was here." One long side of the room had last time looked down via a mezzanine onto a second ballroom below. Tonight, the mezzanine was gone, replaced by a living wall of plants. The other long wall had a marble staircase winding down from above.

"The king likes to change things up. He glamours the ballroom differently for each event he holds."

"But not the ceiling?" The ceiling was glass, as it had been last time, so clear it was as if there was none there at all. Almost like we were standing outdoors.

Jax smiled. "Never the ceiling." He pointed to the staircase, just as Fergus and Willow appeared at the top.

The ballroom was full of people, but few noticed the prince and princess. They were too busy dancing, or drinking, or talking.

I, on the other hand, couldn't take my eyes off them. Willow had added a silver tiara covered in jewels to her hair, while Fergus wore a gold circlet on his head. He looked every bit the regal prince. He found me in the crowd and smiled. My stomach quivered. He was everything I'd been terrified of all my life, a powerful fae who would rule this kingdom one day. I couldn't believe he was the same person I'd talked to about more things than I'd shared with almost anyone else in my life.

He stopped on the top step, said something in Willow's ear, and drew in a breath.

As they made their way down, a voice from the bottom of the stairs called, "Presenting Crown Prince Fergus and Princess Willow."

Almost as one, every guest went silent, looked up the stairs and dropped into a deep curtsey or bow.

Jax pulled on my arm as he bowed, casting a narrowed-eyed stare that told me I'd better do the same. I did as expected, catching Fergus' eye as I rose. His lips twitched, and he glanced away. I knew exactly why he was smiling. I'd told him he'd never get another curtsey out of me. Well, he could be certain that was the final one.

Jax and I made our way toward the staircase where the moment he reached the bottom step, Fergus was detained by three men clapping him on the back. Willow ducked around them, taking my arm and pulling me away. "It's better if he doesn't have to introduce you to anyone. He'll find us soon." By us, Willow meant me and her. Jax had already inserted himself into the circle surrounding Fergus.

"Who are they?" The men talking to Fergus were much older than him, probably closer to the king's age. Fergus laughed as one of them joked about something, yet he seemed ill at ease.

Willow rolled her eyes. "The high lords from the Winter, Autumn and Shadow Courts." The Unseelie courts that fell under the king's rule. "They don't even like Ferg and think he's too soft to be king, but they'll be pushing to have him name one of their daughters as his future queen tonight."

I frowned. "But isn't the point of tonight for Fergus to announce the person he's already chosen?"

Willow shrugged. "It is. But they'll keep trying to convince him their daughter is the one for him right until the day he finally walks down the aisle."

I glanced at Fergus again, deep in conversation with people who only wanted to talk to him because they expected it to help their cause. It made me angry. "Don't they understand that the person they see isn't the person he is?"

Willow watched me for a long moment. "Most people don't understand that about him. Most people don't understand that about anyone." She took a last glance at Fergus then pulled me toward the edge of the dance floor.

My heart raced to the same beat as the music from the orchestra. The dance floor was busy with people dancing closely with their partners and none of the pre-determined moves that had been on show last time. I couldn't focus on anything. Not until I'd found Mother. And so far, I'd had no luck.

Willow put her hands on my waist and started dancing.

I stiffened. "Oh, I'm not—"

"Relax. It's just dancing. This is what we do on a dance floor." She put my hands on her shoulders and spun me around, so I faced away from the crowd. Toward the king. "Is that her? Your mother?"

At the far end of the ballroom, seated on a throne upon a dais a few steps back from the dance floor, Mother sat with her eyes downcast, her hands in her lap. Jeweled clips held her long blonde hair off her face, and though her pale cream dress and silver bracelets set off her golden skin, she looked as if she'd rather fade away than sit where she was. Beside her, the king stared out over his guests. His salt and pepper hair was pulled back at the base of his neck, mostly hidden beneath a heavy-looking jeweled crown. He wore a long black cloak made of fur, and beneath it, he wore black pants and a black shirt, similar in style to Fergus'. His cheeks were hollow beneath his high cheek bones and his blue eyes were cold, reminding me of all the horrible things he'd done. But it wasn't him I was interested in. "Mother," I whispered.

As if she heard me, Mother's head lifted. Her dull eyes drifted over the sea of people, not seeming to see anything before she dropped her head again. On closer inspection, her hands were shaking in her lap.

"That's her?" Willow whispered.

I nodded, my eyes fixed on the woman I hadn't seen for five weeks. Apart from the shaking hands and dull eyes, she looked fine. Unhappy but unhurt, which was better than I'd dared hope. I untangled myself from Willow's arms and took a step toward the dais before she grabbed my wrist and pulled me back.

"What are you doing?" she hissed.

"Getting Mother and getting out of here." I shook her off.

Willow moved in front of me. "Not yet."

Her eyes bore into me, reminding me how stupid I was being. We had a plan. We had to follow it. We would wait until she went to the bathroom.

"It's her, right?" Fergus came up from behind, placing his hand on the small of my back as he spoke in my ear. His breath sent tingles along my spine and his hand sent tingles everywhere else.

Willow looked between the two of us, her lips tightening. "Well it certainly isn't our Mother." There was a note in her tone I didn't understand.

Fergus' shoulders stiffened. He'd told me the first night we met that his mother was dead, but there was something else going on. Something I didn't understand.

I looked between them both but before I could speak, Fergus' eyes turned hard. "Remember how we decided I was a cold-hearted killer? Willow means Mother can't be here because I killed her." He turned on his heel and strode away, the crowd of people parted before him and swallowed him up in his wake.

"Ferg!" Willow called. "That's not what I meant."

I glanced at Willow. Fergus' words echoed in my ears, but I required clarification. "He what?"

"You might want to talk to him about it." She watched the place he'd disappeared.

It was true then. She wasn't denying it. She'd be denying it if it wasn't true.

I glanced at Mother staring blankly at her lap. She didn't look like she was about to get up and go to the bathroom, and if she did, I hoped Willow would come and find us. I started after Fergus, glimpsing his tall form across the other side of the ballroom, head bowed and fingers pressed to the bridge of his nose. I'd come to Unseelie thinking only of rescuing Mother, but I was starting to wonder if she wasn't the only one who needed help. Fergus was used to everyone's judgement, and he was expecting mine. Perhaps it made me stupid, but I wasn't judging.

I pushed past people who didn't part for me the way they had for him. He'd almost reached the exit to the tunnel I'd come through on that first night when I grabbed hold of his hand, forcing him to stop. We stood, almost out the door and away from the racket and kerfuffle of the guests. He stared a moment and then looked pointedly at my hand in his. His voice changed to that low monotone of Xion Starguard. "You must either be very brave or very stupid to take the hand of a murderer."

I met his eyes. "You think I'm afraid of you?" I wasn't. Whether he was Fergus or Xion, he wouldn't hurt me. I didn't need to understand what had happened with his mother to be certain of that.

His eyes—hard as stone—roved over my face before he spoke again, sounding more like himself. "Well, you should be."

"You've had plenty of opportunities to kill me, yet I'm still here. I don't think you will do it tonight." I glanced across at the guests dancing, eating and drinking, and at the king, sitting not far from where we stood. "Not here, anyway."

His eyes were almost slits. "You never know when it might happen."

His eyes kept going to my hand, like he was waiting for me to drop it, to walk away. I gripped him tighter. "Want to tell me about it? I happen to be a pretty good listener." I dropped my voice. "And not just during private pianoforte performances."

His lips quirked, but his smile disappeared immediately. He looked across the dance floor, his Adam's apple bobbing as he swallowed. "It happened the same as with your magic. I was much older than most fae of royal birth when mine came through—I'd just turned three. When it came, I had no warning, just an itchy palm. Mother was the only one with me, we'd spent the day at Lanwick, swimming and playing. I loved going there with her." He shook his head. "How I wish my magic had shown up an hour earlier."

"Because it would have been safer for it to happen at Lanwick?"

He nodded, his eyes falling on something distant and unseen. "Mother was walking me up to my rooms. We were on the same staircase I took you up earlier tonight. She was in front of me, and then ... she wasn't." He pressed his lips together and drew in some deep breaths. "Everything around me turned to rubble, and she fell all the way to the ground." He shook his head. "I think she must have been hit by a rock because her magic should have slowed her fall. No one knew if it was the fall that killed her, or the rock and rubble that landed on top of her once she hit the ground. Either way, the outcome was the same. I killed her when my magic came through. And Father's never forgotten it."

I'd seen the place on the staircase it happened. The place where it seemed to have been fixed up. "But you couldn't have done anything different." I knew what it was like. I'd had no warning either and I couldn't have stopped it happening if I wanted to.

He shook his head, still not meeting my eyes. "You don't know that." His voice was only just loud enough to hear over the music.

"Did you forget that my magic arrived the same way?" He wouldn't meet my eyes, so I moved to stand in front of him, pulling myself up onto tip toes but still wasn't tall enough to put myself in his line of vision. "I know you loved her, and you wouldn't have hurt her if you'd had a choice." He'd spoken of her laughter and the feel of her hair brushing against his face. I'd heard how much he'd loved her from those few words.

"Father has spent almost sixteen years telling me how much I must have hated her to do that to her." There was no emotion in his voice. There was no anything.

How cruel of the king. "Don't you dare let him do that to you. Don't give him that much power."

His eyes drifted down to rest on mine. "You want to lecture me on giving others power over me when you do it every single day?"

I touched my ears with my free hand—the other was still wrapped in Fergus'. I did that. I let people speak to me like they were better than me because I was embarrassed about how I looked. Fergus was the only person who had ever questioned it. "Perhaps it's something we both need to work on."

"Come, Fergus." The king's voice boomed across the ballroom. Though no one stopped their dancing or their drinking, it seemed as if every person tuned in to listen.

Fergus lifted his eyes from mine, swiveling to stare at his father. The exit we stood in was on the same wall as his throne, but we stood behind and out of his line of sight. Or so I'd thought.

"Come. Introduce us all to your future wife." The king watched his son from his elevated height on the dais. Fergus could have run. Should have. He didn't need to tell me he stayed because of me. Because he'd promised to help me with Mother.

With stiff shoulders, he made the long walk across the width of the room to stand in front of the king's throne. I followed five steps behind. When Fergus stopped and spoke, his voice was almost too soft to hear. "I can't."

"Can't?" The king's voice was loud and mocking. It seemed as if the orchestra lowered the level of their music just enough for the conversation to be heard across the room. "Why ever not?"

"Because she's currently in the guest chamber. Waiting until the guests have finished arriving." He drew in a breath and when he spoke again, his voice hardened. "As per protocol."

The king raised his eyes to meet mine I tensed. Fergus shuffled to his left, protecting me from the king's stare with his body. "This is not your date?"

Fergus shook his head. "Of course not. This is..." There was a long pause as he considered how to introduce me.

Had I been able to think of anything to fill the silence, I would have spoken up. Instead, it was Willow who stepped up from behind. us "Father, surely you remember Ashling Overtree? My best friend? You've met her many times."

The king frowned, then nodded. "Of course. Of course." Dismissing Willow and I with a wave of his hand, his gaze returned to Fergus. "It's time."

Fergus looked around the ball room. A light sheen of sweat had broken out on his forehead. "There are still guests arriving."

I glanced at Willow, her panicked eyes telling me all I needed to know. The king wanted the naming ceremony to commence right this moment. It was far earlier in the evening than we hoped.

"There will be guests arriving most of the night." The king didn't bother to hide his annoyance.

"I ... I don't think she's ready yet. Still dressing, I believe." I'd never heard Fergus sound so unsure of himself.

The king considered his son a moment. "You don't think she's ready yet, what?"

Fergus drew in a deep breath and clenched his fists. "Your Highness."

Beside me, Willow mumbled, "Damn it. Father's in a foul mood." I didn't need anyone to explain it for me. I could see that for myself.

King Aengus gripped the arms of his throne and leaned forward. "Could it be that she's not ready yet because she's not here? Perhaps because she doesn't exist?"

The king could have had the conversation in private with his son. That he hadn't was worse than bad.

He didn't give Fergus time to respond. "For months you've been stringing my kingdom along. Stringing me along. Telling us you found someone, using my people—the Wild Hunt who have better things to do with their time—to search for her. When, really, it would seem there is no one."

Fergus shook his head, shook out the tension in his shoulders and spoke in that calm and some-what bored tone I'd only ever heard him use here in Unseelie. "She'll be out when she's finished making herself presentable."

"Don't lie to me!" The king's voice reverber-ated around the immense room and everyone stopped. There was no more music. No talking. Just a great yawning silence waiting for what would come next.

Mother sat staring at her hands as if the king hadn't just yelled at the top of his voice.

The king's voice softened to a whisper. "She's not in the guest chamber. Chester already told me. You are nothing but a disappointment. Out every night with a different woman but unable to choose one to rule with? You think I don't know what you get up to, boy?" His lip curled in disgust.

"You have no idea." Fergus' voice wobbled with his own anger. No one here knew—only me, Willow and Jax—where he spent his nights.

I took a step toward him, but Willow wound a hand around my arm and held me back.

"I can't believe you're my child. You're too soft to rule. I had hoped marrying would settle you and that a powerful woman would make you into someone fit to lead this realm when the time comes." He shook his head again. "We'll make you fit to be the Unseelie King one way or another, boy. And since you won't do it of your own accord, I'm sending you to the Army of Souls. When you return, I will invoke the Choosing."

There was a collective intake of breath from around the room. I glanced at Willow. I knew what the Army of Souls was, and even to the Un-seelie fae, it was bad. Going there would wreck Fergus. But the Choosing I knew nothing about, other than hearing Willow mention it earlier.

Willow saw my confusion and whispered, "It's a competition. To find a wife for the future king."

A competition? That was how the king would find Fergus a wife? The thought disgusted me. I wriggled from Willow's grasp and marched up to stand beside Fergus. "You know nothing about your son. He's already an excellent leader. But you haven't seen it because you refuse to look."

"Bria." Fergus' warning came from beneath his breath, so soft, I doubted anyone else heard.

He didn't need to worry. I wasn't about to spill his secrets. But, as he'd so rightly pointed out, too often I backed down instead of standing up.

Not today.

The king waved his hand, dismissing my comments and looking at his son. "You leave tonight."

Fergus lifted his chin and gave a nod. I doubted anyone else here apart from Willow knew how much he didn't want to go, because every movement he made was easy and carefree as if the news bothered him little.

"You can't send him there. You do not understand what it will do to him!" Someone had to stand up for Fergus if he would not do it himself.

The king's glare turned slowly on me. His eyes swept down my body and back up to my face. "Bria?"

I swallowed. Fergus hadn't been as quiet as I thought when he said my name.

Mother's head shot up, and she stared at me. Under the king's gaze, I willed her not to say or do anything. We'd get her out of here, but for now, we needed the king not to know why we were here.

The king stared at me until I was certain he must be reading my mind. "What gives you the right to tell me what to do with my son?"

Nothing. I had no right. Especially here in Unseelie. But the disdainful way the king looked at his son loosened my tongue. "Someone has to stand up for him. He's had no one to do that for him in fifteen years."

"His own fault," the king spat back.

"Bria." Fergus' voice was soft, the warning unmistakable.

But I wasn't ready to stop. "It was a horrible accident that you've blamed Fergus for all his life. He was just a child. You should have taken some of that burden from him!"

A mocking smile settled on the king's face. "Aww. You mean to tell me the Crown Prince feels unloved?" The smile disappeared and his blue eyes turned icy. "There seems to be no lack of love in his bed every night. Different lovers if I'm correct."

I knew that wasn't true. I knew where Fergus went every night, and the words still stabbed at my heart. I couldn't imagine how it made Fergus feel, and it took all my composure to keep my voice even. "If that's where he needs to find love, good for him. Goodness knows, he got none from you."

There was a collective intake of breath from the fae surrounding me. Mother climbed to her feet, and I willed her not to do anything stupid. I was coming for her. I just needed to help Fergus first.

The king laughed. "I have news for you, Ashling ... or Bria, whatever your name is. None of those women loved him any more than I did. They were all after the same thing I'm sure you are after. The role of queen and all the riches that go with it."

Mother got to her feet. "Bria...?"

Fergus spoke out the side of his mouth. "Bria. Don't answer him. It's not worth—"

I cut him off. Somewhere inside I had the sense I was being goaded, but it still didn't stop the words that came next. "I care for your son and there's not a thing I want from him in exchange." I took Fergus' hand to prove my point, and I was suddenly looking in his eyes. They were the most stunning color—deep brown with tiny flecks of gold—and he was staring at me in a way that stopped my heart.

The king laughed, hard and mocking. "You don't care for him. No one does. Not even his own people."

The king's words hit Fergus like bullets. He flinched with each one.

I squeezed his hand, no longer talking to the king, but to Fergus instead. "It's not true. You know it's not."

His Adam's apple bobbed, and his breath came heavily. His eyes were on me, but he wasn't seeing me. Or hearing me. He was probably replaying in his mind all the hatred his father spewed.

I needed to drown that all out. To make him forget what his father said and to forget about all the people watching with glee on their faces. I wanted to erase the embarrassment he must feel at his father attacking him so publicly. And for him to relax and smile, the way he had when we sat on the picnic rug in the clouds just a few hours ago.

I wanted him to know someone cared about him.

I wanted him to know *I* cared for him.

I dropped Fergus' hand, pushed up onto my tip toes and reached up to hold his face between my palms. "It's not true, Fergus. You are good. You are worthy. People love you." He stared through me, giving no sign he heard. "Jax does. Willow. Me."

His eyes focused. "You?"

I licked my lips and nodded. "Me." Everything around me disappeared, and the world narrowed to contain only Fergus. I didn't think about what came next. It just happened. One minute I was looking at him, taking in his beauty, the next I was drawing his head down and pressing my lips to his.

Fergus froze.

I waited, too. Waited for him to push me away. To laugh. To tell me he could have anyone in the room and ask why he would kiss a deformed fae from the Seelie Court.

But he did none of those things. Time both slowed and sped up. His hands slid around my waist and he dragged me closer. A low rumble from his throat sent a shiver up my spine and made my legs tremble. I melted into him feeling like I'd finally found something I hadn't known I was searching for.

One of his hands moved up my back and caught in my hair, holding me where he wanted me—where I hadn't let myself admit I wanted to be. His mouth moved; fierce, demanding. I pressed closer, demanding the same, my fingers digging into his shoulders. This was right. This was where I belonged. With Fergus.

"Bria!" Mother's voice sounded so very far away. "Bria!" Then closer the next time she spoke.

Fergus must have heard her at the same moment because we both pulled apart. I met his eyes and smiled. And was rewarded with a smile from him. His hand slid down my arm and he wove his fingers between mine.

I came back to myself slowly, dimly aware of gasping from the crowd, followed by their sedate clapping over my ragged breathing. My eyes fell on Mother. Then the king.

Mother.

And the King.

I'd just kissed Fergus in front of them all. What was wrong with me?

"Holy hell." Willow's voice broke the near silence as the clapping died down. "Ah, welcome to the family, Bria."

SEVENTEEN

I SMILED at Willow, my eyebrows drawing together. A purple veil partially shrouded her and everyone else, except Fergus. "W-what?"

Her smile faltered, and she looked from Fergus to her father. "You kissed your bonded mate and united your magic."

I focused on the veil in front of me. She was right. The magenta of my magic had twisted around the blue of Fergus', making the veil look purple. Heaviness settled in my gut. I glanced at Fergus. He kept his hand locked in mine, but he was watching his father, his jaw working. "I don't understand," I whispered.

"You didn't know?" Willow's voice rose with surprise. Her eyes moved from Fergus to me and her shoulders fell. "You didn't know."

Fergus turned to me. "It would seem we are indeed bonded mates. The bond was sealed with that kiss."

I shook my head, dropping his hand and stepping away. "No. You said we weren't. That first day. You told me..." This couldn't be happening. I didn't want this. I didn't want to be linked by some fae magic that chose a partner for me. I wanted to make that choice. Though it made sense of the insane and sudden need to kiss him in front of so many people.

He pressed his fingers to his temples. "That day, I believed we weren't."

My eyebrows lifted. "But since then you've come to believe otherwise?"

He gave a single nod.

"And you didn't think to mention it to me?"

"I didn't see how it could be. A true bond takes a year and a day to mature. For the bond to seal, we would have had to have met before now."

We had met before now. "I saw you. The night my father..." My voice fell away. I couldn't explain without giving away his secrets.

Fergus shook his head, understanding. "Not then. We didn't touch each other that night. I didn't even see you."

"Then when...?"

"I don't know." He closed his eyes, letting out a deep breath before looking at me again. "I could feel ... something between us. I'm almost certain that's why I was drawn to your cottage that first night, and it only grew stronger since then. I wasn't worried because we should have had a year and a day before this kicked in. And I expected you'd be long gone by then. You said you didn't want to stay in Faery." Heartache chased regret across his face. "I'd have told you if I thought there was a chance it would end up like this."

I didn't want to stay in Faery. In my head, I didn't, at least. With my body, I wanted to be next to him, his hand in mine. Stars, I wanted his lips on mine again. I settled for moving to stand beside him even as I told myself those feelings weren't real. They were a spell, made by magic.

"The two of you have met before, Prince Fergus." Mother stood wringing her hands on the other side of the fading purple haze. Her eyes— clearer now—moved between the two of us and the king, and her voice was weak. "Your mother took you to the mortal world when you were very young. She went there to meet me. And Bria."

I glanced at Fergus, knowing Mother wasn't lying. Fergus had mentioned how he'd spent time in Iadrun. He'd also said he recognized Mother but didn't recall how.

The king pushed to his feet. "Fergus. Come here. Now. This is a Seelie trick. We obviously didn't put enough suppressors on her." He cast a disgusted gaze at Mother. "She'd do anything to steal our power."

Mother's eyes narrowed and her fingers curled. The veins on her neck stood out and when she spoke, she sounded more like herself than she had moments before. "Aengus, you know this isn't a trick. If Indira didn't tell you what happened, then look at their magic. There's only one thing that twists it together like that." She stared at the king. When he didn't respond, she slumped back into her seat like she'd used all her energy appealing to him.

The king's jaw stiffened as he looked at Fergus. "It's true. You mother thought it possible she exposed you to your bonded mate when you were young. But she wasn't this Ashling girl." He didn't sound as sure of himself as he had moments ago. "It was Briony Ridgewing." The crowd gasped, and the king nodded. "Yes, the Seelie princess. The Seelie say she died as an infant and I've spent fifteen years searching for her to no avail. I believe her to be dead. You cannot be bonded twice. Therefore, this must be a trick." His voice grew stronger as he spoke, but his eyes flitted between Mother and me, and I didn't think he believed his own words.

I glanced at Fergus. There was no trick. I was Briony Ridgewing. And apparently, I was the bonded mate of Fergus Blackwood. A fate I'd sealed myself because, instead of fighting the magic that made the bond—magic I hadn't known to expect—I'd allowed it to pick me up and sweep me toward the person it had chosen for me.

A knot formed in my stomach. I didn't want this. Not because Fergus was a horrible person, but because I hadn't chosen it. But if the king really wasn't aware I existed, it raised another question. "So, you didn't send me an invitation to your masquerade ball?"

The king's eyes narrowed, and he shook his head. "Of course not. Why would I?"

I glanced at Mother. "Then who sent it? Who else knows about me?"

Mother shook her head, her answer quiet. "I don't know, Bria. I don't know."

The king made a sound beneath his breath that drew our attention. Disdain sharpened his features as he stared at his son. "I'll not allow this. You are too weak-willed to be bound to the kingdom of Seelie. They'll steal your magic and then steal our lands and kill our people." He flicked one hand and from his palm, a ball of midnight blue magic shot toward us. Toward Fergus' heart.

"Fergus!" I grabbed his arm and jerked him out of the way. The ball flew past us and sheared through one of the fae guests to lodge in the guest behind her. Both dropped to the floor like stones, dead.

Fergus was wound tight, his face hard with anger. If the king was going to shoot bolts of magic at us, we should probably get out of here. The exit I'd used the first time I came here was close enough if we sprinted like we never had before. I pulled on Fergus' arm, but he jerked it from my grasp. A ball of light blue magic shot from his hand, aimed at his father. At almost the same moment, magic that was such a deep shade of blue it was almost black, surrounded the king. A shield. Fergus' magic hit and slid off, no damage done.

The king laughed. "You'll have to do better than that if you think you can beat me, boy." Another ball of the king's magic shot toward us.

Behind me, I was vaguely aware of people running and screaming, as in front of me, a light blue shield appeared. Yet in my mind, I was back in our cottage the night the Wild Hunt came for Father. Back then, I hadn't had magic and had never seen it in living color, or perhaps magic just didn't show up in the same way in Iadrun. I'd watched Father glare at the man who came for him. I'd heard the man laugh. It seemed so similar to what I was seeing now. It shouldn't be a surprise, but it was. Father was fae, too, and he'd been fighting that night, using his magic in the same way the king and Fergus were now, I just hadn't known. I'd been angry at him for so long for not trying that night, when really, he'd done all he could to stay with Mother and me. And when that hadn't been enough, he'd let them take him away from us rather than tell them we existed.

If he could fight even knowing he wouldn't win, I could do the same.

I closed my eyes, imagining magic shooting from my palm the same way it had shot from Fergus'. My hand heated as the magic pooled there. I opened my eyes and stared at the king. And let the magic go.

Instead of hurtling toward the king, it shot out the back of my hand, spearing through six fae who hadn't bothered to find a safe place to hide and narrowly missing Willow. I should have spent my time figuring out how to use my magic rather than dancing on the clouds with Fergus.

The king laughed and fired back at us. I imagined my magic encasing us to form a shield like the one Fergus had surrounded us with. The king's magic had cracked Fergus' shield—maybe mine could help keep it strong.

My shield formed.

Around Mother.

I cursed as the king's blast hit Fergus' shield and knocked us both back three steps. Another crack formed in his shield. I didn't know how long Fergus could hold him off, and I was no help.

A blue haze shimmered around Fergus as he conjured another blast of magic, giving me an idea. "Fergus."

He took his eyes from his father for a moment to focus on me.

"Our magic together is strong, right?" That's what I'd always heard, and it could be the only benefit of our unwanted bond. Magic as strong as that of the Unseelie King.

He nodded.

"Good." I focused on my magic, imagining that same blast I'd failed at before. My hand grew warm. "When I say go, throw your magic around mine and aim for your father."

He glanced at the king, then back to me, his forehead creased in confusion.

I lifted a shoulder. "A blast from both our magic might get through his shield." Or it might fly out behind us, shear through the band and shatter the wall of glass at the other end of the ballroom. Either way, it was worth a try.

I didn't give him time to think about it. "Now."

As my ball of magic formed, looking like it was again heading out the back of my hand, Fergus threw his magic over mine. It twisted together, blue winding around magenta, and a purple ball shot out of the front of my hand to slam into the king's shield. He smirked at us as the shield held.

Until it shattered.

A thousand shards of deep blue magic fell around the king, our magic sailing straight through the shield to hit him square in the chest. He took a staggering step back, shock registering on his face at the same moment. Some speed fell from our magic when it hit the shield, probably the reason the king wasn't lying on the ground dead. His tunic was burned through to his skin and blood spilled from his chest. He staggered again, dropping to his knees.

We could have hit him again in that moment and he would have been dead.

Neither of us reached for our magic again.

Fergus stepped toward his father, groaning on the floor.

"Mother!" I pushed past him and up onto the dais, grabbing her hand. She stood openmouthed and staring at the king lying at her feet. "Mother.

Let's go." She looked at me with vacant eyes, all the lucidity from earlier gone. I pulled on her wrist. "Come on." We didn't have much time.

She took a step, her eyes still on the king.

"It's the suppressors. They make her want to stay." Fergus ripped the jeweled necklaces from her neck, the earrings from her ears and the clips from her hair, throwing them on the floor. Then he nodded toward the exit. "Go."

"You're not coming?" It was as if the ball of magic that had ripped through the king's chest was ripping through mine, and I wasn't sure if it was because of the magical bond between us or the friendship we'd grown these past few weeks. I wasn't ready to say goodbye to him yet. Not now, over his dying father's body.

He looked at his father. "I'll be right behind you." He threw me a tight smile. "Promise."

I took Mother's hand, and we ran, but turned as I heard Fergus growl. A line of the king's soldiers advanced on us. He sent a blast of his magic at them. Every one of them fell to the floor.

Behind them, some guests, seeing their king and his guards on the ground, were advancing. No magic shimmered around their bodies, but each of them carried a weapon in their hand; sword, knife, trident. Their steps were careful, like we scared them, but I imagined they'd fight to their death for their king, and I didn't want to be responsible for any more deaths tonight.

I took Mother's wrist. This time, when I pulled, she moved with me.

When I glanced over my shoulder, Fergus was bent over his father, healing the wound he'd made. Saving his life.

A burst of burnt orange magic skimmed past me, narrowly missing. Where had that come from? I didn't think there was anyone else here ready to use their magic.

"Shield!" yelled Fergus.

I didn't even try. I'd already proven my magic didn't work in the same way as his. Several times. Instead, I gripped Mother's wrist tighter and ran faster than I'd ever run.

A yell from behind made me turn.

Fergus was no longer beside his father. Instead, he was facing the approaching fae. A sword appeared in each of Fergus' hands. Jax ran toward him, and Fergus threw him a sword. They walked backward with slow steps, their heads moving to watch the advancing fae.

With a roar, one of the fae charged, and the rest followed. Fergus used his sword like he was born to do it, his feet light and strokes lethal. Within seconds, the first attacker was bleeding on the ground, and Fergus was fighting with another.

Mother pulled on me. "Let's go."

As I turned, I realized why. Four of the fae had broken off the group approaching Fergus and had come round behind us. Two carried daggers, one a carving knife, and the fourth held a metal rod.

I pushed Mother behind me.

"Get out your weapon," she hissed.

"I don't have one," I hissed back, planting my feet as the fae advanced.

"Silly girl. You should always bring a weapon into a Faery ballroom." Seemed like solid advice. Pity it came an hour too late.

"I'll remember that for next time." I eyed the smallest of them. A male who was shorter than me. He carried the metal rod. I imagined he would be fast. Not the fae I should attack first. The biggest of them, who would rival Jax for muscles, carried a dagger. He was who I would attack first.

I glanced over my shoulder at Mother, about to tell her to stay behind me. She pulled something from the center of her hairdo. I caught a flash as she threw it. It was one of those stars that had done so much damage in the forest near our cottage.

The star landed in the neck of the smallest man. He cried out and clutched at his injury.

While his friends stared at the blood flowing from his wound, I launched a roundhouse kick—

something I'd learned to keep the school bullies away—at the big fae. I hit him in the stomach and his mouth flew open as he gasped for air. I didn't waste any further time watching him, lining up the woman with a carving knife. My punch connected with her chin and she dropped like a stone. I turned and kicked the final fae between the legs. I'd long ago learned when bullies outnumbered me, there was no point fighting fair.

Mother's mouth formed a circle. "Who taught you to do that?"

"Taught myself. When I was being bullied about my ears at school." If only I'd fought back against the adults who bullied me in the same way. I grabbed Mother's hand and started toward the tunnel.

Fergus and Jax caught up to us. Another blast of magic shot past and hit the wall in front of us, stone and mortar spraying out in chunks big and small. "Can't you annihilate them, too?" I panted.

Fergus shook his head. "Low on magic. Plus, most of them aren't using their magic. It wouldn't be fair." Because if he hurt them with his magic, only he, Willow or his father could heal them. If he hurt them with a mortal weapon, a fae healer could help them.

We skidded through the door and into the exit tunnel, Jax stopping at the threshold. Light green magic formed around him, and he sent a blast barreling toward the last of the fae coming after us. Though not as potent as Fergus' it had enough kick to knock them off their feet, buying us time. He followed us through the door, and it slammed behind him. Fergus pushed me ahead, but I wasn't going yet.

Unlike the ballroom, the tunnel was the same as it had been the first night I came to Faery. Stoney moss-covered walls, uneven dirt floor and light sconces high on the wall. "Can you seal that door so the guards—or your father—can't follow us through here?" They couldn't be far behind and if they caught up to us in this small space, it would be a blood bath. I just wasn't sure whose blood we'd be bathing in.

He shook his head again. "Father is not a problem. He'll need to sleep a few hours to heal from a near-fatal wound like that. But my magic is almost gone."

I could see that by the color that surrounded him—it was so pale, it was almost white. I turned to Jax. "What about you?"

"Sorry. My magic isn't half as impressive as Ferg's. I'm more of a one-shot wonder." And he'd used that shot when he bought us time.

I glanced over my shoulder. Mother and Willow were already making their way through the tunnel ahead of us. "Could Willow do it? Or Mother?"

"Potentially, they both could, but there isn't enough time to get them back here. We need to take our chances by running." Fergus moved along the tunnel after them, then waited for Jax and me to follow.

I placed my hands on the door. "If you talked me through it, could I do it?"

It was Jax who answered. "I'm not sure you should..."

But I wasn't listening, already pulling at that place inside my chest where my magic came from. My hands warmed, and I looked at Fergus. "Ready?" I would seal this door and give us a chance of getting away.

He nodded.

I glanced at Jax. "If you prefer to leave, I understand." I wouldn't want to stand near my magic after what it had almost done to him.

"I'll wait. I trust you."

I wasn't sure that was wise, but I wasn't wasting time arguing, either. I looked to Fergus.

He nodded to the door. "Close your eyes."

I did as he asked, my hands heating as my magic asked me to release it to do its work. I imagined the door to be an impenetrable wall with no handle or hinges. That it was thick and heavy. I imagined no one on the other side being able to pass through it. If Fergus kept talking, I didn't hear him.

Not until he said, "Bria, open your eyes."

I did, to find the door glowing with magenta magic. I removed my hands. "Did I do it?"

Something heavy banged against the other side and voices shouted.

Fergus nodded. "You did it perfectly."

"Let's go then." My magic on the door was already beginning to fade. I hoped it held long enough for us to get out of this tunnel and across the border.

We ran single file and silent along the tunnel. Tonight had gone so differently from what I expected and there were things I wanted to ask Fergus, but not while Jax was here. I kept quiet and focused on running, and the two of them seemed content to remain the same way.

Eventually, we turned a corner to find ourselves standing in thick woods, the tunnel gone. Mother and Willow stood a few paces in front of us.

"Jax!" Willow squealed. "You made it."

Fergus' eyebrows rose. "Ah, I did too, thanks for noticing."

Willow batted his words away with her hand. "Knew you would."

Jax whistled for his horse, a chestnut mare he called Flame.

Willow sighed. "You can't be leaving already."

Jax looked around, his hair plastered to his forehead with sweat. "What else would I be doing? Where are the rest of you going?"

"Back to the castle for me," pouted Willow.

"Iadrun for us." I smiled at Jax. "Thanks for your help tonight. We weren't getting out without you."

Jax nodded, his gaze shifting to Fergus.

"I might walk Bria to the border." Fergus glanced my way to make sure I was okay with that. I absolutely was. He looked back at Jax. "I'll meet you later for a ride?"

"I'll be waiting." Jax pulled himself onto Flame and lifted a hand. "Nice to meet you, Bria."

"And you, Jax."

He clicked his tongue and was gone, into the air and above Faery on the back of his horse.

Mother nodded her approval at Fergus, looking more like herself than she had when she stood beside the king. "Good job, your Highness."

"For what?" I frowned. There were so many things she could be praising him for; helping her escape, hurting his father, stopping the fae guests that were coming after us.

"The tunnels from the castle have many possible exits if one knows where to look."

I lifted my eyebrows. I'd been in them twice now and never seen an exit except the one into the ballroom.

"It's almost impossible to find a person once they use one. It's especially difficult if you come out into the woods. Like this." She wove her fingers into her hair, kneading her scalp and fiddling with something until she pulled it free. Another iron clip. Another suppressor. She threw it into the bushes, took a deep breath in, then blew it out. "That feels better." The points of her fae ears stuck through the strands of her blonde hair. I doubted I'd ever get used to her looking like that.

"Call me Fergus." Fergus looked at the place the clip had disappeared with disgust. "I'm sorry my Father did that to you, but I don't think we have to worry about anyone following us through the tunnels. Bria sealed the door." He let out a shrill whistle, and Buttercup came bounding up to us, looking less like a hound of hell and more like a huge but pampered lap dog, her tail wagging non-stop. She stopped beside Fergus, looking up with big eyes that demanded he pat her.

Mother turned to me. "Bria. I never thought I'd see you again." She held out her arms.

I ran to her and let her envelop me in a hug, inhaling her familiar citrus scent. When I was a child, her arms around me always fixed everything, but today, her arms couldn't do that. I needed answers before I could ever feel safe with her again. I pulled away. "How can you be certain Fergus and I are bonded? And why did you cut off my ears?"

Her eyebrows shot up. "Cut off your ears?"

Fergus cleared his throat. "Ah. Willow, isn't there something that needs our attention ... um, over there?" He started toward his mythical *over there*.

I put up a hand to stop him. "Don't go. Some of this involves you. You should hear it, too."

He met my eyes. "Only if you're sure."

I nodded. I was.

Mother looked around, scanning the thick woods, scraps of moonlight filtering down between the trees. "We don't have time to stand in one spot. If that door doesn't hold, and if they find the exit we used..."

Fergus shook his head. "They won't find us. And that door will hold."

Mother loosed a deep sigh, looking like she'd rather do anything than answer my questions. Too bad. For sixteen years, I'd thought I was someone I wasn't. It was time she told me the truth. "Long before she became queen, while we were still children, Indira, Fergus' mother, was a friend of mine."

Willow's eyes narrowed. "But you're a Seelie princess. You should be their queen. Why would our mother, the Unseelie Queen, want your friendship?"

Mother shook her head. "That is a long story and one we don't have time for now. Just know that we were friends since our childhood when I would sneak across the border to play with her. Sometimes the young prince—your father—and Myles would join us. We were all such good friends until..." She shook her head and her eyes went distant. "Myles and Aengus were both too proud to get over their argument."

I jolted at the sound of Father's name. She didn't mention him often, but I liked the sound of it on her lips. I cleared my throat. If we didn't have time for the entire story, we certainly didn't have time for fanciful reveries.

Mother sighed and met my eyes. "Your father and I tried for children for so long that I never expected it to happen." She glanced at Willow and Fergus. "And I'm sure your parents believed they'd never have children, either. But when we both had our first children within a few years of each other, I contacted Indira. We hadn't spoken in the longest time, but holding you in my arms, Bria, was the happiest time of my life and I wanted to share it with my best friend."

"So, you did what? Forced her to meet you?" Willow eyed Mother with suspicion. She really didn't think Unseelie and Seelie could be friends.

Mother shook her head. "I didn't need to force her. She missed me as much as I missed her. Both of us knew our husbands would never agree to a meeting, so we each told them we were going to visit family for a month. We left Faery and found a little cottage in Iadrun, close to Holbeck and spent the time getting to know each other again. It was magical." She glanced at Fergus. "You were the sweetest child, Fergus. Blond curls and huge brown eyes. And back then, you would have done anything for anyone."

He had changed little, from what I could tell— except the color of his hair.

"We didn't even consider the two of you could be bonded. Bria was just a baby, and Fergus was only two years old. It never happens that young, and never between Seelie and Unseelie fae." She paused, her eyes distant. "But as Fergus made you giggle in your crib one day, the two of you glowed with magic—blue for Fergus, magenta for Bria. Not much, just a slight haze—neither of you had your magic yet, but there it was, the faintest glow of what was to come. As we watched, it combined, just like it did tonight, to turn purple. Neither Indira nor I wanted what the magic was promising for our children. A Seelie princess matched to an Unseelie prince—no one in the fae realm would have it. If it didn't cause a war between the kingdoms, it would result in your deaths as people tried to stop the match. So, without another word to each other, we scooped you both up and left, back to our old lives." She swallowed. "That was the last time I saw her."

I heard the bitterness, the accusation in her voice. I hoped Fergus didn't.

"I'm sorry," he whispered.

He'd heard it.

I hated that Mother would blame him for something she must know little about. "What for?" I asked Fergus. "If Mother wanted to see her friend again, she could have made it happen before your mother died." I wasn't totally okay with this story. Mostly because it didn't seem like I could blame Mother for any of it. She'd done what she thought best—keeping me away from Fergus by leaving Faery.

Mother nodded. "I could have. Should have." She tried to smile at Fergus. It looked nothing like a smile. "I took Bria back to Seelie where Bria, Myles and I were happy for a few months. Father was away, checking on his kingdom, but when he returned, everything changed. He hadn't yet met Bria. I was so proud of her, so besotted with my new baby, that I ran in to see him as soon as I returned. He took one look at her ears, decided you were too ugly to be part of his family and rule Seelie and banished us from the kingdom."

I frowned. "My ears? You mean you'd already cut them off?"

Mother shook her head. "I never cut off your ears, Bria. I don't know where you got that idea. Like I always told you, you were born this way. Maybe it was bad luck, maybe it was something else. Your ears were never an issue to me. My father didn't agree with me, but your father and I always knew you were beautiful."

"She is." Fergus' voice was soft.

I turned to tell him he didn't need to say the things he thought I needed to hear, but the words died on my lips as I saw the sincerity on his face. It brought back images of our kiss which made my heart stumble. And since it was easier not to acknowledge that, I ignored him. "But everyone thinks you did." Everyone I'd come across in Faery, at least.

Mother couldn't meet my eyes. She stared at her feet, her hands, something behind me in the woods. But never me. "Rumors. Most people never saw you in real life. All they had to go on was the words of others. They filled in the blanks with their own versions."

"So, we lived in Iadrun because we'd been banished?" That wasn't the story I'd heard in Seelie. Or from Fergus. Everyone thought Princess Aoife had died, along with her infant child.

Mother shook her head. "One of my father's advisors convinced him to allow us to stay in Seelie. The advisor thought the people might turn against him should he force us to leave. He eventually agreed we could, so long as I agreed..." She swallowed like she didn't want the words to escape.

"Agreed to what?" I prodded.

"That you would never be queen." She looked at her feet but not fast enough to hide the anger dancing in her eyes.

"I embarrassed him." I touched my ears. I was just like the princess in Selina's favorite story book. Too ugly for my kingdom. No wonder Father hated that story so much.

Mother nodded. "I refused his offer knowing doing so would force us out of Faery and have the same outcome as if he'd banished us, but I would allow no one to think you embarrassed me. You mean everything to me, Bria." She swallowed. "As I was packing to leave, Father called me back down to his throne room and offered me another choice. He didn't want me to go and he could see how much I wanted my daughter to become queen."

Beside me, Fergus tensed as if he already knew what was coming. I doubted he did but perhaps, like me, he sensed bad news.

"The Unseelie Queen had just died, and the Unseelie King was looking for a new bride. My father agreed without consulting me that you would be that bride. He felt it would go a long way to mending the broken relationship with our fae neighbors."

Nausea grew inside me. "But he's old. What would he want with a child?" I couldn't imagine being tied to that man for the rest of my life.

Fergus chewed his bottom lip. "Mother told him about our bond before she died. Marrying you and making you his queen would have killed the bond between us." Fergus lifted his shoulders. "I imagine he would have kept you well away from court and from me as a precaution until you were old enough to take your marriage vows."

Mother nodded. "I didn't want Bria growing up in the Unseelie Kingdom. I'd spent enough time there to know that some behaviors there were downright barbaric." She gave Willow and Fergus an apologetic glance. "No offence."

Willow shrugged. "Barbaric is an accurate term."

"The deal was already made, but I refused to allow it. I had planned to leave the castle that night but didn't get the chance. I ended up faking our deaths by falling from the castle wall into the moat. Everyone thought our bodies were dragged out to sea—never found. Myles found us in Iadrun and we all lived there ever since. The plan worked so well that my own family believed us dead and never searched for us. Aengus was not so gullible. He's spent the last fifteen years looking for us."

"If you were in hiding, why live so close to the border with Faery?" Surely she could have gone somewhere farther away, harder to be found.

She lifted a shoulder, guilt flooding her features. "My magic. I needed to spend at least a few minutes in Faery every few weeks so I could keep the glamour on my ears. If I didn't, my magic would disappear. It worked though ... even Aengus didn't expect we'd stay so close to the border."

Until Fergus and I practically led him there. "You did all this to stop the bond growing between the two of us?" Suddenly, I felt the need to stand up for Fergus. "You don't even know him. He's not like King Aengus. He's—"

Fergus rested his hand on my forearm, watching Mother. "It's not about that, though, is it?"

She shook her head. "No one in Faery wants the two kingdoms united. And that's the only option when the two heirs act on their bond. Each kingdom would have fought with everything they had to stop it. They'd have killed you both. The only way you might have survived was if you both had powerful magic. And when I made this decision, I had no way of knowing how either of you would turn out." She sighed. "Aengus Blackwood knows how to hold a grudge. He already had a grudge with me before all this and refusing his marriage offer insulted him all the more."

No one spoke once Mother finished her story. So many lies, all built one on top of the next.

"I'm sorry," said Mother, looking from Willow to Fergus. "Aengus doesn't come out of this looking so good."

"He never does." Fergus glanced at me, his eyes asking if I was all right.

I was fine. Relieved to have some answers finally. And to know my parents hadn't mutilated me. "So what happens now?" King Aengus would not be happy we'd escaped. And if he'd been hunting us for almost fifteen of my sixteen years, I doubted he'd stop now.

Mother took a deep breath. "We go back to Iadrun, find another village along the border and start our lives over. I'll teach you how to use your magic so you can hide your ears, and no one will know who you are." She looked around as if the king might be hidden in the woods. "And we hope Aengus doesn't find us."

"I'll help. However I can." Fergus didn't need to tell me Xion would not help the king—I knew that already. His comment was for Mother but it brought a stabbing feeling to my heart. I hated the thought of saying goodbye to him. It was stupid because I didn't want to be bonded to him, either. I just wanted to be his friend.

"It's decided then." Mother glanced at Fergus, then Willow. "Thank you for helping my daughter. I can't ever repay what you did for her." Her eyes moved to me. "Come, Bria. We need to get moving."

This was it. Time to say goodbye. I hugged Willow. "Thanks for your help."

"Anytime." She smiled, and it seemed like I'd known her for longer than just a few hours.

I turned to Fergus. There was so much I needed to thank him for but before I could attempt to put any of it into words, he said, "I'd still like to walk you to the Crossing. If that's okay."

I nodded. It was totally okay.

Willow decided to join us, and as she and Mother disappeared around the bend on the trail ahead of us, Fergus slowed, taking my hand and pulling me to a stop beside him. "There's something I need to show you. If you'll let me." He seemed unsure of himself.

I shrugged. "Sure." I was happy to put off our goodbye for a little longer.

Fergus directed me off the main trail to a narrow one that had us stepping over and ducking beneath branches that grew across it. Buttercup bounded ahead of us, before loping back to check we were following.

Fergus didn't speak, but I couldn't stand the silence between us. "Should I be worried about you splitting me up from Mother?"

When he turned to answer, his smile was faint. "Probably."

"What's wrong, Fergus?" He seemed quiet and not like himself.

He looked me over, then shook his head. "It doesn't matter."

That stabbing feeling returned to my chest. I would miss him when I left Faery. Perhaps he felt the same way about me. Or perhaps it was the magic of our bond making us both feel out of sorts. "How did you know?" I blurted. "About our ... connection?"

His shoulders rose and fell as he drew a deep breath, and his pace slowed. He turned to face me.

"The only people who can remove my mask are me ... and my bonded mate."

I stared at him as his words sank in. "You've known since the day you brought me here? Since the first day we met?"

"I suspected. Hoped I was wrong. I never wanted the tie—you knew that." Yes, that was something he'd made perfectly clear. "When I went feral at Mrs. Plimmer because of the things she said about you, I was almost certain it must be true, but I kept telling myself it couldn't be, because we'd never met before. Somewhere inside, I guess I knew." He turned away and ran his hands over his plaited black hair. "That's why I hoped you'd go to Rhiannon. If you were in Seelie, if I never had to see you again, my life could go on, at least for a while, as it always had. But it didn't work out that way. Our connection tells me things, and I sensed you were in danger in Seelie and all I could do was go after you."

I'd felt the same thing when I searched the rubble in the prison for him, like I couldn't do anything but make sure he was safe.

He turned back to look at me. "I'm sorry, Bria. I'd never have taken you to that ceremony tonight if I'd known you planned on kissing me. I thought you didn't want me. That's what you said."

"I didn't plan on kissing you. It just ... happened." Stars. Had I taken even a second to consider it, it never would have happened. "You should have stopped me. You knew what would happen if we kissed." Whereas I had no clue there would be consequences.

He gave a guilty shrug. "It's not that easy. That same magic that pushed you to kiss me, pushed me to kiss you back." He closed his eyes. "Stopping you didn't even cross my mind. You looked so..." He shook his head. "Doesn't matter."

He was right. It didn't matter. None of it mattered, because after tonight, we would keep out of each other's way. "So, if we stay away from each other, we can ignore this ... bond?" It felt like I was ripping a hole in my heart, but I glued a smile on my face and reminded myself it wasn't real. Anything I felt for Fergus over and above friendship was because of the bond. Magic controlled my feelings for him.

He smiled back. It didn't reach his eyes. Or perhaps that was wishful thinking. "That's what I figure. I know someone who can reverse spells. If she can help us, I'll come and find you."

I nodded. I'd do whatever I needed to remove the spell.

We walked on in silence through the dark woods, Fergus carrying a ball of blue light in his hand. The only sound the occasional branch snapping beneath our feet and the buzzing of night creatures. It was Fergus who spoke next. "You saved me tonight. Again."

"I know." I liked how surprised he seemed, but I knew he'd do—had done—the same for me. "I'll add it to the tally."

He threw a smile over his shoulder and pushed off the trail to stop in front of a small pile of stones. "This is the grave of the baby you asked me about."

I sucked in a breath. "Tobias?" Selina's brother.

He nodded. "Taking kids is the worst. I wanted to make sure he was treated the same in death here in Faery as his family would have treated him." He looked away as he spoke again. "I brought his sister here once. Or, at least, Xion did."

"You did?" I breathed out the words, remembering how Selina had said as much the last time I saw her. I'd thought she meant it had happened in her dreams. It had never occurred to me that Fergus would do something so kind. It probably should have. If not at the time, then since. "Thank you." Tears pricked at my eyes. This was where that beautiful little baby lay.

He shrugged like it wasn't the big deal that it was. "You don't have to leave," he blurted. "You could stay on the island. With me. For as long as you want."

Yes.

That single word formed on the tip of my tongue.

Living there with him would be perfect. But there was more at stake than me being happy. I had to consider Mother. Rhiannon now knew she was alive, and I doubted either she or King Aengus wanted her to stay that way. I couldn't hide away on a warded island while she fended for herself. I shook my head. "I'm sorry, Fergus, but I can't. I need to look out for Mother. Plus, I can't imagine how living with you would work when neither of us want any part of the bond." Because that was the actual issue. The more time we spent together, the stronger that bond would grow.

He let out a breath, grinning. At least his mouth was. "Neither can I." He held out his hand. "Come on. I'll walk you across the border. Make sure the king isn't waiting for you."

With his hand in mine as we walked the trail, I was happier than I had been in a long while. Mother was safe. Selina had seen her brother's grave. I didn't have to spend my life in Faery. And the border between our lands was just ahead. Mother and Willow stood beneath a bright light on the guard tower, waiting for us to catch up. Everything would be all right.

Mother and Willow crossed as soon as they saw us coming, talking and laughing like they'd known each other for years. The border guard looked us over but said nothing, dropping his gaze back to the book he was reading.

"Bria!"

I turned and searched the woods of Unseelie at the sound of my name, but there was no one, nothing, behind me. When I turned back, Fergus had already crossed into Iadrun.

"Bria!"

The voice belonged to Selina, I was sure of it. And she was on the Faery side of the border. I wasn't going home without her. "Just a minute. I'll be there in a second," I called to Fergus.

I ran toward her voice. It was coming from the thick stand of trees beside the trail. "Selina!"

"Bria?" She seemed surprised to hear me.

I pushed through bracken and ducked beneath branches, calling her name until I found her in the dim woods. She was standing at the base of a tree and turning in a circle like she was unsure which way to go. When she saw me, her face broke into a gigantic smile and ran to me, wrapping her arms around me in a hug. "I'm so glad I've found you."

She took my hand. "Come. We have to leave this place."

I smiled. She looked good. A little thin, but happy. I guess that was the same for us both. "That's what I'm trying to do. Why are you even here?"

"Looking for you. I came to Faery to visit Tobias' grave then decided it was time you came home." She was smiling so hard, she couldn't talk properly. I was the same amount of glad to see her. "I've been trying to find you."

Aside from happy, she seemed dazed, and a little confused. Faery could do that to humans. I wondered how long she'd been wandering lost, though it didn't matter now. I could get her home. "Let's go."

Buttercup raced up to us, her tail a blur as she wagged it so hard. A few steps from me she stopped, so did her tail. Her lips drew back, and she bared her teeth, a low rumble coming from her throat. The hackles on her neck rose.

Selina backed away with a squeal.

"Buttercup! Stop!" I growled. The snarling stopped. Buttercup looked between the two of us, like she wasn't sure she should stop at all. "It's okay. This is Selina. She's a friend." I didn't know when the hound had decided she liked me enough to protect me. I slipped my hand into Selina's, pulling her back onto the trail. "Come on, you stupid dog."

I half expected to step back onto the main trail to find Fergus there waiting for us. He wasn't. He waited perhaps thirty steps away, where I'd left him, on the human side of the Crossing. A frown creased his forehead, but he smiled when he saw me.

I smiled back.

Buttercup growled again, a low rumbling that set me on edge. I glanced over my shoulder, something moved in the darkness. I gripped Selina's hand and pulled her to walk faster.

Hoofbeats sounded behind us.

Guards.

"Run!" I pulled on Selina's hand, but she was slow, stumbling over her steps.

Mother, Willow and Fergus were lined up on the Iadrun side of the Crossing. Their lips moved, but no sound escaped. Was that normal? I didn't think so but couldn't be sure. I'd never tried to hold a conversation across the border between our lands.

Fergus moved his arm, beckoning me with quick movements that made my heart thud. I pushed Selina ahead and sprinted. Buttercup ran with us, barking as if she were running with the Hunt.

I pushed Selina across the border giving the border guard a quick smile, and followed.

Or tried to.

Where Selina had stepped through without a problem, something I couldn't see stopped me. Something hard and unyielding. It was like I'd run into a wall.

I turned to the border guard, the hoofbeats behind me so loud I could barely think. The king's men were coming. I needed to get to Iadrun. I didn't want to be on this side of the border when they turned up. "Please. I need to get through."

"I'm sorry, Princess. But that won't be possible." He looked back down at his book like this wasn't a matter of life or death.

"Please! I need to leave!"

He lifted a shoulder, eyes on the page.

Fergus walked toward the Crossing like he was coming back to get me, but he halted suddenly. The frown on his face deepened, and he banged his fists against the invisible wall.

My mind reeled. Any moment now, those horses would pop through the thicket and when they did, I was done for.

Think. I had to calm down and think this through. There was a way out of this. There had to be.

The guard? Could I kill him? If he'd built the invisible wall that was keeping me here, would killing him destroy it? I had no weapons and couldn't count on my magic doing what I expected. The chances of injuring him were low, let alone killing him.

As I weighed up my options, a faint white glow formed around his body. He was getting ready to use his magic.

Shield. Fergus' lips formed the word from the other side of the wall.

Yes. That was my best option. I imagined a shield around myself, the same as I'd done earlier but this time, I thought carefully about it forming around me. Nothing happened. I cursed and glanced at Fergus. He pounded on the invisible wall with closed fists and shouted something at me. Something I couldn't hear.

I tried again, concentrating on my magic. Still nothing. Not even a pink glow as I tried to call it up. The guard would use his magic any moment, while I had none left.

I'd used it all.

Buttercup growled, her body vibrating.

Run.

That was all I could do.

I took a step just as the first of the horses pushed through the thicket.

Something—magic, I guessed—hit me so hard it knocked me from my feet. Knocked all the air from me. I lay on the ground, staring up through the woods to the starry sky.

Somewhere far off, Buttercup was going crazy, her barking was all I could hear.

Soldiers on horseback approached, faces wary. One climbed down, gray magic floating around his body ready to attack. In one hand he held a sack. His feet were slow as he crept toward me, as if he expected I might jump up and attack him.

I would, too. As soon as I could breathe again.

He flicked his hand and Buttercup fell beside me. I turned my head to look at her. She wasn't moving. Not breathing. Whatever was wrong with her, I couldn't do anything to help. I couldn't even take my next breath. Couldn't fight.

The guard dragged a sack over my head. Darkness crowded my vision.

Fight back. I had to.

Or I would die.

By sheer force of will, I drew in a breath. Once I'd taken a second, I kicked and bucked as hard as I could.

It didn't matter. Hands—so many hands—picked me up and carried me away. I landed a kick on someone's nose—I heard it crack. They dropped my leg but before I could line up a second kick, someone else took hold of me, shutting my movement down.

They threw me over the back of a horse on my stomach and tied me on.

The sack over my head shifted, and I could see Mother, Fergus, and Willow beating on the invisible wall. Mother was crying. Fergus' fists were curled into tight balls, his face twisted with anger.

And behind them, unmoved and unmoving, stood Selina.

No, not Selina.

Wearing Selina's clothing, and with red magic sparking across her body and her arms raised ready to strike, stood Queen Rhiannon.

Already missing Bria? For a different type of kick-butt heroine, try Maryanne in the Sherwood Outlaws series.

This is a complete series, available for purchase or free in Kindle Unlimited on Amazon.

Reviews are an important way for authors to find new readers and finding them means we can pay our bills a little longer! I'd love it if you would take a few minutes and leave a review for this novel – it doesn't have to be long. Head to the Amazon page for this book to leave your review.

Get the Royals of Faery prequel novella for FREE

Thanks for reading Kingdom of Yesterday's Lies.

If you're not quite ready to leave Faery yet, sign up to my reader list and I'll send you Kingdom of Times Forgotten for FREE! You'll also get a copy of Outcast, the prequel for my Sherwood Outlaws series, also free.

Just head to the link below.

I'm looking forward to meeting you.

https://www.hayleyosborn.com/times-forgotten/

Acknowledgments

Well, 2020 has been an ... interesting year! Unfortunately, for me anyway, global pandemics don't mesh well with creativity, so this novel is at least six months later releasing than I'd hoped. Never mind, it's here now, right?

Thanks to Kat Seelig for reading the first (and very bad) draft of this novel. Your insights and suggestions helped it become what it is today.

Thanks to Melissa Craven for editing, for your encouragement, and for answering questions on US English versus New Zealand English.

Thanks to Daqri from Covers by Combs for this amazing cover. I'm pretty sure I say every cover you design is amazing, but this one is doubly so.

Finally, thanks to my family. To Mum and Dad for being the first to pre-order a copy. To Kelly for loving the first chapter. To Zach and Ashleigh for continuously asking when they can read my next book. To Jacob for answering my tech questions (including Instagram). And to Hayden for believing in me. I love you all and couldn't have written this without you.

Also by Hayley Osborn

ROYALS OF FAERY
Kingdom of Times Forgotten (prequel)
Kingdom of Yesterday's Lies
Kingdom of Today's Deceit (coming
December 2020)

SHERWOOD OUTLAWS
Outcast (prequel)
Outlawed
Outplayed
Outlasted

About the author

Hayley Osborn lives in Christchurch, New Zealand, with her husband and three children, cat and dog.

Online, you can find her at:

www.hayleyosborn.com.

To connect with her on social media, you can find her on Facebook at HayleyOsbornAuthor, on Instagram at Hayley_Osborn_Author or on Twitter at @Hayley___Osborn. Or if you prefer to make contact via email, you can contact her at hayley@hayleyosborn.com.

Made in the USA
Middletown, DE
06 January 2021

30920052R00253